From Josie Lit
bestselling author of *Come Ba*
brand-new generation of romance and adventure—featuring the enchanting family from the trilogy *Dream Island, Kingdom of Moonlight,* and *Castles in the Mist.* Return each month to the exotic world these six young men and women inhabit. Look for the other two books in this tantalizing trio by Josie Litton.

FOUNTAIN OF DREAMS

Amelia and Niel's Story

Meet the first of our trio of couples as their love is tested by a startling secret, divided loyalties—and a dangerous mission.

On sale now wherever books are sold

FOUNTAIN OF SECRETS

Gavin and Persephone's Story

A woman of mystery and a man of honor discover their shared destiny when the sins of the past collide with the deadly danger of the present.

On sale now wherever books are sold

Also by Josie Litton

DREAM OF ME

BELIEVE IN ME

COME BACK TO ME

DREAM ISLAND

KINGDOM OF MOONLIGHT

CASTLES IN THE MIST

FOUNTAIN OF DREAMS

FOUNTAIN OF FIRE

JOSIE LITTON

BANTAM BOOKS

FOUNTAIN OF FIRE
A Bantam Book / September 2003

Published by
Bantam Dell
A Division of Random House, Inc.
New York, New York

Cover image by Alan Ayers
Cover design by Yook Louie

ISBN 0-553-58585-1

Manufactured in the United States of America
Published simultaneously in Canada

OPM 10 9 8 7 6 5 4 3 2 1

With my deepest
appreciation to the readers who
made these books possible.

JOSIE LITTON

Fountain of FIRE

CHAPTER I

England, Summer 1837

SCRAMBLING AROUND THE DAMP, DANK INTErior of a stone crypt while a thunderstorm raged outside and floods threatened, Clio entertained the thought that she would have been wiser to stay in bed. Not that she could have done so. The floods put at risk the artifacts she had begun to uncover earlier in the day. She would not rest until they were protected.

The crypt was beneath the manor house of Holyhood on the southeastern coast of England. It was a remnant of a much earlier residence dating, she believed, from the ninth century. That alone made it an extraordinary discovery and well worth studying, even if no one else thought so.

Scraping away with the garden trowel, working as fast as she could by the light of a lantern, Clio ignored the muddy water sloshing around her boots and carefully placed a shard of pottery in the basket she had brought along. Several more pieces of what she thought might have been a clay pitcher were still in the dirt. Determined to get them all, she kept digging as the rain poured down and the water on the floor of the crypt continued to rise.

It was up to her ankles when she finished. With a sigh of relief, she grabbed the basket and turned to go, only to stop abruptly. Hesitantly, not really crediting what she thought she saw, she raised the lantern higher and peered into the shadows at the far end of the crypt.

A man was watching her. He had thick black hair to his shoulders, hard features, and a slashing grin. Incongruously, he was sitting on the floor on the other side of the crypt. His long legs, bare below a short tunic, were stretched out in front of him. He appeared untroubled by either the rain or the water he was sitting in.

But then, he also looked completely dry.

A finger of ice moved down her spine. Clutching the lantern in one hand, the basket in the other, and her courage in both, Clio took a step forward. "Sir . . . you startled me. . . ."

The man did not respond. Indeed, now that she saw

him more clearly, he appeared to be looking not at her but beyond her, as though something on the opposite side of the crypt in the direction of the stairs commanded his attention.

His keen, intense attention.

The man rose and came toward Clio. He was very tall, well over six feet, and supremely fit. The gleam in his eyes was most disconcerting. . . .

As was the fact that he walked straight through her.

Not around, not past. Through.

Clio screamed. She was not, as a general rule, a screamer. Indeed, if pressed, she could not have recalled the last time she had screamed. She was, however, quite good at it, if the measure of a scream is its volume and duration.

She was still screaming when she gained the ancient stone steps leading from the crypt, took them two at a time, and hurled herself out into the silent garden of Holyhood.

Her lungs finally empty of air, the scream petered out. Bent over, clutching the basket and lantern, she struggled to inhale. Her entire body shook, her heart hammered, and the roiling of her stomach suggested the imminent reappearance of the dinner she had enjoyed several hours before.

That would not do. She was, after all, a princess and princesses do not go about losing their dinners because of encounters with men who are not there.

As reason reasserted itself, she set the basket down

and looked back toward the crypt. In the narrow circle of the lantern light, the entrance to it appeared like a black mouth dark against the storm-tossed night.

"Oh, for heaven's sake." Her imagination was running away with her to a disgraceful degree.

There was no man in the crypt. There could not possibly be. And certainly there was no man who could walk straight through her, not there or anywhere else. To do that, he would have to be a ghost.

Clio did not believe in ghosts.

On her native Akora, she lived her daily life in the same places where people had lived for centuries and even millennia. Her private quarters were in a part of the palace that had stood for over two thousand years. Princesses of Akora through all that time had occupied her very bedroom. Their joys and sorrows, triumphs and tragedies had played out within the same walls where she sometimes lay awake at night, wishing the voices of the past truly could speak to her. Not once had she caught so much as a glimmer of a lingering presence.

There was no man, but there had to be an explanation for what she had seen. To find it, she would have to return to the crypt. The choice did not come easily. The echoes of terror still resonated within her, but they were muted by the impossibility of ever yielding to cowardice. Water was dripping off her nose when she moved slowly back in the direction from which she had come.

Holding the light high, Clio descended one step . . . another . . . The stones were slick beneath her feet. She resisted the impulse to call out. One did not address a figment of the imagination. Even so, she breathed a sigh of relief when she found the crypt empty.

No figment there, just muddy ground and the traces of her digging. She was ready to go, satisfied to put the incident down to fatigue and distraction, when a glint of metal caught her eye. Forgetful of all else, she went to investigate it.

AT THE SOUND OF A SCREAM COMING FROM THE vicinity of the house, the Earl of Hollister turned his horse away from the stables and spurred the big roan gelding back down the gravel path. It was very late. He was wet, cold, and hungry. So, no doubt, was Seeker, who was as good a mount as a man could want and deserved better than to be turned away from a warm stall. All the same, the scream could not be ignored.

The path led along the back of the graceful three-story manor built several decades before on the site of a far older residence. Indeed, if legend was to be believed, there had been a manor at Holyhood for a thousand years or more. William gave that scant thought. His mind was on his widowed grandmother, living alone in the house with only her devoted servants for company.

But his grandmother had the sense to be snug in her bed on such a night, and the scream had sounded like the voice of a much younger woman.

One of the servants come to some harm?

He drew Seeker to a halt near the far corner of the house. The storm that had caught him was passing quickly. Behind it, the moon emerged. By its light, he could make out the entrance to what he knew to be a stone crypt under the house. A faint glow emanated from within the crypt.

Swiftly he dismounted, tossed the reins over a nearby hedge, and moved toward the steps leading to the crypt. He was a big man, broad of shoulder and long of limb. Had he not known to bend his head, he would have struck it on the ceiling above the steps.

Descending the stairs, he paused halfway and took the measure of what awaited him. He had played in this place as a child, arranging toy soldiers, imagining long-ago battles. It was a favorite hideaway on the hot summer days that could sweep over Holyhood despite the nearness of the sea. So far as he knew, no one else ever went there.

Certainly no one would venture there in the midnight hour of a storm-filled night.

Which explained his surprise at the sight of a woman on her knees not far from where he stood. She wore a cloak that draped her body. Her head was bent, but he could see that her hair was long, loose, and a deep, rich red. She was digging furiously.

"What are you doing?"

The woman froze. Very slowly she raised her head and looked at him. The glow of the lantern, the light of which had drawn him into the crypt, fell fully on her face.

For a moment, William neglected to breathe. The woman was . . . beautiful, certainly, but beautiful women abounded in his world. Here was something more. Her features, clearly and delicately formed, appeared illuminated from within. Her eyes were very large, all the more so for being very wide. Her mouth was enticingly full, her chin firm. Stillness settled over her as she looked at him.

"Who are you?" she asked.

"William, Earl of Hollister. Who are you?"

To his surprise, she looked immensely relieved. Quickly, she got to her feet and made a futile effort to brush the mud off her cloak. "William . . . I know you. Or at least I did."

"You have the advantage, madam." Yet there was something about her that was familiar, if only to a small degree. It was years ago . . . a little red-haired girl playing in the garden of Holyhood. She had come with her parents, the Vanax Atreus, ruler of the legendary kingdom of Akora, and her mother, the Lady Brianna, who was related to his own family.

That child grown to such a stunning woman? It

didn't seem possible, yet nature was known to work such wonders.

He came to the bottom of the stairs without taking his eyes from her. Close-up, she was even lovelier, for all that she was clearly wet and bedraggled. "Princess Clio?"

Her smile was immediate and genuine. "Please, just Clio. You know we are not so fond of titles on Akora as people are here in England."

He did know that, or at least he had heard it, for all that he had never been to Akora. His grandparents had made several trips there over the years, but they were among the very few outsiders invited to visit the legendary Fortress Kingdom, which was situated in the Atlantic beyond what the ancients called the Pillars of Hercules.

"Clio, then. What are you doing here?"

"Digging," she said as though it should be obvious. When he continued staring at her, she elaborated. "I have been digging for several days and I've found some wonderful things. When the storm started, I was afraid those still left on the surface or near to it would be damaged, so I came down to get them."

Later he would try to understand why a lovely young woman—a princess, no less—was digging in the dirt floor of an empty stone crypt and what sort of "wonderful things" she could possibly have discovered. Just then, he had other things on his mind.

"I heard you scream."

Her creamy skin brightened as though a tongue of flame had moved over it. "I'm terribly sorry. I was . . . startled."

"By what?"

He half-expected her to mention a rat or something of the sort, when she surprised him. "A man, or at least what I thought was a man. There wasn't actually anyone there." Hesitantly, she added, "When I saw you on the steps, I thought you were him again."

"The man you saw looked like me?"

"There was no man, and no, he didn't look like you, not really. He was as tall as you and fit the way you are, but he was dressed very differently and his hair was much darker. Yours is auburn, his was black and somewhat longer."

"This man who did not exist?"

She made a small gesture, whether waving away her own inconsistency or his persistence, he could not tell.

"I was asleep when the rain woke me," she said, "and I realized the artifacts I had found could be endangered. When I got down here, I think I was still less than fully awake. Under the circumstances, it is not so surprising that my imagination overtook me."

"Perhaps not. What are these artifacts you speak of?"

Proudly she held out her basket. He peered into it and frowned. "Those are broken bits of pottery."

"A clay pitcher, I think. There is writing on them."

"That signifies? . . ."

"I am not absolutely certain of the script, but I think it is Anglo-Saxon, from the era of Alfred the Great."

"That would be old, indeed, but why would it interest you?"

"It's what I do . . . dig up the past." When he did not reply, she sighed. "I don't expect you to understand. People think the only objects from the past that matter are great monuments and the like, not the remains of ordinary life."

"You believe otherwise?"

She nodded and gestured to the basket. "From these, I may be able to confirm that this crypt is as old as I think it is and even what it was used for."

"Storage," William said.

"What?"

"It was used for storage, except for the time when it very briefly became a prison for captured Vikings."

"How could you possibly know that?"

He shrugged. "It's an old story, part of the lore of Holyhood. This is not the time to speak of it. You are soaked through and covered with mud."

She gathered her cloak more closely around herself. "I am aware of that."

"Then you must also be aware that you should retire." He offered his arm.

Briefly, she considered refusing. The glint of metal that had drawn her attention came from an iron bar that was revealed by the water washing down into the crypt. She was eager to examine it more closely, but she knew by experience that being metal, it was likely to come apart in flakes as soon as she tried to move it. Excavating it safely would be a delicate process, not best undertaken by lantern light when she was already weary.

Instead, she covered it again with soil, carefully marking the spot before accepting William's assistance. As they emerged from the crypt, she caught sight of Seeker and smiled. "He is yours?"

"Or I am his. We have not settled the matter." He took the reins with his free hand. The gelding followed them.

"How do you happen to be here at so late an hour?" Clio asked as they approached the back entrance of the house.

"I was delayed coming down from London."

Something hovered beneath his words, but she could not place it. His sudden appearance had shocked her. For just a moment, she truly had thought she was looking at the same man she had seen before. But that was not the case. Besides the difference in dress and hair color, the features were different. Yet both men bore the stamp of strength and determination. Both reminded her of the men of her own family and the men of Akora in general, good men to be sure and warriors to the bone.

"Your grandmother will be thrilled that you are here. Have you come for Racing Day?"

"Yes . . . I have. How is Grandmother?"

"Well, I think. She was very kind to invite me."

They had reached the door. He opened it for her and stood aside. His voice was deep and low. "Goodnight, Clio."

She came only to his shoulders and had to look up to see his face. In the shadows cast by the moon, his features looked hard and unyielding. There was a bleakness about his eyes that surprised her. She glanced down and saw that the left sleeve of his jacket was torn and there was a dark stain of some sort on it. The thought passed through her mind that perhaps he was not as well cared for as he might have been. Softly she said, "Goodnight . . . William."

Her smile seemed to take him by surprise. "My friends call me Will."

"Will, then," she said and turned away from him down the long corridor, up the back stairs, and to her room. Once there, she shut the door behind her and leaned against it, listening to the drumbeat of her heart.

William, Earl of Hollister, master of Holyhood. She remembered him distantly, a boy of eleven or twelve when she had last seen him, a strange being from her perspective as a six-year-old. His father had died suddenly the year before, and she wondered, when she heard someone speak of that, how anyone could survive so dreadful an event. Her own father was ever ready to dangle her high in the sky, take her on his horse before him, or let her come into the studio where he created rare works of art when he wasn't busy being ruler of Akora.

The boy she remembered was gone; in his place was a man she could not drive from her mind. He had ascended to the honors of his title after the death of his grandfather two years before. But he was, she understood, little seen at Holyhood. His presence there now surprised her.

About to step onto the Aubusson carpet, she caught herself and bent over to remove her boots, hopping first on one foot, then the other. Her muddy cloak followed. Looking down, she saw that the serviceable skirt she had thrown over her bed gown was also dirtied. That, too, she removed before making her way barefoot to the small alcove set up as a bathing chamber.

On Akora, she could soak in a tub of hot water produced by the thermal springs that flowed beneath the royal city. But here, every drop of water had to be hauled in buckets up flights of stairs from the kitchens. At such an hour, she would not dream of ringing for a servant, and the thought of making her way back downstairs to fetch a bucket was quite beyond her. Instead, she made do with the cold water still in a pitcher on a stand.

The storm had brought a cool wave of air behind it, more in keeping with early spring than summer. By the time she finished washing, Clio was shivering. She dropped a fresh muslin shift over her head and raced for the bed. Sitting up against the pillows, her knees bent and the covers drawn to her chin, she tried to put the events of the past few hours in some semblance of order.

Thoughts of William—Will—kept intruding, but she forced herself to think instead of the other man, the one who wasn't there. He had seemed so real, yet he could not possibly be. Or could he? . . .

Stranger things had happened in her family.

Oh, no, she would not think of that. Such things had nothing to do with her. In a line of women possessed of strange "gifts" that were as often burdens, she was blessedly ordinary. Not for her were the powers of seeing, calling, and knowing that came in different forms to different women in times of peril.

Her cousin Amelia, who was also her dear friend, had been marked from childhood by an extraordinary ability to know what was in the heart of almost any person. Amelia had married recently and was on her wedding trip in America, otherwise Clio would have sought her counsel. As it was, she had to be content with her own.

The man did not exist, but Will most certainly did. What had brought him back to Holyhood on such a night? His grandmother could not have known of his coming or she would have mentioned it.

London was still officially in mourning for the dead King William IV, scant weeks in his grave, but the city and the nation as a whole were engulfed in surreptitious celebration combined with ceaseless speculation about the new young Queen Victoria. With Akora in the process of establishing diplomatic relations with Britain for the first time in its history, her parents had come to pay their respects to the new monarch.

Clio had hoped to be left at home on Akora, where she was in the midst of a fascinating dig, but, uncharacteristically, her parents had insisted she accompany them. After a fortnight spent languishing in London, a city she could not bring herself to like, the invitation to visit Holyhood came as a blessed release.

But while she was happy to depart London, she could not help but wonder what had driven Will to do the same. It was a question with no answer, for she did not know him remotely well enough to discern his motives. All the same, she was still pondering it when sleep overtook her.

She dreamed of the man who wasn't there. He was standing, his head almost brushing the ceiling of the crypt. As he came toward her, she saw what she had not noticed consciously before—his hands were bound in front of him.

Viking prisoners.

She woke up shivering in the darkness, burrowed deeper under the covers, and dreamed the same dream again . . . and again . . . and again. It chased her through the night.

Sometime toward dawn, she said to the man who was not there, "For pity's sake, go away."

Mercifully he did, and she was able to steal a few hours of true rest before the bright sun of full morning, streaming through the high windows, made further sleep impossible.

Dogged by a headache, Clio rang for the young maid assigned to her and gladly accepted the tea the girl brought. It made her feel marginally better. She bathed, then dressed in a simple gown of white muslin scattered with embroidered flowers and left her hair down, secured by a ribbon at the nape of her neck. Informed that her hostess awaited her in the morning room, she set out in that direction.

Lady Constance was seated at a round table near the windows. In her sixties, two years a widow, she was only just emerging from the intense sorrow engendered by her beloved husband's death. Clio had met her in London and, when it became evident they would both prefer to be elsewhere, had been happy to accept her invitation to Holyhood.

Now, as she joined her at the table, Lady Constance looked up from the pile of newly arrived correspondence she was perusing. Her round face beaming beneath gracefully arranged snow-white hair, she said, "Dear child, did you know my grandson has arrived?"

Slipping into the chair beside her, Clio nodded. "Yes, I did. How wonderful." She did not feel compelled to describe the precise circumstances under which she had gained such knowledge. Lady Constance was a warm and generous woman who effected to see nothing odd about Clio wanting to dig up the older parts of Holyhood. All the same, she was not likely to approve of her young guest roaming about in the middle of a stormy night.

"We breakfasted early and had a lovely chat," Lady Constance said. "William has gone off to speak with the tenant farmers, I believe he said, but I'm sure he'll be back before long and the two of you can meet."

"I shall look forward to it," Clio assured her even as she noted the gleam of anticipation in Lady Constance's eye. Her mother, who adored Lady Constance, had warned Clio that her hostess was an inveterate matchmaker. That might explain why she had no less than two dozen godchildren, the sons and daughters of couples brought together by her design.

Clio had passed the warning off without concern. She had no intention of marrying anytime soon and sometimes wondered if she would ever do so. She doubted there were very many men who would tolerate her fascination with the past, but far beyond that, she was not inclined to settle for anything less than the passionate, loving union enjoyed by her parents and other members of her family.

Determined to deflect her hostess, she said, "I found the pieces of what I think is a clay pitcher. There is writing on it."

"What does it say?"

what she had seen. A woman, or perhaps simply a shaft of light with dust motes dancing in it, which her overactive imagination had somehow assembled into the image of a woman?

She had, after all, been bending over to extricate the iron bar. It was a position that often left her momentarily disoriented when she finally raised her head. This was likely to be just another incident of that.

As for the man who was not there, the combination alone of a stormy night and her fatigue could account for him.

Really, there was no reason to trouble herself or anyone else. She needed to be more sensible about these things.

To begin with, the day was much too lovely to spend crawling around on the floor of a dank crypt. She would tidy herself up and suggest to Lady Constance that they take a carriage ride. Of course, she would return to the crypt before long and remove the bar, but she didn't have to do that right then, not while the echoes of what she had seen were still resonating within her. That wasn't cowardice, it was merely good sense.

"Kene." The word was bitter on her tongue but the truth was worse, she was indulging in the worst sort of foolishness. She knew perfectly well what she had seen in both incidents in the crypt, even if she didn't know what they meant. Nothing good could come from pretending otherwise.

And nothing just then could get her back into that crypt. She sat unmoving in the bright warmth of the sun so long that the finches returned to peck at the lawn near her feet. Without fear, they strayed ever nearer until suddenly the whole lot of them rose into the sky. She was watching them go in one of those extraordinarily unified waves of motion birds manage, wondering what spurred them, when Will came around the corner of the house.

He was on foot and casually dressed in a loose white shirt, dark riding pants, and boots splattered with mud. The sun shone on the thick auburn hair curling at the back of his neck. His brow was high, his nose straight, and his chin firm. His eyes were a deep, rich brown surrounded by lighter bands of gold. There was a small bruise on his lower left jaw that she had not noticed the night before.

She was just wondering how he might have gotten it when he saw her and inclined his head. "Princess Clio, good afternoon. I trust you are well?"

Uncharacteristically aware that he was once again seeing her disheveled and muddy, Clio mustered a smile. "Just enjoying the lovely day, your lordship."

He raised a brow. "I thought Akorans didn't use titles."

She who had a twin brother who had long since taught her to give as good as she got, replied, "I thought we settled on 'Clio.' "

but merely smiled. "Do you intend to remain long at Holyhood?"

Did she? Bored in London, chafing at the tedious social routine, she had thought to go to Hawkforte. Her cousin David was there, looking after the manor, as his parents remained engaged at Court. He had written to say he would be glad of her company, and Hawkforte itself was fascinating.

Unlike Holyhood, where the earlier residences had been pulled down, Hawkforte was built around its own past, the oldest parts of the immense house still in use to the present day. In that, it reminded her of Akora. But she sensed that to dig at Hawkforte, to seek to unearth even more of its past, could be a lifetime's endeavor.

She had only a few weeks before she would be returning to Akora with her parents. Lady Constance's kind invitation had offered a welcome compromise between the tedium of the capital and the too-tempting lure of Hawkforte.

"I don't know," she replied. "Lady Constance has been most kind—"

"Grandmother is always kind, but she has a tendency to overdo. I'm sure you understand that as an elderly woman, she needs a great deal of rest."

"I suppose—" In fact, Lady Constance struck her as more vigorous than many people half her age, but she did prefer the relative quiet of Holyhood to the ceaseless activity of London.

"No doubt she meant well inviting you here, but—"

"Are you suggesting I should not remain?" That didn't seem possible, for they had been getting along so well. The notion appeared to come out of nowhere. She was strangely hurt by it. Yet why should that be? She did not know William of Holyhood, not really, and while she had a proper regard for the opinion of all people, she did not let the approval or disapproval of strangers determine her actions.

"I do not wish to be rude," Will said.

To Clio's ears, the words rang hollow. He spoke them well enough, but they carried no conviction. Rather, she was left with the impression that her feelings were of no high matter to him.

A flutter of disappointment moved through her. She ignored it firmly and stood. "I assure you, I would never do anything to cause Lady Constance the least harm."

He, too, stood, making her once again all too aware of his size and strength. "I am certain you would not do so knowingly."

"Should I receive the slightest inclination that Lady Constance would prefer for me to depart, I will do so forthwith."

"Grandmother is too hospitable to ever suggest that. It would be far better for you to be guided by me in this matter."

"Would it? And what is your guidance, sir?"

"That you allow me to escort you to Hawkforte."

But she had to go, on that he was determined. His passing suggestion that he would trust her was entirely false. It had been a very long time since he had trusted anyone outside his immediate family. He was not about to begin doing so now, and most certainly not with a red-haired, blue-eyed princess who grubbed about in the dirt, saw long-vanished Vikings, and left the scent of honeysuckle lingering behind her on the warm summer air.

He was still breathing in that scent, and enjoying it far too much, when a maid appeared, flushed and wide-eyed with the look of someone caught between excitement and dread, to inform him that he was needed in the house.

CHAPTER III

I BEG YOUR PARDON, MILORD," MISTER JEFFREY Badger said, "but I thought it best to inform you at once."

"Quite right, Mister Badger," Will replied. He stood aside to allow the magistrate to precede him into the study. The room was spacious, lined from floor to ceiling with books, and virtually unchanged since his grandfather's time. On his rare visits to Holyhood, Will found it comfortable.

"Have a seat," he said, gesturing to the wing chairs pulled up in front of the large, leather-topped desk. "May I offer you a drink?"

Mister Badger sat with evident relief. He was a large man, almost as tall as Will himself, with a barrel chest and a broad, beefy face. In his youth, he had served king and country in the Royal Navy, returning after ten years with a sum of money at least equal to all his earnings. Such extraordinary frugality was explained by the pledge he had made to his widowed mother to never let alcohol pass his lips, which, he said, left him with nothing to spend his money on.

Whether this was true or not, it was noted that the magistrate was not a drinking man, but was a figure of considerable industry. Prudent investments in property in and around Holyhood had gained him considerable wealth and led to his appointment as magistrate.

"Lemonade, if you 'ave it," Badger said as he wiped the perspiration from his forehead. Pocketing his handkerchief, he took a deep breath and, for the first time since arriving at Holyhood, appeared to relax a fraction.

"Been a shock, I don't mind tellin' you, but then death by violence always is."

Will took a moment to instruct the footman who came at the summons of the bellpull, then returned his attention to his guest. "No doubt. Would you care to tell me exactly what happened?"

"Dick Smallworthe, the tavern keeper—you know 'im, don't you, milord?"

"I do."

" 'E sent his boy—Pritcher, 'e's called—into the forest to find mushrooms." Badger curled a lip. "Nasty things, those, don't know why Smallworthe would want them, but at any rate, it was the boy who found the body. Came on it in the copse of oak trees about a 'undred feet off the London Road. Near frightened 'im to death, it did."

"Reasonably enough. He brought word of it to you?"

"Eventually. 'E went to Smallworthe first, who had the sense to bring 'im to me. Once I understood what 'e was goin' on about, I rode out with a wagon and brought the body in."

"Where is it now?"

"With Doctor Culpepper, who informed me death was due to the fact that someone cut the fellow's throat, as though I couldn't see that for myself."

Will nodded. "All the same, I assume there will be an inquest, and it's just as well to have Doctor Culpepper's view of the matter. He is, after all, the coroner."

The footman returned, bearing a tray with two glasses of lemonade. Will took both, handed one to Badger, but set his own aside while the magistrate drank thirstily.

When he was done, the magistrate said, "I did a quick check of the fellow's pockets. There was nothin' in them to tell us who 'e might be, but 'e's gentry, for sure, or someone posin' as such."

"Because of his clothing?"

"Right, and 'is 'ands. White and soft, they are."

"It might be useful to make inquiries of the coaching companies and at inns for some distance around here."

"Just what I was thinkin'," Badger said. He was about to go on when he glanced toward the door and promptly stumbled to his feet. "Your ladyship, nice to see you."

"And you, Mister Badger." Sweeping into the room, Lady Constance moved with the straight back and sure gait of a countrywoman who has spent most of her life far from noxious cities and who, not incidentally, would have been mortified to hear herself described as "elderly." She wasted no time addressing her grandson directly. "What is this I hear about a body being found?"

Will stifled a sigh. He had hoped to have a little more time before word got out. "Just how did you hear of it, Grandmother? Mister Badger has only just arrived with the news and I brought him here directly."

The question appeared to surprise the good lady, who regarded the answer as self-evident. "Good heavens, Will, my maid, Tessie, told me right after she got it from Meg, the scullery girl, who had it from Tom and Jack, the footmen, who, likely as not, were loitering about when Mister Badger arrived and heard forthwith what he said to you."

Despite himself, Will smiled. "And this transmission occurred all within the space of—what, ten minutes?"

"Scarcely that," Lady Constance allowed. "Now, is it true?"

"Yes, it is, but there is no reason to concern yourself."

"Of course there is. Was he murdered?"

"Dear lady—" Mister Badger began, only to break off yet again when the lady waved him to silence.

"He was," she declared, "I can see it in both your faces. Do you know, we haven't had a murder hereabouts in well over two decades."

"I thought it must 'ave been that long," Badger said. "And that was a Gypsy, wasn't it, done in by 'is own kind?"

"Which made his death no less grievous," Lady Constance said. With satisfaction, she added, "His killer went to the gallows."

"So will this one," the magistrate assured her. "Assumin' we can ferret 'im out."

"Best do that soon," the lady said. "I do not relish the notion of a murderer running loose amongst us."

"He's hardly likely to be doing that, Grandmother. Since the dead man was a stranger to these parts, it's probable his killer was, too, in which case he will be long gone."

That there was no possibility whatsoever of this being true in no way prevented Will from offering the reassurance. A man did what he had to.

"Perhaps," Lady Constance conceded, "but until I have some certainty of that, I shall caution the staff to stay very close to home. I intend to tell Clio the same. . . . Where is Clio?"

"I'm sure she's fine," Will said quickly. He hated seeing his grandmother distressed, loathed the whole situation and knew there was nothing to be done about it. Far worse might well be coming.

"Have you seen her?"

"Yes . . . I did." That much was true, at least so far as it went. "She was going toward the crypt."

"She can't possibly stay there by herself. Anyone might come upon her and we would never know."

About to point out that the crypt was not only near to but also actually in the house, Will was prevented by his grandmother's swift action. Summoning a footman from the hall just beyond the study, she instructed him to find Clio at once and bring her to join them.

Mister Badger took that opportunity to say his farewells. "Beg your pardon for not stayin' longer, your ladyship, milord, but under the circumstances I think it best to be gettin' back."

"No doubt you are correct," Will said as he walked him to the door. "Kindly keep me informed of any developments."

"Be assured of it, milord."

The footman must have hurried, for he was returning with Clio in tow just as Will and the magistrate emerged from the house. She stopped abruptly, looking from one man to the other. "Is something wrong?"

Her question was directed to Will and he answered it, but not before recalling his manners. "Your Highness, may I present Mister Jeffrey Badger, who is magistrate here? Mister Badger, Her Highness, Princess Clio of Akora."

To give Badger credit, he showed himself to be only moderately flustered. Managing a jerky bow, he stared for a moment at the hand Clio extended—after a surreptitious wipe on the back of her skirt—before grasping it very carefully by the fingertips only and bowing again. He released her at once and took a quick step back.

"Your 'Ighness . . . well, now . . . we did 'ear somethin' down in the village about you bein' 'ere. May I say it's an 'onor, ma'am?"

"Thank you, Mister Badger, that is very kind of you."

"You will hear it all shortly," Will said, cutting short the pleasantries, "so I think it better that I tell you. Mister Badger brought word of the discovery of a body in the forest not far from here."

She stiffened but showed no alarm, only a proper degree of concern. "A body? Someone has died?"

"Been murdered," Badger said. " 'Ad 'is throat cut. But 'ave no fear, ma'am. 'E was a stranger in these parts and likely brought the trouble with 'im."

"I see . . ." She looked again at Will before returning her attention to the magistrate. "When did this occur?"

"Found 'is remains not an hour ago."

"No, I mean when was he killed?"

"Oh, well, as to that, 'ard to say. Doctor Culpepper may 'ave a notion, when 'e's checked him out a bit more."

Badger paused, then added, "Wait now, I just remembered, when we took 'is body up, the ground under it looked dry. Considerin' 'ow 'ard it rained last night, that must mean 'e was done in before the storm arrived."

"So it would seem," Will said. "By the way, I should tell you I was on the London Road last night, pressing for home rather ill-advisedly. The storm took me by surprise while I was yet several miles away."

Mister Badger straightened his shoulders and shot him a very direct look. "I see . . . I also notice you've got a bruise there on your jaw, milord."

Will touched the bruise in question. "A bit of clumsiness on my part. It's possible I passed the body. But, of course, I wouldn't have been aware of anything lying a hundred feet off the road."

"No, of course not . . . You didn't 'appen to see anyone else about, did you, milord?"

"Not a soul. Thank you for calling, Mister Badger."

"Oh, yes, well . . . good day, Your 'Ighness, milord. I'll send word if we learn anything else."

"One moment."

Both men turned. Quietly Clio said, "Had the body been disturbed by animals?"

Will raised a brow at so macabre a question. Badger was considerably more startled. "Ma'am—?"

Patiently she repeated, "Was there evidence animals had time to disturb the body?"

"No, ma'am, not at all. Don't be worryin' about such things. Whoever 'e is, 'e's gone to his Maker as 'ole as a dead man can be."

"I am relieved to hear it, Mister Badger, but my point is that if the body was not disturbed by animals *and* the ground beneath it was indeed dry, it is likely the murder occurred sometime late yesterday evening, just before the rain started. The storm was severe enough that it likely kept scavengers in their dens."

"I 'adn't thought of that," Badger admitted.

"If you would not object, I would very much like to see the place where the body was found."

"I 'ardly think—" the magistrate began.

"It is possible," Clio interjected quickly, "that there may be small, easily overlooked clues that, properly appreciated, could bring us to a better understanding of exactly what occurred."

"Is that so? . . ." The magistrate looked skeptical but not entirely dismissive of the idea. She was, after all, royalty and it was well-known they were always a queer lot, no matter where they hailed from. At any rate, it wasn't really his decision.

"What do you think, milord?" Badger asked, neatly tossing the matter to Will.

He thought it was a damnably poor idea, but one look at Clio was enough to make him reconsider denying permission. She had her chin out the same way she had when he suggested she leave Holyhood. No doubt she anticipated his refusal and was already prepared to contest it.

"Very well," he said, and only just concealed his smile at her surprise. "I will accompany you."

It was difficult to speak through gritted teeth, but Clio managed it. "Indeed. Time being of the essence, I would like to go immediately, my lord."

"I can show you the place," Badger offered.

With no reasonable alternative, Will acquiesced. Mounts were brought and very shortly they rode out, accompanied by the magistrate in his carriage. They went far enough for Will to observe that Clio rode very well.

She sat gracefully in the sidesaddle. Her hair had come loose from the ribbon she had used to confine it and flowed down her back. There was a smattering of freckles across the bridge of her nose. She looked like a lovely woman completely without artifice. Also a very serious one, at least at the moment.

" 'Ere we are," Badger called out when they had reached a spot on the London Road about a mile from Holyhood Manor. The magistrate left his carriage as they dismounted. "We've got to walk now," he said and pointed into the nearby woods. "That way."

Clio hung back a little, looking along the road on both sides before lifting her skirts and going with them into the woods. They were on manor land, amongst trees untouched for centuries. Trunks too wide for a man to get his arms around rose into the sky. The canopy above was such that only filtered light reached the floor of the forest strewn with the dried, crumbling leaves of summers past.

The warmth of the day was left behind as the air cooled rapidly. She shivered and wrapped her arms around herself. Will cast her a swift glance and frowned. Before he could speak, perhaps to reconsider what they were about to do, she went quickly after Badger.

A hundred feet or so from the road, the magistrate stopped. He pointed to a spot between two ancient oaks. "There, that's where we found 'im."

Clio stepped forward carefully. Her eyes scanned the entire area, taking in details both large and small. "How many of you were there?"

"Meself, Smallworthe, who keeps the local tavern, and 'is boy, Pritcher."

"Two men and a boy," Clio murmured. "You carried the body from here?"

"That's right. 'E was a good-sized man and fit, but we managed. Why do you ask?"

She did not answer at once but moved closer,

looking at the spot where the body had lain. Bending down, she touched the leaves, confirming that they were, indeed, dry.

"There is no sign of a body being dragged," she said.

"Like I said, we carried 'im."

"No, I mean dragged by whoever brought him here."

" 'E walked here . . . didn't 'e?" Badger asked.

She stood, brushing off her skirt. "Not unless you believe a dead man can walk. He was not killed here."

"How do you know that?" Will asked quietly. He had not taken his eyes from her. His scrutiny disturbed her, but she was determined not to show it.

She looked to the magistrate. "You said his throat was cut?" At his nod, Clio explained, "There is very little blood here, only a few drops splattered on the leaves the rain did not touch. A man who has had his throat cut bleeds copiously. Therefore, he must have been killed elsewhere." She turned, looking back the way they had come. "The killer had to be a man, and a strong one at that, for he moved alone the body you, Mister Smallworthe, and the boy had difficulty moving together."

"Unless there was more than one killer," Badger suggested.

"That is possible," she acknowledged, "but at the moment, there is no evidence for it. A strong man acting alone adequately explains what can be seen."

"The simplest explanation," Will said softly.

She nodded. "So it would appear." She moved back the way they had come and stopped at the edge of the road. Again, she went slowly, head down, looking.

"What are you seeking?" Will asked.

"Blood, ideally, but I don't expect to find it. The rain will have washed it away. It will also have masked any signs of a struggle."

"Perhaps there was none."

"The dead man was, as Mister Badger said, of good size and fit. Surely he would have fought. Unless he had no warning . . . was truly taken by surprise."

"You think the killer laid in wait, to ambush him?"

"That is possible but not necessarily so. We should not overlook that the killer might have been the intended victim, one who managed to defend himself."

"Self-defense?" Badger asked skeptically. "Why not come forward, then? Why risk being labeled a murderer? If a man owned up to what 'appened and said 'e was only protectin' 'imself, it's likely a jury 'ereabouts would give 'im the benefit of the doubt."

"But a jury would also want to know why those men were on the road late at night with a storm brewing," Clio pointed out. "There are several inns not more than an hour from here, aren't there?"

Will nodded. "You think if their purpose was innocent, they would have put up at an inn and waited for morning?"

"It would seem the simplest explanation." She took

the reins of her horse and was about to mount when Will came up behind her. Before she could dissuade him, he put his hands to her waist and lifted her easily into the saddle.

He released her, but had not moved away when Clio bent over slightly. Her hair fell before her, brushing over Will's shoulder. The shimmering red-gold mass formed a veil, shielding both their faces from view. Very softly, so that Badger could not hear her, she said, "You were on this road last night, milord."

"As you heard me tell Badger."

"And you saw nothing untoward?"

"Nothing."

She straightened, looking down at him from the height of the horse. Her gaze was hard and direct. "I would like to believe that, milord."

"Do you have any reason to do otherwise?"

She continued to stare at him, taking his measure. Wind moved in the branches high above them before she said, "Not yet."

He was still looking at her when she touched her heels to the horse's sides and rode on down the long road.

WHY WAS SHE DOUBTING WILL? HE HAD BEEN on the road near the time when the man must have been killed, late at night and with a storm brewing.

But so close to home, it was understandable that he would want to press on rather than put up anywhere. There was a tear on his sleeve and a bruise on his jaw, but neither meant he had been in a struggle, much less involved in a killing.

He wanted her to leave Holyhood. That, at least, was clear, and the reason he gave—concern for his grandmother—seemed weak. A man who had killed—for whatever reason—might be eager to limit the number of people on hand to wonder what had happened. But there were several hundred people living at Holyhood and in the nearby village. Surely one more—herself—could not make any difference.

She rode on a little farther, ruminating yet also alert to her surroundings. The forest was a pretty place. Under other circumstances, she would have enjoyed it. At a crossroads, Badger took leave of them, proceeding into the village.

Clio and Will turned toward Holyhood. The earl rode beside her, his big chestnut horse gleaming in the dappled sun. Silence drew out between them, broken suddenly when a rabbit darted from the cover of the underbrush and dashed across the road.

Both horses were far too well trained to bolt from it, but Clio's mount startled just a little even as the chestnut took a few quick, eager paces before being brought under control by Will. "Easy fellow," he said softly.

The horse obeyed, settling down again, but not without one last look toward the woods.

Shortly thereafter, the chimneys of Holyhood appeared above the treetops.

The horses' hooves rang in the brick-paved courtyard of the stables. Clio dismounted quickly before Will could move to help her and handed the reins to a groom. After the events of the previous night, the morning, and now the afternoon, she wanted a pot of tea, a hot bath, and a few hours to herself.

What she got was a very large, very strong man standing directly between her and the path back to the house. So directly that when she turned away from the horse and took a step, she bumped right into him.

He steadied her with a hand to her elbow. "Clio . . ."

Determined to ignore the *frisson* of pleasure that ran through her at his touch, she said, "Thank you for your escort, my lord. Now if you will excuse me—" Pointedly, she looked at his hand. He appeared to be no fonder of gloves than she was herself, for his hand was bare. It was also large, tanned, and with long, blunt-tipped fingers.

He stepped back, releasing her, but did not move entirely out of her way. "I regret that I upset you earlier."

She noted that he did not actually withdraw his suggestion that she leave; yet he did seem to be trying to offer some sort of amends.

In turn, she said, "There is no need to apologize for being concerned about your grandmother."

A bit wryly, Will said, "She seems very fond of you."

"As I am of her."

"Even so, I do request that you refrain from wandering about anymore in the middle of the night. At least until this matter is resolved."

As she had no intention whatsoever of going anywhere at night—the crypt was daunting enough now in the full brightness of day—Clio was content to agree.

Having gained her assurances, Will stepped aside and allowed her to proceed. Doing so, she fancied she felt his gaze lingering on her, but did not look back.

CHAPTER IV

WHAT PRECISELY DID YOU SEE?" LADY CONstance inquired. She spoke, not with unseemly eagerness, but with an obvious degree of interest.

"Very little," Clio replied. She had bathed and changed into more suitable clothing before joining Lady Constance in the conservatory. It was, in her opinion, one of the most pleasant parts of Holyhood, being a large, airy room with high windows overlooking the garden. Unlike much of the rest of the house, which in keeping with the wealth and position of the Hollister family was furnished luxuriously, the conservatory was outfitted in a utilitarian fashion with large, sturdy worktables and shelves holding plants, gardening tools, bottles, flower presses, and other equipment.

Lady Constance was in the process of making a lilac wash, excellent for cleaning delicate fabrics. Clio stirred the crushed soapwort leaves and lilac florets as her hostess added a bit more rainwater to the mixture.

"The body had been removed, as you know," Clio said. "The ground where it had lain, was dry; Mister Badger was right about that."

"While you were gone, Tessie brought word that a riderless horse wandered into the village. It carried a saddlebag, but the contents revealed nothing about the identity of the dead man."

Lady Constance's maid continued to be a fount of information, or so it seemed. "Do people normally travel about with nothing whatsoever to identify them?" Clio asked.

"I suppose it depends. Certainly, when I'm out and about here, it would never occur to me that I ought to take anything along that would signify who I am."

"Because everyone here knows you?"

"Yes, but there are many other places where I would be known to at least someone. However, if I were traveling in foreign parts, of course I would have letters of introduction and credit with me."

Clio nodded. "The man appears to be a stranger."

"Then I take it as odd that there was nothing on his

person to identify him and nothing to that end in his saddlebag."

"There might have been, and such documents could have been removed."

"By the killer?" Removing the pot from the heat, Lady Constance set it aside to cool and wiped her hands. "Dear me, what a thought. Bad enough to kill someone, but then to riffle his pockets—"

"Are there any highwaymen operating in the area?" She had heard of such people, who frequented the roads of England in certain locales, preying on travelers.

"Certainly not. Will wouldn't stand for it for a moment and, frankly, neither would I. The population hereabouts is quite law-abiding, which makes this all the more difficult to understand."

Seeking to reassure the older woman, Clio said, "Mister Badger—and Will—are certain to get to the bottom of it."

Lady Constance cast her a glance that could only be described as shrewd. "Do I gather that you and my grandson met before this morning?"

Startled, Clio almost dropped the sieve she was about to use to fill bottles with lilac wash that had already cooled. "What would lead you to believe—?"

"Will is hardly high-nosed, but his manners are impeccable. Yet he did not wait for me to introduce him to you, as would be proper if you had not already met."

With a sigh, Clio said, "I suspect I will never fully

understand the complexities of British etiquette or its pitfalls."

Lady Constance smiled. "Do I take that to mean you are caught out?"

"I did fail to mention that your grandson and I had conversation last night."

At this, her hostess appeared genuinely surprised. "Last night? But it was after ten o'clock when we both retired. I presumed you went right to sleep."

"So I did until the storm woke me. I was concerned about water coming into the crypt and damaging items left exposed there."

"Good Lord, I had no idea you were roaming around the place in the wee hours. Really, Clio, you must not do that again."

Both Hollisters, it seemed, were of one mind in this regard. Ruefully, Clio said, "Be assured I will not. At any rate, I encountered Will—he has requested I call him that, by the way—as he was returning home."

If she had hoped to distract the good lady with that bit of news, she failed. Lady Constance was silent for a moment before she said, "I didn't realize he arrived here in the middle of the night. I thought it was very early this morning."

Sensing the direction of her thoughts, Clio said, "He has already informed Mister Badger of when he was on the road."

"Of course he would do that," the older woman said

quickly. "Pressed on despite the storm, did he? That's very like Will."

"He wasn't in London when we both were there, was he?" She had heard nothing about the presence of the Earl of Hollister. Had he been in London, she thought Lady Constance would have mentioned it.

"I believe he was in Scotland," her hostess said, "but I'm not really sure. Will's comings and goings are his own affair."

She seemed resigned to that, or at least not concerned about it. They continued filling bottles with the lilac wash until all of it was safely stored away. It was mid-afternoon by then, and Clio was thinking of returning to the crypt when Lady Constance said, "I'm going into the village. Would you care to come with me?"

Ordinarily, Clio would have agreed at once, but Will's concern about his grandmother stopped her. Perhaps Lady Constance would do better to rest. But when she suggested as much, the response was entirely predictable.

"Dear child, I am hardly an invalid! If the day comes when I can't put up a bit of lilac wash *and* take a pleasant ride into the village, I shall hardly know myself."

With that settled, Lady Constance gave the bellpull a tug and informed the young footman who appeared that she would require her carriage. It awaited her when, a short time later, the ladies came down the front steps of the manor house.

To Clio's surprise, there was a familiar face in the driver's seat, one she would have expected to see at Hawkforte rather than at Holyhood. "Bolkum . . . is that you?"

The short, broad-shouldered, and very hairy man of indeterminate age tipped his hat and smiled. "It is, indeed, Your Highness. Lady Constance, how d'you do?"

"Well enough," she replied as the footman handed her up into the open carriage. "Where is Trencher?"

Trencher was her usual driver, and, like Bolkum, a man of less than impressive stature, but extremely strong and utterly dependable. The plainspoken of the world might describe both men as "troll-like" and there was a certain truthfulness to that. However, it in no way diminished their natures.

"Slipped an' fell under a bridge, he did," Bolkum replied with a look somewhere between amusement and disgust. "I happened to be visiting, come down for Racing Day, an' he asked me to step in for him, as it were. Hope you ladies don't mind?"

"Not at all," Lady Constance assured him. Looking at him more closely, she added, "I must say, Bolkum, as rarely as I see you, you never seem to change."

"Kind of you to say, my lady," he replied and, having confirmed that Clio was also snugly seated, tapped the reins lightly.

As the carriage set off, Lady Constance leaned her

head a little closer to Clio's and murmured, "He truly does look just the same as he did a quarter-century ago when I first met him at Hawkforte."

As softly, Clio answered, "I seem to remember my cousin David mentioning that Bolkum and another servant have been at Hawkforte forever."

Lady Constance nodded. "The other would be that Mulridge woman. Dour-looking sort, for all that your dear aunts adore her. She rather reminds me of a raven."

"What was that you said, mum?" Bolkum asked over his shoulder. "Having trouble with the ravens hereabouts?"

Lady Constance moved a little way apart from Clio and smiled brightly. "Not at all, Bolkum, no trouble whatsoever. I trust everything is well at Hawkforte?"

"Couldn't be better, mum. Everything's just as it should be. I did hear that wasn't quite the case here, though."

"You are referring to the murder?" Clio asked.

The back of his shaggy head nodded. "If that's what it was. Never wise to be jumping to any conclusions."

As she had brought up the possibility that the killing might have been in self-defense, Clio could hardly disagree.

They continued on into the village along a road lined on both sides by leafy oaks that formed a canopy above their heads. The air smelled of wildflowers, hay, and the nearby sea. The scents and the play of light and shadow through the branches of the trees reminded Clio of Akora, but instead of inspiring a yearning for her home that she was so accustomed to feeling whenever she was away, it made her feel oddly content.

Quietly she said, "This truly is a lovely place."

"I think so," Lady Constance said agreeably.

The carriage drove round a corner of the road and they saw the shore laid out for a mile and more. Waves crashed against a pristine beach gleaming with white sand. Cormorants circled overhead, calling raucously.

The beach was only a mile or so from Holyhood and offered good anchorage. On impulse, Clio asked, "Do you suppose the Vikings landed there?"

"The Vikings?" Lady Constance looked puzzled for a moment but recovered herself quickly. "Oh, the Stolen Bride. They could have. It's quite close to Holyhood, isn't it, and I suppose they would have wanted to make a quick escape."

"Best anchorage in these parts," Bolkum informed them from the driver's seat. He glanced toward the shore. "A smart man—and believe me, the fellow who led those Vikings was a *very* smart man—couldn't have picked a better place."

"You know the story, Bolkum?" Clio asked eagerly. If he did, perhaps he could shed some light on the extraordinary events in the crypt.

He glanced again over his shoulder and grinned. "You could say that. Happened a long time ago, to be sure, but there's still those hereabouts that remember it."

"My late husband was quite interested in the tale," Lady Constance said.

Bolkum nodded. "I remember talking about it with his lordship. It all started here at Holyhood but it ended at Hawkforte, at least so far as it ever did end."

"There really was a bride?" Clio asked. "And she really was stolen?"

"Oh, yes," Bolkum replied. "And he really was a Viking, hell-bent with vengeance on his mind. Changed it, though, once he met her."

"What happened to them?"

"Oh, many things. I could tell you—" Bolkum cleared his throat. "Least, that's the tale. She had a brother, you know. He was lord of Hawkforte and Holyhood both, there being only the one manor back then."

"What did her brother do when she was stolen?"

"Went in search of her, brought her back to Hawkforte, but she didn't stay for long. The Viking came after her. Legend has it two great armies—one Saxon and the other Norse—faced off there, but they didn't fight. They made peace instead."

"I suppose the tale has been much embellished over the years," Lady Constance said, not without regret. The romance of it seemed to appeal to her.

Bolkum shook his head. "No, that's just how it happened. Her niece wrote the story down. It's still there at Hawkforte somewhere."

"I would love to see it," Clio said, and made a mental note to ask David if he knew the whereabouts of such a work. If it existed, it would be extraordinarily rare and valuable beyond price.

Further discussion of the subject was forestalled as they approached the village of Holyhood. To their left was the church built in Tudor times, with the adjacent vicar's residence and graveyard. A little farther on they passed the Seven Swans Tavern, a whitewashed building with twin bow windows in front, framing a battered wooden door. Older even than the church, the tavern was sagging a bit around the eaves.

On such a fair day, benches were set out in front for thirsty drinkers wishing to sun themselves. There were many people about, but very few of them were sitting. Preparations were well under way for Racing Day.

Clio could see tents already set up on the far side of the village near the field where the races would be held. Banners and pennants flew from them. Wonderful smells floated from the brick ovens out behind the bake shop, challenged by equally tempting aromas from the cook fires set up in front of many ordinary shops whose owners made a few extra guineas each year, preparing food to tempt the crowds that assembled for Racing Day.

A very stout woman, her sleeves rolled up to reveal

arms that would not have shamed a blacksmith, was turning roasts of beef over a spit while shouting directions to a gaggle of children. Spotting Lady Constance, she called a greeting.

"Milady, can I tempt you with a bit of this good beef before it all goes down the gullets of strangers?"

Descending from the carriage, Lady Constance did not hesitate but went directly to the woman and smiled at her kindly. "Thank you, Betsy, but no. Once started, I fear I would be hard-pressed to stop, so good is your beef."

Pleased, the woman might have flushed; it was hard to tell, given how ruddy her face was from the fire. She turned her attention to Clio and, when introduced to her, nodded.

"I thought you must be she, Your Highness. Everyone's talkin' 'bout you comin' here. Leastways, they were talkin' 'bout it till that poor feller in the woods came to such misfortune."

Without pausing for breath, or even changing the direction of her gaze, she reached out, seized a small child who was about to make off with a roasted potato from the fire, and said, "Let that cool 'fore you eat it, Pulver."

The child nodded and scampered off, startling a nearby horse in the process. The animal, hitched to a post outside the Seven Swans, shied slightly before settling back down.

As the horses had shied on the road back to Holyhood when the rabbit darted by.

That small event, so ordinary and of no possible consequence, lingered in the back of Clio's mind. She had no idea why, nor did she have any chance to puzzle it out before she saw Will emerge from a gracious little house set near the center of the village. He was accompanied by a young man of medium height with sandy hair, dressed in the manner of a gentleman. They spoke for several minutes before the young man took his leave and returned to the house.

Will walked down the narrow path and out the garden gate, whereupon he saw both ladies.

"You wasted no time seeking out Doctor Culpepper, I see," his grandmother said when he had greeted them. "What is his rendering?"

His gaze on Clio, who affected not to notice, Will said, "Just what is to be expected: death by violence. The perpetrator is unknown and must be sought."

"And the man himself," Clio asked quietly, "is there anything more to tell whom he may be?"

"Not a hint. The working assumption is that he was a stranger come down for Racing Day."

"Don't most people travel to such events with friends?"

"Perhaps he thought he was doing so," Lady Constance suggested. Spying a lady of her own years leaving the milliner's shop on the other side of the street, she picked up her skirts. "I simply must speak with Lady Hillary. Will, do show Clio about the village."

And she was gone, neatly leaving the two of them together.

"She's quite good at that," Will said when they were alone. Or as alone as it was possible to be in the midst of a village in which every man, woman, and child seemed to have found occupation outdoors.

Surprised that he would speak so frankly of his grandmother's matchmaking tendencies, especially to a woman he wanted to be free of, Clio said, "I don't wish to delay you. No doubt you have far more pressing matters to attend to."

He raised a brow. "That sounds like a royal dismissal, Your Highness."

Undeterred, she faced him squarely, "As I recall, it is you who is given to dismissing people."

He had the grace to look just a bit abashed. Not much, to be sure, but even that small degree surprised her. All the same, he recovered smoothly.

"As you are still here, *Clio,* may I suggest we make the best of it? I would enjoy showing you around the village."

Though she could not quite bring herself to believe that, neither could she be so churlish as to refuse the arm he offered. On it, she strolled with him down through the center of the village and along a shady lane fringed by hedgerows and trees.

Cottages were placed to either side, each seemingly

with a garden more superb than the last. Vivid delphiniums and dahlias vied with trellises heavy with roses, lush peony bushes, and here and there, immense stalks of sunflowers, their heads hanging slumberous in the sun.

At the end of the lane stood an ancient thorn tree, its long sprays of branches covered with snowy blossoms. Beneath the thorn was a small, dark pool that reflected the tree against the vivid blue sky. Not for the first time, Clio wished she had some talent for drawing beyond the sketches she made of the objects she found.

The thorn tree was behind them and the field lay directly ahead when a rabbit darted from the underbrush. It was small, brown, and quick, just like the rabbit on the road.

"There seem to be quite a few rabbits around here," she said.

"I suppose." His hand tightened on hers, which rested on his arm. "Is something wrong?"

"Your horse and mine both shied when we encountered a rabbit on the road coming back from where the body was found."

He smiled gently. They stood almost exactly between the shadows of the lane and the brilliant sunlight of the field. "Horses will do that," he said.

"Yes, they will—" Horses would shy at anything that surprised them and even more so if they caught a scent of danger.

A scent . . .

"Nothing untoward happened last night when you were on the road?" she asked.

"I've already told you; nothing."

But by his own accounting, he had passed the spot where the dead man likely lay not very long after being killed. And not very far from where his blood must still have soaked the ground, not yet washed away by the rain.

Seeker had not reacted at all? Smelling blood, as he surely would have, the horse signaled no alarm?

A chill went down her spine.

"Did you know," she said with deliberate calmness, "my mother's family on Akora are horse-breeders. Some of my happiest times have been spent with them. They've taught me a great deal."

Will gave no sign that her sudden change of subject surprised him. He merely nodded. "Did they? What sort of horses do they breed?"

"All sorts, but some are bred for war. You know what is said on Akora, that we prepare for war so as to have peace?"

"A wise policy." They continued walking out into the sunlight, but she did not look at him again. The field lay ahead. Dozens of tents were up and a stand was being erected.

To Clio's eye, it looked like the descriptions she had read of medieval tourneys. She had to remind herself that the man at her side was no chivalric knight. To the contrary, he might be as far from chivalrous as it was possible to get.

"Do you breed horses for war?" she asked.

"Here in England? Yes, of course we do."

"Was Seeker bred for that?"

"Not likely. He was born with a weak leg, although he's overcome it very well. However, I've never even raced him."

"What about hunting?" She assumed that he hunted, for surely all English gentlemen did, but Will surprised her.

"I haven't hunted in years. It bores me."

Yet he seemed a hunter to her—in the agility and grace of his body, which she really shouldn't notice but did anyway, in the keenness of his gaze, and in the sense she had that he was not a man who would shirk from dealing death.

A hunter, not of foxes or deer, but of men?

And of a woman, should it come to that?

The horse had no training for battle, was not even a hunter. Nothing in its experience would have inured it to the smell of blood. And the smell must have been very strong there on the road in the night.

"Your hand is cold," he said, and led her farther away from the shadows.

They lingered a little while longer on the field, observing the preparations for the coming day, before returning to the village and rejoining Lady Constance.

Clio rode back with her in the carriage, while Will stayed behind to talk with Mister Badger.

He arrived at the house shortly after they did and accompanied them in to supper. Lady Constance kept the conversation flowing, but with scant help from either her grandson or her guest. Clio found herself able to think of little else but the man seated across from her and what role, if any, he had in a brutal death. For his part, Will appeared preoccupied.

He excused himself before long, leaving the ladies to their tea. When Clio went up to bed a short time later, the door to his study was closed.

She opened the door to her room, thinking only of her need for a good night's rest, when the thought instantly vanished from her mind.

The room she was stepping into, the very one she had left only a few hours before, was not there. In its place was a room she had never seen before.

CHAPTER V

SHE HAD OPENED THE WRONG DOOR. THAT HAD to be it. Tired as she was, her mind full of the events of the day, she had mistaken another room for her own.

The simplest explanation . . .

Except a quick glance up and down the corridor, lit by lamps in wall sconces, confirmed that she was standing at the door she had been coming in and out of since arriving at Holyhood the previous week.

She should have been looking at a spacious, feminine room with a high ceiling embellished with crown molding; an Aubusson carpet in shades of ivory, rose, and spring green; and a canopy bed hung with silk. And she was, she could see all that.

But the bed was in the wrong place, between the windows rather than facing them, and the bed hangings were green rather than the ivory they should have been. There was still a large chair in front of the fire, but it was a different chair from the one she had sat in just the evening before, and there was no footstool.

Myriad other differences leaped out at her. The dressing table was the one she knew, but the items on it most definitely were not her own. The decorative paper on the walls was wrong. The lamps beside the bed were not those she remembered.

What in heaven's name was happening to her?

Without taking her eyes from the room, she backed away from the door, leaving it open. Abruptly, she twisted around and ran down the corridor. She got only a few yards before stopping in front of another door. Thrusting it open, she peered inside.

Not her room, not anything remotely like it. She was not mistaken. She was not! She had gone to the right room only to find it horribly wrong.

Looking down the corridor, she could still see the door to "her" room looming open. Rather than approach it again, she turned in the opposite direction and walked toward the stairs. Clutching the curving banister, she took each step with care, all too mindful that she was perched on the keen edge of panic.

At the bottom of the stairs, she paused, trying to

decide what to do. Lady Constance had gone to bed, and besides, she wouldn't dream of troubling her hostess with her little . . . lapse. Yes, that was a good way to think of it. Just a little lapse.

If the boundaries of time dissolving and visions of the past appearing real could be considered in such terms.

Of what use could what was happening to her possibly be? Her Aunt Kassandra had seen visions of the future, of obvious help in avoiding a terrible crisis that had been about to descend on Akora. But the past? . . . What good could come from seeing that?

She should think of it in other terms. Visions of the past could be invaluable to her in the work she had chosen for herself. Imagine being able to see what had actually gone on years and even centuries before.

But no gift had ever been granted for personal gain. Down through history, the gifts came only when there was dire need for them.

The past . . . something about the past threatened the present. Was that it? But if it was, how could she possibly hope to discern what such visions meant? In the last twenty-four hours, she had seen—it now seemed—snatches of a world that had existed more than nine hundred years before, and one that could only have existed sometime in the past half-century when the present Holyhood was built.

The crypt and the bedroom, what could the two possibly have in common? What could connect the man and woman she had seen, with whoever had lived in "her" bedroom?

She was still pondering all that when Will stepped into the center hall. For a moment, while yet he was unaware of her, she studied him. He looked torn between anger and frustration, and tired, very tired. Seeing her at the bottom of the steps, he stopped abruptly, his expression becoming guarded.

"Clio . . . is everything all right?"

She nodded automatically. "Yes, of course—"

He came toward her, his stride long and sure. He had taken off his jacket and loosened his collar. The sleeves of his shirt were rolled up. Tall, lean in the hip and broad through chest and shoulder, he reminded her all too well of the statues she had always admired. Ancient statues of gods and men who often appeared indistinguishable, so perfect were they in face and form.

"I thought you had gone to bed," he said.

"I did, but then I didn't. That is—"

"Did you want something?"

No man who looked the way he did should be permitted to ask that question. And he most certainly should not be allowed to do so after provoking suspicions of his own involvement in a terrible crime.

She took a breath, seized hold of what was left of her self-possession, and said, "No . . . yes."

That was a great help. Hurrah for her; she had succeeded in amusing him.

Smiling, Will asked, "Would you like me to guess?" Without waiting for her reply, he said, "Perhaps you came in search of a book."

So that she could lie awake attempting to read in the room that was not hers? "No, I don't think so."

"Not a book. Grandmother may have some of those ladies' journals that seem so popular."

The monthly magazines with elaborate sketches of gowns that fashionable young woman simply must be wearing, advice on matters of the heart, and articles on the management of servants? She hardly thought so.

"Sherry," she said. "I came down for a glass of sherry." If nothing else, it would help her sleep.

He looked suitably surprised, but did not reject the idea out of hand. Instead, he opened the door to his study and stood aside for her to enter.

She did hesitate—he might, after all, be a murderer. But in all honesty, she had trouble entertaining that notion, and besides, she was not about to turn away out of fear. It was bad enough that she fled from her "lapses"; she would not retreat from the challenges of her own time and her own reality.

The study was familiar to her; she had perused the books kept there shortly after arriving at Holyhood and had found many of interest. Now, stepping into the room, she saw that the fire and several lamps were lit.

Papers were spread out over the top of the desk. Will went over to them, gathered them up, and put them away in a leather portfolio. That done, he indicated the pair of wing chairs facing the fire. They matched a similar pair near the desk.

"Please sit down. I'll get your sherry."

She did as he said and was surprised to find the fire pleasant. As she was discovering, English summers could be cool, especially once the sun went down. She was staring into the flames when he returned with a small crystal flute halfway filled with a dark golden liquid.

Taking the chair next to her, he raised the glass he had brought for himself. Not sherry, she saw, but an inch or so of something amber.

"Whiskey," he said in response to her silent inquiry. "I developed a taste for it in Edinburgh."

"What took you there?"

"Business. I have interests in mills in Scotland."

She nodded and sipped the sherry. It was rich and warming. Slowly, the sharpest edges of shock softened a little. "Those are 'factories,' aren't they? I've heard of such places. They're spreading everywhere."

He shrugged. "The factory system is a more efficient means of using resources to produce wealth. Ultimately, it can benefit everyone."

"But I have heard that people are being made to work under terrible conditions, merely to survive."

"Some people are," he corrected quietly. "Not those who work for any business in which I own an interest. It's a difficult battle to convince some that workers who are treated fairly will ultimately be more productive, but it's a battle I intend to win."

She did not doubt him. Will Hollister struck her as the sort of man who would not be readily defeated in any endeavor he undertook. Aware that she was staring at him, she was not prepared when he said quietly, "Would you care to tell me what is troubling you?"

Her hand tightened on the crystal flute. She had thought to try—however she could manage—to draw him out on the subject of the killing and attempt to come to some conclusion, at least in her mind, about his involvement. Yet the temptation to be honest with him, even to confide in him, was startlingly powerful. Not unlike the man himself.

Slowly she said, "Obviously, I am concerned about the man who was killed."

"And who did it?"

Clio nodded. "And why. Why is always important."

"So it is, yet I have the impression there is more behind your present disquiet. The incident in the crypt, perhaps?" When she did not reply, he continued, "My grandmother has the greatest respect for your family. I haven't had the opportunity to get to know any of you, until now, but she has told me stories, some of them rather strange, frankly."

"What sort of stories?" Clio took another sip of the sherry, biding for time as she tried to decide exactly how much to reveal to him. That she was considering revealing anything at all surprised her. She had no reason to trust Will Hollister, yet the temptation to do so was proving surprisingly strong.

"Your grandmother was a cousin of my grandfather's," he said. "Is that right?"

With the benefit of having grown up in a family at once extremely old and intricate in all its many branches, she said promptly, "Yes, it is. You and I are distantly related. We share the same great-great-grandfather."

"According to my grandmother, your mother has a strange gift, I suppose you'd call it. It's hard to credit, but supposedly she can . . . summon the wind?" His tone was frankly skeptical if not outrightly disbelieving.

"*Could* summon it," Clio corrected, aware that so matter-of-fact a response was not likely to be what he had expected.

"You're saying it's true?"

"It was true and they are called 'gifts,' you're right about that, even though they are more often burdens."

He took a swallow of his whiskey and put the glass down on a small round table next to his chair. "May I ask what you are talking about?"

She set aside her own glass, took a breath, and said, "As you know, Hawkforte, Holyhood, and Akora are all intertwined. Hawkforte and Holyhood were once one manor belonging to the same family. Now they belong to different branches of it. A member of that family went to Akora in 1100 A.D. and married an

Akoran princess. Far more recently, in the generation just before us, those ties were further strengthened by the marriages not only of my parents but also of my aunts and uncles."

"The last part I know," Will said, "but genealogy has never been my strong point." Yet he was giving close attention to what she said.

"From what I have learned recently, I believe it's possible that the 'gifts' first appeared right here at Holyhood with the woman known as the Stolen Bride. They've appeared many times since, always in circumstances of great danger."

He leaned forward, resting his arms on his powerful thighs, his hands clasped together as he regarded her. "That's what is troubling you."

His leap of understanding did not surprise her. She already knew he was a highly intelligent man.

"You are concerned about what happened in the crypt," Will went on. "About the man you saw."

"Not just a man," she said quietly, having come to a decision. For better or worse, she would tell him what was happening to her. Perhaps his response would prove instructive, although she was hard-pressed to think how.

"The next day, I also saw a woman. And a short time ago, when I went upstairs, I opened the door of my bedroom, to find it wasn't the room I've been staying in." At that memory, the warmth of the fire and the sherry seemed to fade a little.

"Excuse me?"

She could hardly blame him for being confused; she was herself. "It was the same room in certain ways but things were changed around in it. I think it may have been an earlier version of the room from several decades ago."

"You think you're seeing the past?"

"My Aunt Kassandra saw the future, which had obvious benefits. I'm not sure what I'm seeing or why." Daringly, she added, "But I think this has to do with the man dead in the wood."

"Circumstances of great danger?" He was quoting her.

"No other explanation makes sense to me."

Will stood and walked over to the fire. Leaning against the mantel, he looked at her. "Forgive me for being blunt, but you could be hallucinating. Wouldn't that be a simpler and therefore more likely explanation?"

She had thought of that, frightening though it was. "If I were, it would mean I was undone in my mind, yet I see no evidence of that. I seem to be functioning normally in all other ways." After a moment, she added, "Believe me, I know how strange this is, but given my family's history, the simplest explanation is that the same thing that has happened to other women of my line is happening to me, and for the same reason."

"What do you propose to do about it?"

"I propose to stay at Holyhood and find out what is happening." She looked at him directly, well aware that she was handing him an opportunity to insist she leave. When he remained silent, she said, "You said you wanted me to leave for the sake of your grandmother—"

"But you don't believe that?"

"Your concern appears to be misplaced. Lady Constance is well able to order her own life."

He did not disagree. "Has it occurred to you that perhaps I wanted you to leave for your own sake?"

The flames reached a bubble of sap in one of the burning logs and caused it to explode with a sudden crack.

"My own sake? Do you think I am in danger?" From him perhaps?

Will turned so that the fire etched the hard, pure lines of his face. Looking at her directly, he said, "I did not murder that man."

"I am glad to hear it." Her voice sounded thin, at least to her own ears. She reached for the glass of sherry again and drained it in a single swallow. The liquor burned her throat and brought tears to her eyes. She blinked them away. "At any rate, I cannot leave."

"Why not?"

She stood, smoothing the skirt of the silver-blue muslin gown she had worn to supper. English clothes were very different from those she was accustomed to on Akora, but she thought they had a certain charm.

Hairstyle, however, was another matter. She heartily disliked the current fashion for heavy loops curled over each ear. Instead, she had left her hair down, restrained only by twin pearl clips that held the red-gold strands away from her face.

The clips were a present from her parents on the occasion of her sixteenth birthday, now eight years in the past. She had other jewelry suitable for a princess of Akora, but the clips were among her favorite pieces.

A princess of Akora . . .

"It would be cowardly," she said.

Was there any possibility that he would understand? Courage was bred into her, the gift not only of her parents but also of all the generations before them from both Akora and Holyhood. To betray it would be to betray herself in the most fundamental way possible. Before she would do that, she truly would die.

Will seemed to think better of whatever he was about to say. Instead, he asked, "Would you like another drink?"

She shook her head. "No, thank you. I must go back upstairs."

"To the room that is not yours?"

The reminder of what was happening to her, lifted a corner of the blanket of comfort that had settled over her while she sat and drank sherry in the company of the man who said he was not a murderer.

"Likely, all is back in order now."

"Let's see." He walked over to the door.

"You don't have to—"

"Yes, I do," he interrupted, cutting off her protests. To be fair, they were halfhearted.

Her skirt brushed against his legs as she passed him. Moving up the stairs, she was vividly aware of him directly behind her. Her heartbeat quickened. She told herself it was in anticipation of what she would find when she reached her bedroom, and knew that was not entirely true.

The door to the room stood agape, as she had left it. She walked swiftly down the hall, not giving herself time to think. At the entrance, a soft sigh of relief escaped her. The bed was where it ought to be and hung with ivory silk, not green. Her own belongings were on the dressing table. Everything was as it should be.

"There doesn't seem to be anything amiss," Will said. He shot her a quick glance. "You are certain of what you saw?"

"Absolutely, but I can understand why you would think otherwise." Indeed, what sensible person would not do so, no matter how she tried to explain about the women of her family and their "gifts"? She straightened her shoulders. "Goodnight, Will."

He made no move to go, but instead took her hand in his, lifting it to receive the light, seductive touch of his lips. His head still bent, he met her gaze.

"Sleep well, Clio."

She was a woman of Akora, daughter of a land where passion and sensuality rode on every ray of sunlight and drifted on every moonlit cloud. Her education would not have been considered complete without a thorough—if entirely theoretical—grounding in the art of pleasing men.

But no amount of theory could possibly have prepared her for the impact of the master of Holyhood. The effect the man had on her was really quite unfair.

To right the balance, just a little, she smiled beguilingly. "Pleasant dreams, Will."

CHAPTER VI

WILL STARED AT THAT SMILE AND THE EXquisite mouth that shaped it. His interest in that mouth—and the woman to whom it belonged—had been growing moment to moment as they sat together in the study, but he hadn't actually intended to act on it. He was well accustomed to strong desires and the need to control them lest they control him.

But now all that seemed to have slipped his mind. Hardly aware of what he was doing, he straightened, still holding her hand, and drew Clio to him. She looked startled, which was good, but not resisting, which was better yet.

For all that it was considerably more dangerous.

He laid her hand flat against his chest and stepped toward her. She withdrew; he followed, his hand still covering hers. When her back touched the wall, she stopped abruptly. Bracing both arms on either side of her head, he effectively but gently trapped her.

A gleam of defiance shone in her eyes. "Is this wise?" Only the tiny quaver in her voice revealed that she was not as calm as she wished to appear.

"I've never kissed a princess," he said lightly, the better not to alarm her.

She did not appear to be alarmed. To the contrary, she merely said, "I've never kissed an Englishman."

He raised a brow, wondering at the extent of her experience, then quashed the thought as ungentlemanly. Besides, other matters preoccupied him.

Telling himself he could withdraw any time he chose, he brushed her mouth with his, savoring the soft fullness of her lips. She made a small sound he took to be encouragement. Truth be told, he didn't need any. Again, his mouth touched hers, harder this time, no longer coaxing. Her lips parted just enough to admit the searching tip of his tongue. Hers darted away, then returned, shyly to be sure, but very pleasantly.

No, more than that, far more. Merely being near her in the study had aroused him—she was, after all, an entrancing woman—but suddenly he was shockingly, painfully hard.

He lowered his arms, his fingers brushing the soft curve of her cheek before his hands closed on her, his thumbs pressing just above her navel. Tenderness fled, replaced by driving need.

He tasted her deeply, his mouth slanting over hers, drawing from her the response he demanded. For a moment, she stiffened and raised both hands, pressing against his chest. But in the next instant, her arms slid up around his neck and she kissed him fully.

The woman could kiss, he had to give her that. How exactly she had acquired such expertise he did not wish to consider, if for no other reason than the effort was beyond him. When her small teeth nibbled at his lower lip, the effect was a jolt straight to his groin.

His brain, accommodating thing that it was, cheerfully excused itself, deferring to the merry fellow more than ready to assume control. They were alone in the hallway, her bedroom only a few feet away. A handful of steps, a discreet kick, to close the door behind them, and—

He'd have her naked and under him in no time at all, and then . . .

No, no, that was wrong! She was a guest in his country and under his own roof—

She was fire in his arms, the scent of her skin like sun-warmed honeysuckle filling his breath. He was rock hard, near to bursting, and if he didn't get inside her soon—

What the hell was he doing! She was the daughter of a royal house, already suspicious that he had killed a man, and now he was going to do what—seduce her? His brain might have bowed out, but his instinct for survival was made of stronger stuff.

Survival? Who cared about that? Only the next few minutes mattered. All right, more than a few. A man had his pride. She'd be purring—

For God's sake, he really was mad!

Abruptly, Will pulled away. He was breathing hard, his blood surging, and if he didn't get out of that hallway damn fast—

"My apologies, madam. It seems I underestimated your appeal or perhaps my own susceptibility . . . or both. Not that it matters. Pray, go to bed."

She stared at him uncomprehendingly. Her cheeks were flushed, her mouth swollen. She looked like a woman who belonged on smooth linen, naked, with her legs apart.

"Your . . . susceptibility?" She sounded as though the words threatened to choke her. Never a good sign where the fair sex was concerned and the wise man's signal to withdraw.

"We can discuss this in the morning, if you insist. Goodnight, Clio."

With a hand to her shoulder, he turned her toward her room. The moment she stepped inside, he reached around her for the doorknob, seized it, and closed the door firmly.

Even then, he had to wrench himself away before the temptation to go straight through that door overcame him. Striding down the hallway, he did not slow until he gained his own quarters.

HER BREATHING RAGGED, HER HEART RACING, Clio pressed her fingers to her lips, where the memory of Will's kiss lingered. She had been kissed before by several—not many, just several—Akoran warriors seeking to draw her interest in the time-honored fashion and she had enjoyed the experiences so far as they went, which was, to say, no further.

But this— This was—

Well!

She certainly had not expected this.

Nor had she hoped for it.

She had done nothing to lure Will Hollister into kissing her. Nothing except smile and wish him pleasant dreams. All right, she had done something, but only a very little.

Apparently, the man did not require much in the way of encouragement.

An irrepressible smile spread across her face. She dropped her hand, straightened her shoulders, and tried to compose her features into a semblance of seriousness. A glimpse in the mirror above the dressing table confirmed that she had not succeeded.

This would not do. There were grave matters afoot—the dead man in the wood, the seeming awakening of a "gift" within her. Such was not the time for frivolous self-indulgence.

Except there was nothing at all frivolous about Will Hollister or the way he made her feel.

Every inch of her skin seemed sensitized, so much so that she could scarcely bear the touch of her gown any longer. Removing it, her chemise, and her stockings, she put them away and went through her usual nighttime toilette before extinguishing the lamps.

She left the window curtains open, allowing moonlight to flood the room. The maid had turned down the bed earlier, but now Clio pulled the covers all the way down to the foot, leaving only the sheet in place. Even that felt uncomfortable when she slipped beneath it. After a few moments, she tossed it back and let the cool breeze from the windows wash over her.

The breeze was soothing, but not enough to ease her. Her nipples ached and there was a tight coiling in her lower abdomen that would not lessen. She moved restlessly on the bed.

Her difficulty was obvious and she did not shy from acknowledging it: Will had left her painfully aroused. For the first time in her life, she experienced not merely vague desire but the specific need for one man and one man only.

Fine, let her remember this and be far warier of him.

After a time, cooled by the breeze, she drifted into a light sleep from which she roused sometime in the wee hours of the night to find that she was shivering with cold. Hauling the covers up from the foot of the bed, she huddled under them and waited for dawn to come.

WILL, TOO, WAS AWAKE TO GREET THE DAWN, and in no better a frame of mind than was Clio herself. He'd done some incredibly stupid things in his life—the time he got drunk with David Hawkforte and the two of them damn near fell off the roof of Holyhood sprang to mind, and then there was—

No point dwelling, suffice to say, he obviously had not been in full possession of his faculties the night before. Even before he walked out into the hall to find Clio looking frightened and uncertain. He'd had to find out what was wrong and, of course, it was only right to walk her back to her room.

It was what happened after that that made him doubt his sanity.

Done was done, there was no point dwelling on it. He simply would keep his distance from the lady who was far more dangerous—on several different levels—than he had suspected.

Besides his ill-advised attraction to her, there was the matter of her strange "gift." If there was anything to it—and he was far from convinced of that—the likeliest cause was the danger he himself had brought to Holyhood.

That he deeply regretted the necessity of doing so, went without saying. As did the fact that, to date, nothing was working out as he had intended.

His grandmother was supposed to be in London, where he had understood she intended to remain despite her lack of fondness for the city. She had wanted to take the measure of the new young queen, so she had told him, and besides, Holyhood held too many memories of her dear departed William for her to be truly happy there.

Yet she had returned all the same, and brought Clio with her. An elderly woman, generally predictable and sedate in her behavior, inclined to retire at a reasonable hour, could be kept safely out of the way.

A far younger woman, given to wandering about in the wee hours, was another matter entirely. Especially when she was having strange visions that led her to believe something was very wrong.

Clio would not leave, he realized that now, and she had to be kept from awareness of what was happening. His best hope was to distract her—but how? Will was pondering that as he shaved, dressed, and went downstairs.

It being Racing Day, most of the servants were excused from work, and the few who were on duty would be done as soon as the morning chores were completed. A maid informed him that Lady Constance was breakfasting in her room and would join him shortly. He requested a simple meal and sat down to peruse the paper, but broke off quickly when Clio appeared.

She stepped into the parlor, saw him, and hesitated. For a moment he thought she might withdraw and moved without thinking, to prevent that.

"Good morning," he said, rising, the paper forgotten in his hand.

She was wearing a day dress the same shade of yellow as the daisies in a bowl on the breakfast table. Bands of white lace circled her waist and the bottoms of the short sleeves. She looked young, fresh, and wary.

"Will," she murmured, not taking her eyes from him.

"Come in," he said quickly and, setting the paper aside, drew out a chair for her. "Grandmother will be down shortly."

It was a clever ploy, reassuring her they would not be alone very long. Or perhaps she wasn't the one who needed reassuring. His heart leaped at the sight of her and too easily he remembered the sweetness of her mouth against his.

"I'm not really hungry," she said, but she did take the chair he offered. She also did not look at him again, but kept her eyes straight in front of her.

He resumed his seat. Silence drew out for several

moments. Birds were chirping just beyond the windows. They quieted when a cloud moved across the sun.

"Should I apologize for what happened last night?" Will asked.

She did look at him then, and frowned slightly. "Why would you do that?"

The Englishwomen of his acquaintance would not have needed to ask. They would have been far too occupied assessing the situation and determining how to turn it to their advantage. Perhaps he had been meeting the wrong sort of woman.

"For taking liberties?" he suggested gently.

She unfolded her napkin and smoothed it out on her lap. "You did not take anything that was not given."

And that, it seemed, was that. A maid entered, to inquire as to what Clio would like for breakfast. The young woman was leaving when Lady Constance arrived. She looked from one to the other, smiled and said, "My, it certainly is a lovely day."

Holding out a chair for his grandmother, Will could not help but think that, lovely or not, the day promised to be a long one.

SHE PROBABLY SHOULD HAVE ANSWERED HIM DIFferently. Certainly he seemed to expect some other sort of reply. But really, what was she to say? If he had done something wrong, so had she, and they should both apologize to each other.

From where came this sense that only the man was responsible? Even on Akora—where, heaven knew, men liked to think of themselves as being in control—it was understood that both parties to a romantic encounter were equally responsible for what occurred.

Like as not, she would never understand the English, for all that her mother had been one of them. Not that it mattered. She would be returning to Akora soon, and if she visited England again, it would be rarely.

A sudden twinge of regret darted through her. She looked up at the spreading oak branches above the road the carriage moved along and tried to understand her own feelings.

She would miss England? How could that possibly be? She barely knew it.

"You seem very far away, dear," Lady Constance said beside her. The older woman gestured to the passing scene—the trees and hedgerows, the sky dotted by fluffy white clouds that looked as though they had been painted on, and the sea, visible just as a sliver glimpsed here and there. "It's far too nice a day to be woolgathering."

"I'm sorry, it's just that I didn't sleep particularly well." An understatement; she had drifted between dreams of embarrassing frankness and empty wakefulness.

"I hope you aren't troubled by this business with the dead man. He was a stranger, nothing to do with us. It's likely Will is correct and the odds are that his killer is long gone."

I did not murder that man.

The words surfaced suddenly in Clio's memory: Will Hollister's assertion of innocence.

Murder. He had not said, "I did not *kill* that man."

A distinction without a difference? Perhaps, but it would have occurred to her immediately had she not been so distracted by him.

"Dear—?"

They were coming into the village. Clio roused herself to note that far more people were about than she had seen the previous day. The high street was crowded with carriages, wagons, and single riders, as well as many men and women on foot. All seemed to be streaming toward the field where drums could be heard being loudly beaten, as children dashed about squealing with excitement.

Bolkum, who once again was driving the carriage, maneuvered through the crowd and brought them right to the edge of the field. Hopping down from the driver's seat, he extended a hand to assist first Lady Constance, then Clio.

"Well, now, ladies, here we are, and a fine time to be had by all, I'd say. If I'm not mistaken, his lordship's in the thick of it already."

He gestured toward a crowd of men gathered

around several kegs of ale. Will's head could be seen above the rest. He had gone on before the carriage and appeared to be enjoying himself. Yet it did not escape Clio's notice that despite his seemingly relaxed mood, he was paying close attention to everything going on around him.

"It's so good to see Will spending time with the people here," Lady Constance said as she took Clio's arm. Together, they began walking across the field in the direction of the stands set up beneath a wide awning. "He's been away far too much."

"What keeps him away?" Clio asked. She hoped she didn't sound overly curious, but the truth was, anything to do with Will interested her greatly.

"Business, I suppose. My dear late husband was no spendthrift, but he made some investments that did not work out as well as he would have liked. Will has remedied that and gone quite a bit further. He seems to have an excellent sense of this very changeable age in which we live."

"What does he do when he isn't seeing to business?"

"I don't know," Lady Constance said candidly. "He has a seat in the House of Lords, of course, but I am not aware that he has made any particular use of it. Politics do not seem to engage him. However, he is acquainted with the Prime Minister."

"Is he?" Clio had met Lord Melbourne and was impressed with him. She knew also that the British Prime Minister was well regarded by her family.

"The extent of that acquaintance, I could not say. One hears things . . . But Will had always been rather closemouthed about his dealings."

"Discretion is an admirable quality," Clio observed.

"I should say so. However, there were times when I have thought he carried it a bit too far."

This was the closest Clio had ever heard Lady Constance come to criticizing her beloved grandson, and it hardly seemed serious. They had reached the shaded stands where two seats had been left free for them down in front.

Settling into one of them, Lady Constance observed, "Quite a good turnout, I'm glad to see. Last year it rained. We still had a crowd, but not like this."

"How long has there been a Racing Day here?"

"Centuries, I would think. People come from all over, even down from London. It's very exciting for a place where normally it's unusual to see even one or two people one doesn't know."

"I suppose it would be."

"William and I used to host house parties for Racing Day. We'd bring down a load of people from London and have a wonderful time. Since his death, of course, I haven't done anything of that sort."

"Perhaps you will again one day."

"Perhaps," Lady Constance allowed, but she sounded far from convinced. However, she was not a woman to allow even her private grief to intrude upon the happiness of another.

"I do hope you will enjoy yourself, my dear, and please, don't think you must keep me company every moment. There are a great many activities planned in addition to the horse races. I daresay you might enjoy participating in one or two of them."

"I hadn't realized they were open to participation."

"Oh, most certainly. See over there; I believe they're setting up for one now."

Looking in the direction her hostess indicated, Clio saw several men bringing onto the field what appeared to be planks of wood hammered together and supported in the back by thick wooden braces. The planks were painted with white circles in the form of bull's eyes. When they were in place, weighed down by large rocks added to the braces, one of the men walked off a distance of about thirty feet and, using a small pot of paint a boy held for him, drew a line parallel to the wooden planks. Before he had finished, other men were gathering nearby. Clio could not fail to notice that they all carried axes.

"An axe-throwing contest?" she asked.

Lady Constance nodded. "Do you have such things on Akora?"

"We have contests of every imaginable sort. Women like to test their skills, of course, but nothing seems to please men more than to compete against one another, whether they win or not."

"So I have observed," her hostess said with a smile.

A group of men, boys, and a few women was clustered off to one side, busy assessing the competitors and laying bets, when Will strolled up. He exchanged greetings with the men, shook his head once or twice, then shrugged and joined the rest in line.

"Does he mean to compete?" Clio asked.

"That would seem to be the case." Lady Constance sounded surprised but not at all displeased. She leaned forward eagerly when her grandson's turn came.

He was using a borrowed axe and weighed it carefully in his hand—taking its balance, Clio thought. Several of the men called out advice and encouragement.

Standing at the line, Will planted his feet firmly apart, flexed his knees slightly, and drew back the arm that held the axe. It flew through the air straight and true, spinning until it struck the wooden plank, the head of the axe burying itself precisely in the center of the bull's eye.

A cheer went up from the assembled crowd. Will grinned, walked over to the axe, and freed it. He went back to the line to await his second turn.

"I'm always surprised by the things Will can do," Lady Constance mused. "Neither my own dear William nor our son, Will's father, were interested in such pursuits. Will seems to be something of a throwback to an earlier era."

Apparently so, for shortly thereafter, he landed his second bull's eye. More bets flew fast and furious as the odds turned in favor of the lord of Holyhood. A short time later, the contest was concluded with Will the victor, but only by a narrow margin. Several of the other men were very skilled with an axe, just not quite skilled enough. He accepted the congratulations of the crowd good-humoredly, but refused his winning purse, giving it instead to the vicar, who was clearly well pleased.

Other contests followed, some serious, others not at all. The three-legged race occasioned much hilarity, as did the spitting contest. Stripped to their waists, men wrestled.

Clio pretended not to be disappointed that Will was not amongst them. Her interest revived when she saw archery targets being set up. To her surprise, there were several young women taking up positions in front of them.

"Go on," Lady Constance said kindly. "I'm sure you want to."

"I would not wish to intrude."

"You'll be doing no such thing. They'll be delighted to have you join them."

And so they were when Clio went over, still a little hesitantly, and introduced herself. The young women already knew who she was and quickly recovered from their surprise at meeting royalty so informally.

They were, Clio learned, two sisters and a cousin, all ladies of the landed gentry, with family holdings in the area around Holyhood. They were named Lady Faith,

Lady Hope, and Lady Charity. Once Clio bade them to use her given name, explaining that titles were rarely mentioned on Akora and she was unused to them, they reverted to what she guessed was their normal exuberance and warmth.

"What our mothers were thinking of, we will never know," Hope, the tallest and eldest of the group proclaimed, referring to their own names.

"They pretend not to remember," Faith added.

"We bear it as best we can," Charity said with a grin. She handed Clio her bow and the quiver of arrows. "Do you know how to shoot?"

"I've had some instruction," Clio acknowledged.

"Are you any good?" Hope asked bluntly.

"Passingly, why do you ask?"

"Because we would love for one of us to beat the men," Charity informed her. She tilted her head ever so slightly toward a group of young men standing a little distance away, watching the ladies and nudging one another.

"We've been practicing in secret for months," Faith confided. "And we've improved tremendously, but we fear none of us is quite good enough, at least not yet."

"We would be if we had a good instructor," Hope insisted. "But none of the older women here know a thing about archery, and asking a man to teach us would defeat the purpose."

"If we did win," Charity said, "they'd just say it was because a man taught us."

"Or they'd claim they had gone easier on us," Hope said with a snort. "One of us has to win decisively."

Clio had no wish to discourage them but she felt compelled to say, "You do realize that a man is likely to be able to shoot farther than a woman can?"

"This is a contest for accuracy," Faith said, "not distance. The targets will be fifty feet away."

Fifty feet did not seem very far. Still, Clio had heard enough tales of English bowmen to be hesitant. When she said as much, Hope laughed. "Those fellows"—she indicated the cluster of young men watching them—"aren't bowmen, although I suppose some of their forefathers might have been. They don't even hunt with bows. They merely assume they can best us because we are women."

That was enough for Clio. The assumption of superiority seemed to be a failing common to many young men. Her own dear brother and twin, Andreas, had passed through it.

She had bested Andreas in archery, albeit several years ago. There was nothing to say she couldn't best other young men. Even so, she wished she had the benefit of even a little practice.

Her first shots hit the target, but nowhere near the bull's eye. Faith, Hope, and Charity all did better. At that rate, she would place last amongst the women, much less be able to best very many of the men.

But with her muscles loosened and the habit of old skills returning, her fourth shot came very near the center of the target. So near, that several of the young men took notice and began attending more carefully to their own shots. What had begun as an expected rout the men did not take very seriously, became earnest.

Truth be told, Clio had not been drawn to the physical training the young women of Akora underwent. She would much have preferred to be left with her books and her digs. But her female cousins and friends had drawn her out, encouraging and cajoling, until she actually began to enjoy the experience.

She also discovered that the same intense focus she could bring to unearthing the past was very helpful when it came to placing the tip of an arrow precisely where she wished it to go.

Right in the dead center of the bull's eye.

Again.

A cheer went up from Faith, Hope, and Charity, as well as from several other women who had gathered to watch. For their part, the young men looked chagrined but still unconcerned.

That changed several rounds later when Clio stood third amongst all the competitors, behind two young men—brothers from an outlying farm—whom she suspected did have experience hunting with bows, Hope's assurances not to the contrary.

The women were urging her on and the men were staying mostly silent, apparently at a loss to deal with the situation, when, from the corner of her eye, she saw

Will standing nearby, watching her. Until then, she had not been aware of him. Now she had to drag her attention back to the targets and fight the temptation to look in his direction again.

She did not look, but she was vividly aware of his presence all the same when she took aim, inhaled, sought the stillness within herself that her archery instructor has always claimed was present and—

—amazingly enough, found it. A calm, quiet pool at the center of her being, set apart from all else. In the hush that seemed to spread out from it to every part of her body and beyond, she drew the arrow back, sighted down its shaft, steady . . . steady . . .

Straight and true, the arrow flew to the exact center of the target. A great cheer went up but was cut off quickly when the first of the brothers stepped up to take his shot. He and the brother who followed both landed bull's eyes.

When the totals of all their shots were added up, theirs outstripped Clio, who remained third. She felt a twinge of disappointment, mollified by the knowledge that the two men who had come in ahead of her were genuinely skilled archers.

Faith, Hope, Charity, and the other women who rushed forward to congratulate her were unbridled in their glee. When she reminded them that she had not actually won, they brushed that off as inconsequential.

"You bested every dunderhead but two," Faith said, speaking for them all, "and truth be told, that pair isn't so bad. The rest of them won't soon forget being beaten by a woman."

Far from resenting her performance, those she had beaten seemed overcome by curiosity. They pressed forward to meet the strange being who had accomplished such a feat. Introductions proceeded at far too swift a pace to be burdened by an excess of propriety.

Clio soon found herself conversing with half-a-dozen strapping young men who peppered her with questions about what she thought of Holyhood, whether this or that rumor they had heard about Akora was true, how long she intended to stay, how she had learned to use a bow, and the like. Occupied answering them, she noticed only belatedly that Faith, Hope, Charity, and the other women had drifted—or been pushed—to the side, leaving her alone in the circle of males who made no secret of their admiration.

Being no stranger to that particular phenomenon, and having far too good sense to take it seriously, Clio was enjoying herself when she happened to glance past the attentive circle and notice Will lounging against the side of one of the many stalls offering food and drink. His arms were folded across his chest, his smile was sardonic, and his gaze did not waver.

Having caught her eye, he straightened and walked the short distance across the field to where she stood. The circle of young men parted for him as grass bends before the wind.

"Clio," he said, inclining his head. "The races are

about to start." He held out his hand in a gesture at once commanding and compelling. That it was also entirely natural to him did not escape her notice.

She took his hand and went with him, away from the young men who remained, forgotten, behind her.

CHAPTER VII

"DAMNATION," LADY CONSTANCE MUTTERED. She turned slightly, as though to avert her gaze—or avoid someone else's.

Beside her, Clio broke off watching the horses coming out for the next race. "Is something wrong?"

"Nothing . . . I hope. It's just that I've seen someone I'd rather have not."

Clio took a quick peek in the direction her hostess had been facing but saw nothing of note. Unless . . .

A group of elegantly garbed men and women had arrived on the field. There were a dozen in all and they appeared to be together. The women carried lace parasols to protect their complexions from the sun and fussed over the mud, making a show of lifting their skirts to avoid it while grimacing exaggeratedly. The men appeared little better, affecting a manner Clio could only think of as supercilious. All were dressed far too elaborately for a day in the country.

"Who are they?" she asked.

Beside her, where he had been since they joined Lady Constance in the stands, Will said, "The tall man carrying the cane is Lord Reginald Mawcomber. The blonde woman is his wife, Lady Catherine. The shorter, round fellow is Lord Peter Devereux. His wife is the woman with all the ringlets, Lady Barbara. The rest are the usual cluster of their hangers-on and sycophants including, I see, Sir Morgan Kearns, Lady Catherine's lover; Lady Felicity Cardwell, Devereux's mistress; and—"

"Can that be? They not only are unfaithful but blatant about it?" Although she had heard of such things, she had trouble believing such behavior really occurred.

"I'm afraid so," Lady Constance said. "Of late, there are signs of a turning away from immorality and excess, but if that really is happening, it has yet to affect the likes of our visitors."

"What are they doing here?"

"Come for the races, I suppose. With the social round suspended since the death of the king, that lot would be casting about for amusements. Pity they thought of Holyhood."

"Will they be staying with you?"

Her hostess looked genuinely appalled at the prospect. "Heaven forbid. I cannot abide them. Besides, Reginald is a renowned yachtsman, as he never fails to tell anyone who will listen. He is the proud owner of a cutter said to be outfitted with every luxury. No doubt, they came down on it and are staying on board."

"If that fails to suit them," Will said dryly, "there's always the Seven Swans."

That, at least, was some reassurance, for the more she observed the two couples and their half-dozen friends, the more she hoped to avoid encountering them any more closely. They had the mincing, affected manner of the bored aristocracy, the inheritors of landed wealth who saw no need and made no effort to extend themselves in the least. She had left London in part because to suffer the company of such people day after day and night after night was a torment to be wished only on the very worst of enemies.

And now they were here, or at least some of them were. The bright day, hitherto so enjoyable, dimmed a notch.

"They can't really be avoided, can they?" she asked.

Lady Constance replied, "I fear not. They are bound to see us."

A moment later, they did. There was much pantomiming of delight and amazement on the part of the visitors who wasted no time mounting the stand.

"My dear Lady Constance," ringletted Lady Barbara

exclaimed. She had an artificially high, trilling voice that made Clio wince. "How wonderful to see you! I said to Reggie on the way down, 'I do wonder if Lady Constance will be in residence at Holyhood.' But we had no way of knowing, and now to find you here is such a happy event." She smiled broadly.

"A most welcome occurrence," Lord Reginald agreed. His attention focused on Clio even as he inclined his head to Will. "My lord, I don't believe we have had the pleasure—"

Will made the introductions with a marked lack of enthusiasm. Clio contrived to be polite. She was well schooled in dealing with all manner of people, but the new arrivals tasked her patience, all the more so when they showed themselves inclined to linger.

"Are you enjoying the countryside, Your Highness?" Lady Felicity Cardwell inquired. She was a woman in her late thirties, striving to be taken for a decade younger. In the light of a cloudless day, the rouge on her cheeks stood out harshly.

"I much prefer it to London," Clio replied. Discretion and diplomacy were all well and good, but there were limits to how much of either she would expend on this lot.

Lady Felicity raised her severely-plucked brows in a practiced expression of surprise. "Truly? I cannot imagine why. The countryside can be amusing, I admit, but surely a certain *ennui* sets in before very long."

As the most likely cause of boredom was the continued presence of Lady Felicity and the rest, Clio did not reply directly. Anything she could have said would provide tattle for the bunch, who no doubt would relish reporting to all and sundry that the Princess of Akora was a rustic cow.

With a smile so false it threatened to crack her face, she said, "I do hope you won't stay long enough to be afflicted."

Lady Felicity was still attempting to decipher whether this was an expression of interest in her well-being or her departure when Lady Constance sighed deeply, pressed the back of her hand to her forehead, and murmured, "Oh, dear . . ."

Will was at her side in an instant, steadying her. Clio did the same. "Lady Constance," she asked urgently, "are you all right?"

With a weak smile, her hostess said, "Fine . . . fine . . . I'm afraid the sun has been a bit much for me—"

"We should get you back to the house, Grandmother," Will said firmly. He sketched the barest nod to the others. "You will excuse us."

Whether they would or not was hardly an issue as he and Clio together assisted Lady Constance back to her carriage. Before they reached it, the good lady seemed much revived.

She disengaged herself from them, smoothed her skirts, and sighed again, this time with relief. "Forgive me, but I thought it only a matter of time, and very little of that, before they tried to wangle themselves an invitation to dinner." With a fond glance at Clio, she added, "The lure of a princess would overcome even the tedium of dining with a stodgy old soul such as myself."

"A clever old soul, don't you mean?" Clio said, gladdened that Lady Constance was well and also grateful for her ploy.

Equally pleased, Will said, "I assure you, Grandmother, they will not set foot in Holyhood. If you are truly well, I will take my leave. I promised Mister Badger I'd have a word with him about the inquest."

"When is it to be?" Clio asked as he handed both ladies up into the carriage.

"Tomorrow."

Was it her imagination or did a shadow move behind his eyes just then? She could not be sure and had no chance to study him more closely before he closed the carriage door and gave Bolkum leave to go.

But she did glance over her shoulder, watching as he walked away, and was surprised to see that he appeared to be headed back in the direction of Lord Reginald and the others.

DESPITE HER INSISTENCE THAT SHE WAS PERfectly well, Lady Constance did allow that a rest before dinner would be welcome. She parted from Clio in the center hall of the manor house with the suggestion that she might consider a little lie down for herself.

Although she could scarcely claim to have slept well the previous night, the thought of trying to do so again held no attraction. Instead, Clio went to her room only long enough to change into sturdier clothes, then returned to the crypt.

After hesitating very briefly at the entrance—and telling herself not to be a ninny—she marched down the stone steps and got to work excavating the iron bar. Once freed from the soil, it looked very much like what she had thought it might be: a bar used to secure a door. The verification that the crypt could have been used as a prison reminded her of her strange visions there and brought a prickle of unease to the back of her neck.

She looked up, half-expecting to see the mystery man or woman, but no one appeared. With a small smile of relief, she returned to studying the bar. A short time later, a sound caused her to look up again.

A small boy was sitting cross-legged on the floor of the crypt not ten feet away from her. He was absorbed in arranging a row of toy soldiers.

"Hello." Her voice quavered just a little. She cleared her throat and tried again. "Would you like to help—"

The boy continued setting up the toy soldiers. He did not respond in any way to what she said or show any awareness of her presence.

There was something familiar about him, his eyes, the set of his chin and cheekbones, his hair, and the way he held his head. She looked more closely, scarcely breathing. It couldn't be . . . could it?

"Will—?"

The boy glanced up suddenly. So startled was she that Clio almost fell over backward. He listened for a moment, then frowned and began gathering the soldiers back into the wooden box beside him. When he was done, he jumped up and walked toward the stairs.

Before he reached them, the boy vanished.

Clio straightened up slowly. Her heart was pounding, but not so badly as it had done after the earlier visions. Perhaps she was learning to cope with what was happening to her.

The boy was Will. The moment he moved, she'd known for sure. Will at about nine or ten years of age. How extraordinary. And how strangely wonderful. She had received a quick, tantalizing glimpse of the child he had been. Would a son of his look like that? Would he enjoy playing with toy soldiers?

What would it mean to have such a child of her own?

She would not, could not succumb to such thoughts. Instead, she concentrated on what had just happened and what it might mean.

Four visions of the past, separated by centuries, but coming ever closer to the present. Was that a meaningless coincidence or did it signify something?

Did it mean that the danger, whatever it was, was drawing nearer?

Her head was throbbing. She emerged from the crypt to find the sun slanting westward and realized that she would have to hurry in order to be presentable at dinner.

That she wished to be presentable, and rather more, had nothing whatsoever to do with her anticipation of Will's presence. That was fortunate, as she entered the dining room to find not Will himself but the note he had sent, explaining that he was remaining in the village and would not be home until later.

Lady Constance made a show of unconcern but was quieter than usual and accepted Clio's suggestion that they both retire early with an apologetic smile. "I had a lovely time today," her hostess said, "but I have to admit, such events tire me more than they used to."

"You are more engaged with life than many people I have met decades younger than you," Clio said sincerely.

"Thank you, my dear. May I say, I find your company invigorating. Having you and Will here together—" This time her sigh was filled with wistful yearning.

Clio was discovering that Lady Constance wielded sighs much as the jockeys on view that day had wielded their crops, to prompt in the right direction and discourage lagging. She was also far too sensible to overuse that particular tactic.

An hour later, having selected a book from the study, Clio was in bed. She read for a short time before turning off the lamp. Her eyelids grew heavy as she watched the curtains fluttering gently at the windows, their color washed out by moonlight. Sleep hovered very near when she was startled back to alertness by the sound of a horse's hooves on the flagstone behind the house.

Rising, she tossed off the covers and went swiftly to the tall window. The night was so bright that she could see the long moon shadows cast by the trees. Far out beyond the woods and fields surrounding the manor, she could just hear the muted crash of waves against the shore.

A rider moved along the gravel path behind the house. Man and horse together were a dark silhouette against the moonlit night, but she had no trouble recognizing Will. Tall, broad-shouldered, his back very straight despite the lateness of the day, he handled Seeker with the easy grace of a true horseman. Even as she wondered what had kept him in the village, she could not help but savor the sight of him.

I did not murder that man.

It was, of course, essential that those words prove true. Whatever her personal desires—and those were making themselves very clear even now as she watched him—pride and honor assured she would never allow herself to become committed to a man capable of a vile crime.

Killing, now that was a different matter. The taking of life was always regrettable, to be sure, but there were circumstances under which it was entirely justifiable. So she had been taught since birth in the land rightly known as the Fortress Kingdom. Akora had preserved its sovereignty for thousands of years not only by the kindness of geography that set it apart from the rest of the world, but, just as importantly, by the fierce determination of its people never to be conquered.

All her instincts told her that Will Hollister was an honorable man. But instincts could be wrong, especially when clouded by passion. Torn between the need to believe the best of him and the fear that she could not, she considered going back downstairs on the chance of encountering him. They could talk, she could ask what kept him in the village, perhaps she would gain some greater sense of what lay behind his eyes in those times when they appeared so shuttered.

Perhaps he would kiss her again.

The yellow dress . . . it was pretty and she could put it on quickly. No need to fuss with her hair, just a quick brushing and—

Stop! Who was this temptress urging her to do what reason dismissed as foolish?

Forget reason; there would be plenty of time for that when she was old and gray. In the meantime, live! For once in her life, forget about focusing on every single little detail and see the big, luscious, oh-so-seductive treat just waiting for her to—

Whether or not she was in danger of falling in love with a man who was a murderer was not a *little* detail!

Did she have no faith at all in her own judgment? She *knew* he wasn't a murderer. And if he had killed that man, like as not he had a very good reason.

She *knew* no such thing and if he had killed that man, she had to know why.

Ask him. Go downstairs and ask him.

The yellow dress was over her head and she had her arms into the sleeves when she realized what she was doing and groaned. Inside, the temptress laughed.

Straightening the dress, Clio paused for breath. She couldn't go on arguing with herself, and returning to bed to toss and turn had no appeal. On the other hand, she could go downstairs to look for another book and if she just happened to encounter Will, as she had the night before, they could talk.

Only talk. This time she would be on her guard, mostly against her wayward self, who was not going to lead her into anything she did not want to do.

Absolutely not.

A little perfume wouldn't hurt.

Kene! She snatched her hand from the crystal perfume bottle and marched—not walked—out of the room.

Her pace slowed as she reached the top of the stairs. Will's quarters were in another wing of the house; he might already have gone to bed. She would feel foolish wandering about looking for him.

Of course, if he had retired, there was nothing to stop her from knocking on his door. After all, she only wanted to talk, didn't she?

The sense of being split in two between reason and desire was becoming intolerable. She was about to give up the whole venture and go back to bed, even if that meant sitting up all night reading, when a sudden sound from the vicinity of the center hall brought her up short. Standing in the shadows of the upper landing, she peered down.

Will had not retired for the night. He was coming from his study, shrugging a jacket on as he walked and checking something under the jacket at the small of his back. He reached the front door, opened it, and disappeared outside, closing the door behind him.

The grandfather clock on the landing showed the time to be almost midnight. Will had come to Holyhood in the midnight hour with a dead man on the road he took. Where now was he going? And what was he about?

She had to know. For once, reason and desire were in agreement.

If she took the time to return to her room for a wrap, she would have no idea of which way he had gone. What she had on would have to do. Hurrying down the stairs, she cracked the door open and slipped out.

The night was calm and clear. Moonlight filtering

through the leafy branches of the trees illuminated the gravel path leading along the back of the house. Quick though she had been, there was no sign of Will. At a loss as to which way to turn, she went in the direction of the crypt. Her guess proved correct when, a few minutes later, she caught sight of a dark shape leaving the path and moving off into the woods beyond the house.

Clio hesitated but only briefly. Having gone this far, she was not about to turn back. Her thinly soled shoes, comfortable in the house, were not well suited to hurrying over rough ground, but she managed all the same. Her main concerns were keeping quiet enough to be undetected, while at the same time not losing sight of Will and possibly becoming lost in woods she did not know.

He emerged from the other side of the trees onto a narrow path that ran along the cliff overlooking the sea. Without the concealment of the woods, she was far more likely to be seen if he happened to glance back. Even so, she would have to take the chance.

She had left the trees and was following after him when suddenly, without warning, he was no longer in sight.

"Will? . . ." She spoke without thinking, but softly, restraining herself from calling out. Cautiously, she continued to move along the path. Below, waves crashed against the beach. Large boulders dotted it, looking like slick, black hulks rising up out of the sand. Nearby were the long fishing skiffs riding at anchor. At this hour, only a few crabs moved about, skittering back and forth near the surf.

A cloud moved in front of the moon. The light dimmed suddenly, casting the world into near total darkness. For just an instant, Clio felt the knife-edge of panic stab at her. She was fighting it, determined to remain calm, when panic hardened into full-fledged terror.

She was grabbed from behind, hurled to the ground, and crushed beneath the large, overwhelmingly powerful body of a man.

Frantically, she struck out at her attacker. She had been trained on Akora, taught to defend herself, but truth be told, she had not paid all that much attention to the lessons and had never had the faintest reason to apply them. Until now.

Even so, she knew exactly where to kick him. The problem was that he knew, too, and easily prevented her from doing so. His grip was hard, his strength unrelenting. To her horror, he secured both her wrists in one hand and turned her over onto her back.

Her hair fell over her face, momentarily blinding her. She twisted her head back and forth, still fighting desperately to get free, even as she realized her efforts were futile. A horrible sense of hopelessness rose in her but she could not give up.

She arched her back, trying desperately to throw him off, and stopped only when she heard the harsh growl of his voice at her ear.

"Just what the hell do you think you're doing?" demanded Will.

CHAPTER VIII

WILL, THANK GOD!" CLIO EXCLAIMED. IN AN instant, she went from terror of an unknown assailant to overwhelming relief. That the man pinning her to the ground did not appear inclined to let her up made no difference.

Nor did the fact that she still had no idea why he had left Holyhood at so late an hour or, indeed, if he recently had killed another man. Regardless, she could not deny that, rationally or not, with him she felt profoundly safe.

Will got to his feet and dragged her upright. Just then the moon emerged from behind the cloud and shone directly on his face. Clio swallowed hastily as she confronted the evidence of his anger. She did not believe she had ever seen a man quite so enraged.

"Will—?" She said his name again, but far more tentatively.

He took a breath, another, she saw him struggling for control and uttered a silent prayer that he would achieve it. Slowly he exhaled and loosened his hold on her, but only a little.

"I asked you what you are doing here," he said, his voice low and hard.

The sudden urge for a stroll in the moonlight? A craving to see the sea at night? Sleepwalking? A litany of possible excuses—all lies—flitted across her tongue.

She raised her head and looked at him directly. "Following you."

"Following—? Are you out of your mind?"

"Not to the best of my knowledge, but given what's been happening to me, I suppose we at least have to entertain the possibility."

He closed his eyes for a moment, shook his head as though in a vain effort to clear it, and glared at her. "Do not—*do not*—attempt to make light of this."

"A man who is afraid," her mother had told her in what now seemed a long ago and far simpler time, "will often express that fear as anger, especially if the fear is for a woman he believes has put herself in danger. It is best under such circumstances to be patient and soothing."

With hindsight, Clio wished she had listened more carefully to her mother and her aunts as well, all founts of wisdom on the subject of men. But she had, at least, absorbed some of their excellent advice.

"Of course I won't make light of it," she said, speaking softly. "But you are hurting me and I would appreciate it if you would stop." She was exaggerating, if only a little, but thought that pardonable under the circumstances.

His hands dropped from her like stones. In the instant before his face hardened again, he looked genuinely dismayed. "I'm sorry," he said, "but your being out here right now, doing this, is beyond belief."

"I was worried. Will, please try to understand. I keep seeing the past, and I know it means something bad is happening or will happen. One man is dead already and I can't escape the sense that his death is only the beginning."

He took hold of her arm again but far more gently. Even so, she knew better than to try to pull away. Nor, truth be told, did she wish to do so.

"So you thought," he said, "assuming any thinking at all was involved in this, that the best thing to do was to follow me? Out into the night? Alone, knowing that a killer is loose? All that seemed reasonable to you?"

"It seemed necessary. I'm sorry to have upset you but—"

"No, no 'but'. You have no idea of the position

you've put me in, and I have no time to try to explain it to you."

"Then let me go. I'll return to the house. We can talk about all this in the morning."

"You'll return? I'm supposed to trust you to do that?"

"You can trust me," she said, rather offended that he would suggest otherwise.

"Trust you to be exactly where you should not be, doing exactly what you should not be doing. I knew the moment I set eyes on you that you were trouble. I tried to convince you to leave, but what I should have done was insist. Hell, I should have tossed you out on your ear!"

"Well, if that's the way you feel—" She wasn't the sort of thin-skinned person who took offense easily, but hearing the man who had taken a leading role in her dreams of late speak of her in such terms was undeniably wounding.

"There is no time for this," he said. "You're coming with me."

"I think not."

"Had you thought sooner, neither of us would be in this predicament."

What the hell should he do?

He couldn't let her go; the situation was much too dangerous. Although Clio did not know it, they were far from alone on the seemingly deserted stretch of coastline. Leaving her to her own devices would be akin to depositing an innocent little dove in a circle of hawks, although she'd likely take his head off if he suggested such a comparison.

By the same token, he couldn't keep her with him. That would plunge her into even greater peril.

He had to find some place to leave her safely until he could collect her. Assuming he lived long enough to do so.

And if he didn't—he'd faced that possibility some time ago and did not shirk from it now—it had to be some place she could get out of on her own eventually.

Fortunately, he knew the area well, having explored every inch of it as a boy, and recognized his best—not to say only—option.

"Where are we going?" Clio demanded as they turned away from the path onto a trail that was little more than flattened grass. It ran down a portion of the cliff that angled gently toward the beach, making it possible to descend without having to hold onto bushes or slide over rocks.

"Some place safe, I hope." He scanned the base of the cliff, searching for what he knew had to be there. In the moonlight, the slightly darker streak against the face of the cliff was almost impossible to discern. Anyone who did not know to look for the entrance to a cave could walk right by it without noticing its existence.

Clio did not realize where they were going until

they were almost at the cave entrance. When she did, she balked, digging her heels into the damp sand.

"Why are we going in there?"

With very little time and none of it to waste, Will scooped her up in his arms, ignored her protests, and carried her into the cave. He had to bend to clear the low overhang and once inside, the roof almost brushed his head.

It was pitch-black inside, except for the thin sliver of moonlight that illuminated a small chamber. At the far end was a rock ledge jutting out several feet above the floor of the cave. Will set Clio on it.

Before she could anticipate what he was about to do—and resist—he grasped hold of the bottom of her dress and ripped it off. Not all of it, just the bottom foot or so, but the distinction eluded her.

"What are you doing!" She lashed out, trying to land a blow where it would do the most good—or the least, from his point of view. He was able to block her, but only just. The lady was quick.

"Making sure you don't wander off," he said even as he grabbed hold of both her arms, wound the strip of fabric around them, and secured her to a thick stalagmite rising from the floor of the cave.

"You're out of your mind! You can't do this!"

"I just did. Now listen to me, this is important." When she still railed against him, he shook her lightly. "Listen! In less than an hour, the tide will come in. At its height, it will come into this cave and reach partway up toward this ledge. If you stay right where you are, you won't have a problem. I'll be back for you as soon as I can."

As he spoke, Will stripped off his jacket and draped it around her shoulders. "It may get a little cold in here," he said apologetically.

If he didn't make it back, fishermen would be on the beach come dawn. He had every certainty that she would shout loud enough for them to become aware of her.

"Don't do this, Will! I know you're angry, but—"

"It isn't anger that's driving me," he said truthfully. "I can't send you back to the house alone; you might never make it, and I can't take you with me. This is the safest place for you to be."

"Then don't leave me tied!" She yanked hard at her bonds even as she pleaded with him to release her.

Will's stomach knotted. He hated doing this but could see no alternative. Best he steel himself and be gone. "Try to relax," he said, the words hollow even to his own ears.

"Relax? Relax! You'll pay for this, Will Hollister. I swear I'll . . . I'll—"

Apparently, she couldn't think of anything bad enough to threaten him with. Amused by that—and all too aware he might be going to his death—he leaned over suddenly and kissed her hard.

She struggled for a moment but quickly softened

against him. The swift, darting touch of her tongue against his made him groan. He tore his mouth away.

"Let me go, Will, please. Whatever this is about, we can face it together."

He was tempted, heaven help him, tempted by the passion that flamed between them, but even more by the thought of what it would be like to share this burden with her, to have the benefit of the strength and courage she so obviously possessed.

Before that lure could prove too much, he set her firmly aside and went out into the night.

Clio stared at the gap in the cave wall through which Will disappeared, as a numbing sense of unreality settled over her. Half-expecting to awaken from a strange dream, she tugged again on the strip of cloth securing her to the stalagmite. It remained firmly knotted.

The rock ledge was hard beneath her legs. Will's jacket, draped over her shoulders, was warm and smelled pleasantly of him. Her senses were not deceiving her; he'd really done it. He'd left her tied up in a cave while he went off to do who-knew-what, intending to collect her afterward. He'd neglected only to pat her on the head and tell her to "stay." Or had the kiss been the equivalent of that?

The man definitely did not realize with whom he was dealing.

She puffed out her cheeks in exasperation, got up on her knees, and wiggled closer to the stalagmite. Akora was filled with caves and they were filled with stalagmites, as well as their first cousins, the stalactites that hung from cave ceilings. Both were the deposits of water laden with minerals, and both were often embedded with crystals.

Crystals could have very sharp edges.

She tested the side of the stalagmite with her finger, nodded in satisfaction, and got to work. Sturdy rope would have been hard to cut through. Muslin, even twisted in layers, gave far more readily. It took effort and patience, but she was well accustomed to expending both. Before the largest waves, harbingers of the incoming tide, could do more than spill a thin sheen of water over the cave floor, Clio was free.

Jumping down from the rock ledge, she yanked off her useless shoes. The ribbon of moonlight was moving beyond the gap in the cave wall. In another few minutes, she would not have been able to find her way out.

On the beach, her toes digging into sand still warm from the day, she looked in both directions along the shore. In the direction from which they had come, the beach stretched on as far as she could see. The other way, it ended about fifty yards farther on, where a portion of the cliff face jutted out far into the water.

Back the way she'd come, then. Trudging along the beach, she kept her eyes and ears alert for any sign of Will, while entertaining herself with thoughts of the horrible things she would do to him. One of the advantages of having a brother, and a twin at that, was that she had ample experience dealing with males given to overstepping themselves.

Even so, none of her ways of retaliating against Andreas—frogs in his bed, sour milk in his cup, pepper in his handkerchief—seemed remotely adequate. She would have to invent a truly special vengeance for Will Hollister.

But first she had to find him.

She would also be wise to take the situation very seriously. This was not a game they were playing and she might be walking into genuine danger.

Slowing her pace, she sought the shadows along the cliff wall and moved with greater care. The night air grew cooler and she was glad enough to have Will's jacket. Shivering slightly, she stopped and looked around.

Aside from the almost full moon riding high over the water, there was nothing to be seen. She appeared to be entirely alone on the beach. Alone except for—

Was that a light up ahead, near the base of the cliffs?

Clio approached it gingerly. Near where she saw the light, the cliffs seemed to rise to their highest point, looming over her. No one could have climbed down directly to that location with ropes, and she saw no evidence of such. But a little beyond the light, the cliffs sloped down as they had where she and Will descended to the beach. There they could be navigated easily.

She moved forward again. The light was coming from another of the caves that might very well dot the shoreline. She could not make out if there were any footprints nearby, but even if there were, the incoming tide would wash them away quickly.

Slowly she drew closer to the entrance to the cave. Pressing her back against the cliff wall, she held her breath and listened intently.

There were voices coming from the cave. Men's voices, if she was any judge. One of them might be Will's but she couldn't be sure.

She inched a little nearer and listened again. Two . . . no, three voices and now she did believe one belonged to Will. Unable to resist, she eased her head very carefully around the break in the cave wall and peered inside.

The cave was larger than the one she had left and set higher up on the beach so that the tide did not reach it. Several lanterns were lit, giving her a clear view of what was happening inside.

Will stood to the left, leaning against the cave wall. At first glance, he looked relaxed, but she was not fooled; he was tightly coiled, ready to strike.

At whom?

There were two other men, both facing Will. One was in his twenties, the other looked to be fifty but he might have been younger. They wore the garb of city men—loosely fitted trousers and jackets paired with checked waistcoats and high-collared shirts. The younger had a bowler hat on, the other was bareheaded.

To Clio's eye, they appeared ill at ease in their garments, as though they usually dressed differently. The younger man pulled repeatedly on his collar, while the older kept arching his shoulders. Even so, they looked like a good many of the men she had seen at the Racing Day festivities, come down from London or the surrounding towns, anonymous in their sameness.

"Weren't sure ye was comin'," the younger said, addressing Will. He had a plug of tobacco in his cheek and directed a stream of yellow spittle onto the floor of the cave.

"Any reason why I wouldn't?" Will asked quietly.

"Platt's just sayin' we wasn't sure," the older man said. He smiled, revealing teeth untroubled by hygiene. "Terrible shame 'bout Toffler. Ye're sure it's 'im, o'course?"

"I saw the body myself. It's Toffler." Will looked at the pair. "He had his throat cut."

"Bloody 'ell," Platt muttered.

"Quick death," the older man said. "Not t'be sneered at in this troubled world."

Platt looked unconvinced. "I swear, McManus, ye've ice water fer blood."

"An' a good thing I do. This is no time t'be losin' our 'eads." He turned to Will. "Are ye certain ye've no idea wha' 'appened t'poor Toffler?"

"I know he got his throat cut."

"Aye . . . well, are we all set, then?"

"You know we're not and we won't be until I speak to Umbra."

McManus shook his head. "There's no need fer that. 'E trusts us t'get the job done. All ye 'ave t'do is tell us when an' where."

"He may trust you; I do not. And I do not relish being recruited by a man I have never met face-to-face. I made it clear that he had to come with you."

"An' 'e did," Platt said. "Least 'e's nearby waitin' fer us t'give the signal that all's as it should be."

"Then give it and let's get on with this."

"There's just one problem with that, mate," McManus said. He began walking toward Will, his right hand slipping beneath his jacket.

Behind him, Platt grinned and moved toward the entrance to the cave, blocking it.

Clio pulled back sharply, afraid he would see her, but a moment later she resumed peering around the entrance. What she saw, sent a bolt of fear through her.

McManus had drawn a pistol. He pointed it directly at Will.

" 'Ere's the problem," McManus said. " 'Fore Toffler left London, 'e sent word t'Umbra what 'e'd found out 'bout ye. Toffler was supposed t'kill ye, but looks like 'e bulloxed the job. Ye got 'im instead."

Will shifted slightly away from the wall and moved his feet farther apart. Clio knew exactly what that meant. She had seen warriors in training do it often enough when she and her girlfriends hid in the tall grass watching them.

"I thought that might be the case," Will said. "You understand, there was no telling whether Toffler had tipped the rest of you or not. If not, it was still worth coming, on the chance Umbra would be here."

McManus nodded. "Too bad fer ye that ye bet wrong."

"What are ye wastin' time talkin' to 'im fer?" Platt demanded. "Let's kill 'im an' be done with it. Sooner we get out of 'ere, 'appier I'll be."

McManus shrugged, raised the gun, and took aim.

Clio screamed. A good, rich, bloodcurdling scream. In the midst of it, she hurled herself straight at a very surprised Platt.

Everything seemed to slow down. She saw Will, looking stunned, in the instant before he leaped forward and grabbed McManus's arm. The two men fought for the gun even as Platt rounded on Clio and came straight at her with a knife.

She did exactly what she had been taught to do, dropping to the ground, tucking her head close to her knees and rolling out of harm's way. In an instant, she was back on her feet. Platt was still reacting, turning around to face her.

She didn't hesitate but lifted a large rock from the floor of the cave and threw it straight at him. The rock hit him square in the chest, momentarily knocking the breath from him. Unfortunately, he still held on to the knife and recovered enough to come at her again, roaring in rage.

"Goddamn bitch, ye'll pay fer that!"

She tried to sidestep him and would have made it had her foot not caught on the torn hem of her dress. Stumbling, she was right in the path of the knife when Will let out a roar of rage, slammed his fist into McManus's jaw, and made a long, diving tackle across the cave, to knock Clio out of Platt's reach.

While she was still on the ground, trying to get up, Will reached right past the knife, took hold of Platt, lifted him into the air, and hurtled him straight at McManus.

Grabbing hold of Clio with one hand and seizing a lantern with the other, Will ran for the entrance to the cave. There he stopped, hefted the lantern, and threw it at the two men who had regained their feet and were coming toward them. The lantern struck them both, spilling oil and fire. Instantly, their clothes ignited.

Clio could still hear McManus and Platt screaming as they struggled to put out the flames while she and Will raced down the beach.

"They'll be after us in minutes," Will said as they ran, "and McManus still has the gun." Clio could scarcely breathe, much less talk, but she did manage to nod. She understood what he was telling her; there was no time to try to reach Holyhood, not with an armed man on their heels. Their only hope was the concealed cave.

Running below the rising tide line, their footprints were quickly erased. They reached the cave through water already coming up to Clio's knees. With the moon having moved on, the interior was pitch-dark. Blinded, they splashed through the waves until they reached the ledge. Will boosted her up onto it and followed her quickly.

His jacket had fallen from her during the struggle with Platt. Instinctively she went into Will's arms, grateful for his warmth and strength. His hand stroked her back gently.

"How long do you think we will have to stay here?" she murmured.

Her head resting against his chest, she felt the deep resonance of his voice when he spoke softly. "McManus isn't stupid. He'll send Platt toward Holyhood on the chance we made for there and stay here himself, keeping an eye out."

"He can't do that forever." At least, she sincerely hoped not. While Will's nearness kept the chill at bay, she didn't much relish being trapped as they were.

"He'll be driven off at dawn," Will said, "when the fishermen come. He can't afford to be seen."

"I suppose not." Whether from the shock of what had happened or simply the exhaustion of the long and eventful day, she yawned loudly.

Will shifted slightly and she imagined him looking down at her. Amusement laced his tone. "Am I keeping you awake, Princess?"

"Sorry, it's just that—"

His arms tightened around her. "For God's sake, Clio, you don't have to apologize. You've been through hell."

"I wouldn't go that far, although it certainly has been . . . eventful."

A deep rumble made her cheek vibrate. It took her a moment to realize that Will was laughing.

"Eventful?" he said. "Is that how you'd describe it? When I saw Platt coming at you with that knife—" He broke off and for a moment said nothing at all, at least not with words. The strength of his embrace communicated a great deal.

At length, he said, "Just where did you learn to react the way you did, dropping to the ground and rolling out of the way?"

"Oh, that, it's just normal training."

"What sort of training?"

"The usual, what every girl on Akora learns—literature, mathematics, music, dance, art, sports, self-defense, one or two other things."

"Self-defense? I don't understand. Isn't there a saying about Akora: Where warriors rule and women serve?"

"Oh, yes, that's said." She saw no reason to explain that between what was said and the reality of how people lived, lay a huge gulf.

"But isn't there also some sort of prohibition against any man ever hurting a woman?"

"Most definitely." On that score, there was not an eyelash's difference between word and deed. "It is one of the central tenets by which we all live."

"I see . . . I think. So why do women need to know how to defend themselves?"

She thought about that, having never really done so before. Slowly, she said, "Because it is not good for any group of people to be completely dependent on another—not for food, shelter, or even safety. The women of Akora trust and honor our men, but it is also important for us to have confidence in ourselves as women and to know that we are never helpless, not in any situation."

"Including being tied up and left in a cave for your own safety?"

It was her turn to laugh, if wearily. The warmth of Will's body was causing the last of the tension to seep from her, and making her aware that she had no strength left.

Even so, she managed to say, "If you want to keep someone captive, don't tie her to a stalagmite. They have sharp edges, excellent for cutting."

A deep sigh escaped him. "You are a complicated woman."

"Thank you, I think. Who was Toffler?"

Her abrupt change of topic, done deliberately to take him off guard, rendered him silent. Finally, into the darkness of the cave, Will said, "He was the man whose throat I cut."

CHAPTER IX

THERE, HE'D SAID IT AND NOW HE WOULD DEAL with however she reacted. Lying in the darkness of the cave, holding Clio in his arms, Will struggled against the images of the past hour that still flashed over and over through his mind. Already he suspected that as long as he lived, he would never forget the sight of Platt coming at Clio with a knife. Beside that, nothing else—McManus, the gun, nothing—mattered very much.

Braced for an expression of disgust, if not outright fear, he was unprepared when she asked only, "Why did you kill him?"

Relief flowed through him. A woman of beauty and passion, possessed of a keen mind and the will to use it, no longer seemed a misfortune. "Toffler found out I wasn't what he thought I was: a disgruntled nobleman more concerned with wealth and power than with honor. He followed me to Holyhood, intending to kill me. We fought and I killed him instead."

"Then it was self-defense and you told me the truth when you said you had not murdered him."

He nodded, breathing in the fragrance of her hair close beneath his chin. She was warm and soft in his arms, the shape of her body clearly discernible through the muslin of her dress. It occurred to him that the Princess of Akora did not wear a corset.

This would be an excellent time to concentrate on something—anything—else. But that was damned difficult to do in such confined, not to say private quarters, while holding her. The desire that had flared between them surged again. Will did his best to ignore it, but with little success.

She yawned again and he hoped she would drift into sleep. It was hours yet before they could leave the cave safely. She had to be exhausted after all that had happened. It would be far better for her if she could sleep.

But a moment later, Clio asked, "Who is Umbra? What is all this about?"

He dragged his mind away from tempting thoughts of how they could be occupying themselves. She had a right to know, having almost lost her life because of the answer, but still he hesitated. Only two people beside himself knew the dire threat at work in England in that seemingly bucolic summer of 1837. If Will succeeded in his mission, it was a secret that would never be revealed. But if he refused to tell her, there was a high likelihood she would simply persist in trying to find out for herself. He had already learned the hard way the perils of underestimating the lady.

And then there was the fact that she was a princess, the daughter of a royal house that, like as not, had kept secrets of its own.

Slowly, he said, "I don't know who Umbra is, but I'm trying to find out."

She stirred and sat up a little. The moonlight was gone but faint starlight filtered into the cave. Now that their eyes had adjusted to it, they could see each other, if only dimly.

"What does he matter," she asked, "and what does he have to do with the others—Toffler, Platt, and McManus?"

"They work for him. Umbra, whoever he is, is of interest to the British government, that is to say, to the Prime Minister, Lord Melbourne. Melbourne charged me to discover his identity."

"I didn't realize you worked for Lord Melbourne."

"Not many people do realize that. David Hawkforte knows. In fact, we've done some missions together."

"David undertakes missions for the Prime Minister? I had no notion of that."

"Does it really surprise you?" Will asked. "After all, he is a member of the family known as the Shield of England."

She was silent for a moment, recalling what she had heard over the years of the role the Hawkfortes played in protecting the kingdom they had served for so very long. Quietly she asked, "Are you also part of that shield, Will?"

He pondered his answer for a moment, then said, "Hawkforte does not stand alone."

"Holyhood and Hawkforte were once one, were they not?"

"That is true, and in certain ways, they have remained one. My grandfather, for example, was considered a mild-mannered man, but there were episodes in his life that would surprise those who thought they knew him well."

"Including Lady Constance?"

"I doubt that; I think Grandmother knew. Very little gets past her. At any rate, once Platt and McManus realize they aren't going to find us, they'll have to tell Umbra what has happened."

"Platt said he was somewhere in this area." She gasped softly. "Could he be Mawcomber or Devereux?"

The same thought had occurred to Will but he said only, "It's a possibility. At any rate, I must report to Melbourne that our efforts to ferret out Umbra have failed. He has eluded us this time."

"Why must you find him? What is he doing that merits risking your own life?"

She had come to the crux of it; he could delay no longer. Trust her or not, the die had to be cast.

Will sat up against the rock wall, drawing Clio with him. In the darkness of the cave, with the waves lapping softly beneath them and the air filled with the scent of the sea, he vastly would have preferred to forget the world outside and concentrate only on the woman herself. She enchanted and enticed him, drawing him as no other woman had ever done. He wanted at once to protect and possess her, to keep her safe from all harm and forget all else but her. The first might be possible, assuming the lady herself cooperated. The second definitely was not. Grave matters touching upon nothing less than the future of the kingdom called him to duty.

His arms close around her, as though to shield her from the shock about to strike her, he said, "Umbra, whoever he is, has set in motion a plot to kill the new Queen."

Clio gasped and stiffened against him. "Kill Victoria? Are you serious?"

"I'm afraid so. You understand, you must not speak of this to anyone?"

"Of course not, but what? . . . how? I can scarcely think . . . This is monstrous. Aside from the personal tragedy, it would be terrible for England. Thank heaven Melbourne found out, but how did he do so?"

"There was a previous attempt, of which the Queen is unaware. Toffler was involved and he was identified. A search of his quarters, done surreptitiously, revealed instructions signed with the name 'Umbra.' The script and wording indicated it was written by a man of education, but beyond that we know nothing."

"And Toffler was left free in the hope that he would lead you to his master?"

Will nodded. "I was put in his path and presented as disgruntled, with access to the Queen, a man who could be turned."

"No one who knows you could possibly believe that," she declared stoutly.

Her faith in him pleased Will, but he was swift to correct her. "I've been as effective as I have been, working for England, because I am generally believed to be a man on the lookout for his own advantage, unhindered by much in the way of principles."

"Lady Constance has no such thought of you."

"My grandmother is fiercely loyal and, as I said, very little gets past her. I was contacted directly by Umbra when I let it be known I was privy to the Queen's schedule. Staging the attack at the right time and place would, of course, be critical to its success. The first one failed because guards appeared when they were not expected. At any rate, my only contact with Umbra has been by letter. I insisted on a personal meeting and arranged for it to occur here under the cover of Racing Day."

"Your grandmother deciding to come to Holyhood must have been an unwelcome surprise, and my own presence even more so."

"It was a complication," he acknowledged.

"To put it mildly. Will, what is to be done?"

He settled her more snugly against him, trying to ignore the inevitable effect her closeness had on him and hoping at the same time that she would not become aware of it. "To begin with, we both should get some rest."

"I cannot imagine being able to do so," Clio declared, but a moment later, she yawned again. Her words slurring a little as weariness overtook her, she said, "Do you think Augustus Frederick is behind it?"

"I don't think he's Umbra, if that's what you're asking. The Duke of Sussex is far too much in public view to carry on the secret life of a mastermind plotting to kill a queen, and frankly, I don't believe he has the disposition for it under any circumstances."

"If Victoria dies and does not leave a child to succeed her, Augustus Frederick will become king." The way she spoke the name of the man who, at the moment, was next in line for the throne told Will that Clio was well aware of the duke's reputation.

"That is true," he said. "Clearly there are hopes that the Queen will wed soon and that she will prove fertile. Until then, England will be at risk."

"And possibly not only England." Fatigue wore her down, but her mind still functioned well enough. A generation ago, her beloved Akora had faced the threat of an invasion from England, connived by ambitious men willing to stop at nothing to achieve their ends. That had been prevented, but it was not beyond the realm of possibility that the threat could reemerge should Augustus Frederick take the throne.

"What is that?" Will asked, unsure of what she had said.

But Clio did not reply. The tumultuous events of the day—and night—had finally caught up with her. She slipped into sleep with no awareness that she did so.

But she did, at some deep level, remain aware of the arms that held her and the strong body against which she rested. Her dreams were mere fragments, as though her mind itself was too weary to muster more, but they were also pleasant.

Deep in the night, Clio rose from dreams into the realm between sleep and wakefulness. Not fully awake but no longer asleep, either, at first she did not know where she was. Her head rested against something smooth and hard; she was warm but there were no covers over her; looking down she saw tiny sparkles gleaming against darkness, as though the sky had become inverted and she soared above it.

Something terrible was happening. Awareness of that, although not of what it meant, jolted her to greater wakefulness. The remnants of sleep dissolved, replaced by memory.

McManus and the gun, pointed at Will. Her terror that the next breath would bring the crack of a bullet and the blossom of red over the chest of the man she loved.

Loved? She scarcely knew him.

No, that was not true. She knew his courage, his honor, and his passion. His commitment to duty, his gentle care of his grandmother, his dedication to his country. In calm, uneventful circumstances, years might be needed to learn so much of a man. But since the first moment she looked up from the floor of the crypt and found herself gazing into the eyes of Will Hollister, time itself had careened forward, carrying them both with it. She suspected that he had learned as much about her as she had about him, and that they were in no way strangers to each other.

And from that came love? She admired him; that was without question. She desired him; there was really no point trying to deny that. But love?

If she left this cave and never saw Will Hollister again, she would—

—be devastated. Everything in her rebelled at even the notion of losing him.

She tried to sit up a little, hoping that would clear her brain, but the moment she moved, he tightened his arms around her. Even in his sleep, it seemed he wished to keep her close. That was rather nice.

Out there in the darkness, like as not, McManus lingered. Platt might have given up and rejoined him by now. They would not be able to remain much longer but they would, wherever they went, still be a danger, as would Umbra. It was not impossible that she or Will, or both of them, could die. Indeed, only a few short hours ago death had seemed all but inevitable.

A shiver ran through her, but hard on it came determination. Life offered no guarantees, only opportunities. She had one such now.

What she was contemplating was beyond the pale. Throw caution and propriety to the winds and follow her heart? What would her family say?

Her parents had wed scant months after meeting, and following a courtship that might best be called tumultuous. Clio knew few precise details about it, but she did know that her mother had a tendency to smile whenever she reminisced about those days. And between her parents shone the steady, unmistakable glow of loving passion that illuminated their lives.

The same could be said for her Aunt Kassandra's marriage to Royce Hawkforte, and her Uncle Alex's marriage to Joanna Hawkforte.

As for her cousin Amelia, suffice to say that upon her own return to Akora and her reunion with the man who was about to become her husband, Niels Wolfson, Amelia had confided to Clio that as great as her expectations had been for love's pleasures, they paled before the reality.

In short, she did not come from a family of shrinking violets.

Even so, the circumstances were hardly the height of romance, at least not in its more conventional forms, and besides, the man himself might not be willing.

Now there was a thought. He'd seemed willing enough when he kissed her outside her bedroom door. Of course, he'd then walked away.

Was she truly willing herself to leap from the world of innocence into the realm of passion? She didn't actually know, but lying in his arms on the rock ledge, staring down at the twinkle of reflected starlight in the dark water of the tide, Clio was very tempted to find out.

But just how to go about doing so? Theoretical knowledge was all well and good, but when it came to actual application—

She reached out a hand and very tentatively touched the hard wall of his chest. His skin beneath the linen shirt felt smooth and warm. It emboldened her to go a little further, pressing her palm just above where she could feel the slow, steady beat of his heart.

Will slept on. She didn't know whether to be glad of that or not. Before her courage could desert her, she drew herself up and very lightly kissed his mouth.

Nothing, absolutely nothing.

Well, of course, he must be exhausted, what with the events of the last few hours. Like as not, he wouldn't wake at all. Which made it perfectly safe for her to kiss him again, a little more daringly this time, and while she was about it, stroke the hard muscles of his thigh lying so close to her own.

She had never touched a man in such a manner, although she had imagined doing so. The tips of her fingers tingled where they touched him and she suddenly felt more than merely warm.

Perhaps this wasn't a good idea after all, or perhaps it was the best idea she had ever had. Uncertain which was closer to being true, Clio drew back a little. Or at least she tried to do so. The instant she moved, so did Will. Before she could draw breath, he reversed their positions.

His hands cupping her face, he looked down at her. In the faint light she could see the curve of his mouth. He was smiling. "Am I dreaming?"

Belatedly—and vividly—aware that he was fully aroused, Clio shook her head. "No, I don't think so." Her voice shook just a little.

"Then we're both awake?"

"So it seems."

"And you know what you're doing?"

"Well . . . yes, of course—" This did not seem the optimum time to admit her uncertainty.

He might be awake—he certainly thought he was—but he was also dreaming. There was an air of unreality about the whole encounter—the escape from death, the danger that lurked, but here in the cave nothing seemed truly part of that world. Yet he knew that it was; he could not allow himself to forget that.

He was thirty years old, a man who had known his share of women and perhaps a few extra. He liked women, genuinely enjoyed them, but he had always looked on the fair sex as an excellent source of relaxation and release, nothing more.

Until now. Somewhere in the back of his mind he had known—or more correctly, hoped—that he would meet a woman someday who was different. A woman he could not rise from a bed and forget. A woman who would put her mark on him as surely as he put his on her.

He had just never imagined that when he finally met that woman, it would be in a time of peril, or that she would be a princess from a foreign land wreathed in mystery and myth.

So be it. He could wish the circumstances were different, but he would not take the chance of losing her, or having her change her mind, or any of the other fears that flared within him. He was suddenly vulnerable in a way he had never been before and his instinct was to protect himself.

But also to protect her. A rock ledge in a dark cave? She deserved silk and satin, candles and romance. She deserved to be wooed.

And she would be, the first chance he had. In the meantime, life was too precarious and chances for happiness came too rarely. When they left the cave, the demands of the world would wrench them apart. He had no idea when they would come together again. He resisted that, wished to deny it, but could not. That left only this moment to claim her and leave no doubt in either of their minds to whom she belonged.

He touched her mouth lightly with his own, once, again gauging her response. It was hesitant, but warm and definitely willing. Kissing her repeatedly and deeply, he drew up her skirts, baring her long, slender legs. She trembled at his touch, as soft sounds of pleasure came from her. He sensed no fear in her and no hesitation. Either would have caused him to draw back immediately. Instead, the last slim restraints keeping his passion in check dissolved.

With fervent gratitude for the blessing of shared passion, he turned, taking the roughness of the ledge against his back. She rose above him, her hands braced on his shoulders, straddling him. He heard her gasp when she felt his erection straining against the fabric of his trousers.

"Oh, my . . ." Her voice was breathy, a thread of sound, filled with astonishment.

He laughed faintly, for his breath was tight and his heart pounding. "Easy, sweetheart, I'm too close to the edge now."

"Edge? . . ." She broke off when he cupped the back of her head, drawing her down commandingly to receive the swift plunge of his tongue. At the same time, he reached for the fasteners along the back of her dress.

They were the usual complicated sort women favored. He fumbled with them before giving up and using both hands. She helped, their hands brushing and tangling until finally the dress slipped from her shoulders and pooled around her waist. Beneath it she wore only a silk chemise.

He groaned deeply and dragged the chemise up over her head. It fell discarded on the ledge as his callused palms rubbed over the hard buds of her nipples. She was shivering now, in the grip of passion, and he could feel her heat through his trousers. Feel also when she tugged urgently at his shirt, their mouths still locked, baring his chest.

Slow . . . go slow . . . sprout wings and fly . . . He had about as much chance of either. He hadn't felt like this at fifteen. Hell, he'd never felt like this. Shards of light flared behind his eyes. He was consumed with hunger for her. Only a faint remnant of reason, and the certain knowledge that there would be a morning after, prevented him from ripping off the buttons that secured his trousers. No man wanted to face the world with his . . . Enough. Freeing his erection brought a flicker of relief, but that vanished in a heartbeat.

He slid a hand down into her silk drawers, stroking her. She cried out, her back arching. Carefully he lifted her, easing her down onto him. She was hot, slick, and exquisitely tight. His teeth clenched as he fought the pleasure coiling within him, driving him deeper and deeper into the oblivion of ecstasy.

That shattered abruptly when he breached her innocence. The sudden reminder of the full magnitude of what he—what they—were doing, shocked him enough to restore some faint measure of control. He managed, barely, to hold himself still, trying to give Clio time to adjust. When she began to move against him, he thrust into her slowly and deeply, drawing her with him, her soft cries the goad that drove him to hold on, not to let go, to give her everything and more. The sweet convulsions of her body, when they came, wrung a groan from him and shattered what little was left of his restraint. He clasped her hips, holding her against him, and drove hard into her yet again. His release was a fierce, consciousness-shattering explosion of life force that seemed to go on and on without end.

AN UNKNOWN TIME LATER, CLIO RAISED HER head from its resting place on Will's chest. She lay with her dress bunched around her waist, one hand on his thigh, her fingers brushing that which had lately so enthralled her.

Had she truly done what memory and the lingering resonance of pleasure deep within her body said she had done? Seduced Will Hollister? Whoever would have guessed she could manage it or that she would be so very well seduced in turn?

A soft smile played across her mouth, where she

seemed still to feel his kiss. Even as the rational side of her mind reminded her that she had taken an irrevocable step some might consider utterly wrong, her heart said otherwise. In a cave close by the sea, she had seized a moment of love and glory that came to few lives. Come what may, she would cherish it forever.

But now the tide was turning, the sandy floor of the cave where reflected starlight had twinkled, gleamed darkly as the retreating waves left it exposed. Through the narrow crack in the cliff wall, she could make out the first faint hint of dawn.

Moving carefully, and a shade gingerly, she disentangled herself from Will and attempted to adjust her clothes. The absence of her chemise puzzled her for a moment, until she found it mainly by touch where it lay on the ledge. The fabric was cool against her still-heated skin. She donned it quickly and pulled up the top of her dress. In the confined space, she could not manage to secure the fasteners up the back; they would have to wait.

A faint breeze against her legs led to the discovery that her drawers had not fared as well as the chemise; they were torn. She removed what was left of them and let them go. They drifted onto the cave floor from which the next high tide would claim them, her offering to Venus who, it was said, was borne from the sea. She rather thought the goddess would appreciate the gesture.

Will stirred just then and she was suddenly self-conscious. Tugging down her skirt, she angled her legs over the side of the ledge and jumped down lightly. Her bare feet landed on the soft, wet sand. She stood for a moment, adjusting her garments.

"Clio—?" He sounded like a man just awakening from sleep and not entirely certain of his reception.

She took a breath, smelling the sea, and schooled herself to matter-of-factness. "Down here. The tide is going out again."

A few moments later, he joined her. His clothes appeared in better order than her own and he was running a hand through his hair. He looked rumpled, unshaven, and glorious.

"If you wouldn't mind," she said and turned her back on him, indicating the gap in her dress.

His touch on her bare skin made her inhale sharply as pleasure echoed deep within her. Managing the fasteners as best he could, Will asked, "Clio . . . are you all right?"

"Of course." She had hoped to sound assured and perhaps even sophisticated, but thought she fell short, landing somewhere in the vicinity of bravado.

Clearly, Will was not fooled. He finished fastening her dress, put his hands on her shoulders, and turned her around to face him. Without preamble, without even the tiniest shred of warning, he said, "Clio, marry me."

CHAPTER X

WILL HAD NOT MEANT TO PROPOSE SO ABRUPTLY but he knew exactly what had spurred him. The way Clio was standing with her back to him, ready to walk away as though nothing of any particular importance had occurred, triggered his instinctive need to claim her even more emphatically than he had already done. Even so, in the moments that followed his sudden offer of marriage, it was difficult to know which of them was more surprised.

"Will—" He could see her more clearly now. Her eyes looked very wide, her lips were slightly parted. If he started kissing her again—

—they would never get out of the cave.

Of that, Clio was entirely sure. Of that and nothing else. Never had she expected this, not so abruptly or under such circumstances. Yet she knew perfectly well what she should say.

"I'm honored by your proposal, Will, but I think we should postpone any decision about our own futures until the future of the Queen is secure."

That was what she should say, or words to that effect. That was the sensible, rational, intelligent thing to do.

Or failing that, she could fall back on the tried-and-true query of any woman faced with such a moment: "Why do you want to marry me?"

But that was a question intended to prompt assurances of his undying love and esteem. Such a declaration, if and when it came, should be entirely at his own initiative, not her prodding.

And so, she said what she truly felt. "I would be honored to be your wife, Will, but never would I wish you to think you were tricked into marriage."

Her bluntness took him by surprise, but he rallied quickly. What, after all, was one more surprise on top of all those she had provided already? "You have not trick—"

She pressed her fingers lightly to his lips, stopping him. "I followed you last night, not once but twice, and it is fair to say that I began what happened between us."

"You were a virgin," he said as though that freed her of responsibility, when she knew perfectly well that it did no such thing.

Her hands covering his, she stepped away from him. "And you were wonderful. But morning comes and we must go." Deliberately, she sought to move his attention to other matters. "McManus and Platt are likely fled by now, don't you think?"

Think? He remembered how to do that . . . didn't he? She wouldn't accept his marriage proposal, but she thought he'd been wonderful. He was flattered and confused at the same time.

A horrible possibility occurred to him. "You aren't promised to some Akoran, are you? Because if you are, you have to realize I won't just stand aside and—"

Even in the dim light, he could see her cheeks flush. Calmly and with dignity, she said, "I am promised to no man. If I were, he would command my absolute loyalty."

He was properly corrected and relieved at the same time. That was something, at least, but damned little. He stared at her as the light deepened, trying to discern what was in her mind and, far more importantly, in her heart. Though she returned his gaze, she revealed nothing. The best he could do—and he found it profoundly inadequate—was to say, "This is not settled, Clio. If you expect me to forget what has happened, you are mistaken."

She inclined her head but did not reply. In the back

of his mind he wondered if she was giving him the last word, to mollify him. On that unsettling notion—and the womanly wiles it suggested—he strode from the cave, going ahead of her to make sure the way was clear.

She followed moments later and together they walked up the sloping path to the top of the cliff. He helped her the last bit, offering his hand. She took it and allowed him to assist her onto the road. The morning breeze riffled the red-gold strands of her hair. Her eyes looked even bluer than usual, rivaling the almost cloudless sky. At quick glance, she appeared to be a young lady out for an early stroll. But a keen gaze would see her dishevelment, including the several inches missing from the bottom of her gown.

"Grandmother is an early riser," Will said as they regained the woods and continued on toward the house.

Clio took the reminder for what it was—a warning—and nodded. "I'll use the back stairs." She spoke matter-of-factly but inside, she felt as though a small bird had taken up residence beneath her breasts and was trying to flutter its way out. Her legs barely held her and the stickiness between her thighs was a steady reminder of how very far she had transgressed.

They reached the gravel path and she stopped, aware suddenly that she was barefoot. Will saw her predicament and did not hesitate. He lifted her into his arms and continued on steadily toward the house.

"This is not wise," she said with little conviction. The comfort of his strength was undeniable.

He shrugged the broad shoulders she had clung to in passion's fury, her fingers digging into his warm, taut skin. "If we are seen now, the particulars scarcely matter."

But they were not seen as they reached the back door of the house where he set her down gently. He stood inches above her. His gaze was hooded and his dark brows were drawn together. "Are you certain you're all right?" he asked.

Was she? No, not truly. She was deeply shaken and felt as though the control she had so far managed to exert over herself was about to snap. Even so, she said, "I expect Lady Constance will want to attend the inquest. Unless you object, I would like to go with her."

"I have no objection. Mister Badger and I have discussed the matter and agreed there is no reason for me to be called as a witness."

She understood what he was telling her—he would not be required to perjure himself for the sake of his country.

She was turning toward the door, about to go in. He stopped her with a hand on her arm. As she looked up at him again, he said, "I make my own choices, Clio, and I don't hold anyone but myself responsible for them afterward."

Her breath caught. She teetered between the mad desire to accept what he had so gallantly if impulsively offered and the certain knowledge that this was not the time or place. "Then we are alike, you and I," she said finally and went from him before she could think better of it.

Alone in her room, and knowing the maid would expect her ring at any moment, Clio hurried to strip off her torn dress and bathe quickly in the cold water left over from the night before. That done, she threw a bed gown on over her head and jumped back into the bed she felt as though she had left a lifetime ago.

Leaning back against the pillows, she stretched luxuriantly. Truly, there was nothing like a night spent on a rock ledge—even with such memorable company—to make a woman appreciate her bed. With very little effort, she could go on sinking into it until she sank right back into dreams.

That would not do. Before the urge could get the better of her, she leaned over and tugged the bellpull, summoning the maid.

THE INQUEST INTO THE DEATH OF THE MAN LISTED in Magistrate Badger's records as "unknown" was called in the largest building Holyhood boasted apart from the manor itself, the church. A long, narrow table had been set up in front of the altar. There Mister Badger sat, his plumb face gleaming in the warm air, heated further by the press of so many people gathered together. To his right sat Doctor Culpepper and to his left was the vicar, Doctor Samuel Prescott, a small, innocuous man who on this occasion was functioning as secretary.

Everyone else faced them from the pews, the choir loft, and even along the stairs leading up to the belfry. All the villagers were present, as were a great many outsiders who had come for Racing Day and lingered, drawn by the excitement of violent death.

Only those immediately in front—Clio, Will, and Lady Constance among them—heard Doctor Prescott's muttered aside that were he to achieve so good a turnout of a Sunday, Heaven itself would peal forth in delight.

Lords Mawcomber and Devereux, as well as their ladies and their hangers-on, were also in the front pews. Efforts at conversation were kept mercifully brief, cut short by Mister Badger calling the inquest to order.

"Now, as we 'ave an unknown personage dead by violence," the magistrate informed the crowd, "we are gathered 'ere today to determine the circumstances of 'is death insofar as we are able." Without further ado, he called the first witness. "Pritcher, be a good lad, then, an' come forward—"

The boy who approached the bench was of an age when growth comes in sudden spurts, bringing awkward, ill-controlled limbs, spotty skin, and self-consciousness. Under the combined scrutiny of so many eyes, he blushed fiercely and wrung his cap between his hands.

To his credit, Mister Badger dealt with him gently. "Just tell us what 'appened, lad. No need to be concerned."

The boy cleared his throat, kept his eyes on the magistrate, and said, "Mister Smallworthe sent me after mushrooms in the woods. It bein' a fair day, I was goin' along, doin' wha' he tol' me, when I saw somethin' lyin' up ahead. I went a little closer an' made out it was a man. I called out but he didn't answer, so I crept nearer an' it was then it came t'me he was dead."

Badger nodded encouragingly. "Good, good, what did you do when you realized that?"

"Ran fer Mister Smallworthe, sir."

"You didn't touch anything?"

"Oh, no, sir! Couldn't pay me t'do that. Right disturbin' it was, seein' someone lyin' dead all in a heap t'way he was."

"Did you see anyone else about?"

"No, sir, not a soul. Dead quiet it was in the woods, 'cept fer the birds an' such."

"That's fine, then, Pritcher," Badger said. "Take your seat."

The boy did, with such heartfelt relief as to wring smiles from some of those in the pews. He was followed by his employer, a short man with wide shoulders, thinning black hair brushed forward toward his brow, and a piercing glance whose stiff, high collar appeared to be giving him difficulty. To Clio's eye, he bore a startling resemblance to the late Emperor Napoleon Bonaparte in his declining years, allowing that the emperor had been neither British nor a tavern keeper.

"Tell us what 'appened, Mister Smallworthe," Badger directed, "in yer own words, if you please."

Smallworthe proceeded to do so, making plain that the arrival of Pritcher without the mushrooms he'd been sent to gather and going on about a dead man in the woods was not the sort of thing a man of Mister Smallworthe's standing wished to have happen on that day or any other. All the same, he knew his duty, which was why he'd gone straight to Mister Badger and accompanied the magistrate into the woods, where he'd helped to recover the body. He had no notion who the man was or why he'd come to his end where and how he had. If it was all the same to everyone, he had a business to get back to running.

"In due time, Mister Smallworthe," Badger said when the tavern keeper was done. "We'll 'ear from Doctor Culpepper next."

The physician's evidence was by far the longest and most detailed. The audience hung on every word as he described the slash across the unknown man's throat, which had partially severed his head and caused his life's blood to drain from him "so that he was almost entirely exsanguinated, which is to say, rendered free of blood." In addition, there were several other marks, particularly on the man's hands, that suggested there had been a struggle. Death, when it came, had been swift and there would have been no opportunity to cry out, the fatal blow having also severed the windpipe.

Seated beside Will, Clio reached out a hand and gently covered his. He squeezed her fingers but kept his eyes straight-ahead.

At length, Culpepper was done. Badger gave the audience a moment to recover before he said, "Is there anyone else 'ere present who wishes to testify?"

Will did turn his head then, to glance in the direction of Mawcomber, Devereux, and the others. Neither they nor anyone else spoke.

Badger nodded. He and Culpepper leaned their heads together and conferred. After several moments, the magistrate straightened up and addressed the assembly.

"I expect it's plain to all what we 'ave 'ere. 'Death by violence' is what we came in with an' it's what we've got now. The matter will be referred to the proper authorities an' what will be, will be. What's left for us is to bury the feller—that'll be right after this inquest, by the way—say a prayer for 'im, if you're so inclined, an' put the matter behind us."

Having delivered this eminently sensible advice, he slammed his gavel down on the wooden board and adjourned the proceedings. The audience filed out with a well-satisfied air.

Will, Clio, and Lady Constance were standing in

front of the church, waiting for their carriage to be brought round, when Lady Constance murmured, "Oh, Lord, here they come." She immediately did her best to assume the guise of an elderly woman not in the best of health.

Clio did not have to ask whom she meant. Mawcomber and the rest were descending on them with the clear intent to engage in conversation. They were all as elaborately dressed as they had been the day before, and were—without exception—smirking.

"So amusing when the lower orders try to parrot their betters, don't you think?" Lord Mawcomber inquired as he twirled his cane. He directed his observation to them all, but his gaze focused on Clio. "Tell me, Your Highness, how would such a matter be dealt with on Akora? Would some rustic have the ordering of it?" His manner left no doubt what answer he expected. Clio was pleased to disabuse him.

"Most likely," she replied as pleasantly as she could manage, which was to say not very pleasantly at all. She had encountered Mawcomber's type before—arrogant, supercilious, amoral—but was always struck afresh by how unpleasant such people were. "At least half the population of Akora is made up of country people, including two of my beloved grandparents. The 'rustics,' as I suppose you would call them, do all sorts of things—grow food, raise animals, serve in the military, help to run the government, to name a few."

"Really?" Lady Barbara affected the high-pitched

drawl popular among certain elements of the nobility. "How terribly exotic. I had the great honor of meeting your parents a few weeks ago. Your father—the Vanax, he's called?—is such an impressive man, so obviously born to rule. I would think people would simply realize that and let him do it."

Clio nearly bit her tongue, thinking what her father would say in response to such a blindingly ignorant remark. He was the kindest and most patient of men, at least where she and her mother were concerned, but on rare occasion his speech could be downright earthy.

"My father does not rule," she said at length when she trusted herself to speak. "The Vanax serves Akora and its people."

"Serves?" Lord Devereux looked startled by the mere thought. "What an extraordinary notion." Despite the high heels augmenting his boots, he stood inches shorter than Clio and had to look up at her as he said, "Of course, you don't mean it literally." His knowing look suggested he, for one, was far too well versed in the ways of the world to be taken in by such a pretty statement, however much he understood it was politic of her to say it.

"Actually, I believe Her Highness does mean it," interjected the tall, well-built man whose smooth features would have appeared bland were it not for the restless energy evident in his eyes. Sir Morgan Kearns might be Lady Catherine's lover, but he did not hesitate to look at Clio with unfettered admiration.

She frowned as much from instinctive distaste as the desire to disabuse him of any notion he might entertain in her direction. The man did not precisely make her skin crawl, but he came very close.

"Akora is an exceptional place, is it not, Your Highness?" he inquired.

Before she could reply, Will said dryly, "Unless you're planning to attend the burial, I think you'll find there's little more excitement to be had here at Holyhood."

Lady Barbara pursed her lips and sighed. "I daresay you're right, my lord. We should return to London. Even under the present gloomy circumstances, it remains . . . well, London." She looked brightly at the others, as though encouraging their agreement.

Her husband, Lord Devereux, ignored her, rather pointedly to Clio's eyes. "Are you returning to London, Your Highness?" he asked.

"My plans are as yet uncertain." That was true only in the broadest sense, but she preferred to leave the impression that London was not on her immediate horizon. Heaven forbid that one or all of them should think to call on her once she returned to the city.

Mercifully, Bolkum arrived just then with the carriage and they were able to make their farewells. They were on the road when Will said, "I will be returning to London this afternoon."

Lady Constance looked regretful but not surprised.

"I had hoped you could stay longer. However, of course, I understand."

Clio had anticipated the announcement but was startled all the same. She had thought he would find some way to explain to his grandmother why Clio would be returning to London as well.

He did realize she would be doing that, didn't he? Surely he didn't imagine she would remain at Holyhood while such dire matters were afoot?

Yet he said nothing of her own departure and did not respond when Clio looked at him quizzically. No further mention of London was made during the remainder of the ride back to the house. Scarcely had they arrived and left the carriage, than Lady Constance went off to the conservatory, leaving Will and Clio alone in the hall.

Before either could speak, a footman appeared, saw them, and quickly withdrew again. The reminder that there was no real privacy where they were, was enough to prompt Will to open the door to the study and stand aside for Clio to enter.

She did so, but only a little way. Her hat, a pretty confection of soft green silk and straw that framed her face, was making her head ache. She unfastened the ribbons holding it in place and set it aside.

Watching her, Will said, "I will be back as quickly as possible."

"I had thought to go with you."

The very idea seemed to surprise him. "It is far too

dangerous. Bad enough that you were involved last night. I cannot countenance any further risk to you."

"But I can help. The visions I have been having—"

"The visions, yes. I understand you believe they have some part in all of this, but Clio, be reasonable; there is no connection between anything you think you've seen of the past and what is happening now."

"Not so far, but that may change, and when it does—"

"If it does," he interrupted, "it makes no difference. The danger would remain the same. I cannot allow you to go."

"Allow me—?" She spoke softly but her emotions were of an entirely different order. Allow her? She was twenty-four years old and accustomed to making decisions for herself. Did he imagine she was a child, or one of those seemingly meek and pliant women who sought only to please?

If he did, he had a very grave misunderstanding of her.

She was pondering that—and all it meant—when he asked suddenly, "Have you thought any more about what I said?"

"About us?" She looked away, instinctively seeking to shield the turmoil of her thoughts. No doubt he believed he was acting from the best of motives, but she could not accept that. Quietly she said, "This isn't the time."

He went to her but stopped several feet away. Keeping his hands clenched behind his back, Will said, "Perhaps not, but I would have no misapprehension between us, Clio. I intend to make you my wife."

She cast him a quick, slanting look before averting her gaze. "Do you? I daresay I shall have something to say about that."

"Of course you will, provided what you have to say is 'yes.' "

That sounded well enough, but he knew perfectly well it was mainly bluster; her family would not force her into an unwanted marriage. There was always kidnapping. At Holyhood, home of the Stolen Bride, it could be considered a tradition.

Astonished that he, a hitherto sensible man, would contemplate such an action, Will made a strategic retreat. He went up to his rooms to pack and write a letter. It was short and to the point: In the event of his death, and should Princess Clio Atreides be delivered of a child, he, Will Hollister, claimed that child as his own and bequeathed to him or her his fortune. Happily, that fortune was unentailed and he could do with it as he liked. However, he could not bequeath his titles, not in the absence of matrimony. Even so, he had the consolation of knowing that a child of his making would be well provided for.

He left the letter, signed and sealed, in the drawer of the bedroom desk. A short time later, having taken leave of Lady Constance, he rode out from Holyhood and did not look back.

Clio watched him from the window of her room. When he was out of sight, she let the curtain drop, smoothed her hair and went downstairs to the conservatory. There she found her hostess, placing rose petals in a press in order to extract their oils.

"I thought I would leave for London in the morning," Clio said.

CHAPTER XI

LADY CONSTANCE TURNED THE SCREW ON THE press a little tighter, wiped her hands and said, "*We* shall leave, my dear. I have no notion what my grandson is up to and I don't expect you to tell me, but on the slim chance that he could require assistance, I prefer not to be so far removed."

Clio began to reply, found she could not, and contented herself with a hug that made Lady Constance laugh and embrace her in turn. The two women stood for a moment in the warm, fragrant air of the conservatory before parting to attend to their separate tasks—

Lady Constance to order her household for her departure and Clio to make her own preparations.

In mid-afternoon she returned to the crypt, not with the intention of continuing to dig, but drawn there by the thought that she might gain some further insight into the "gift" that had overtaken her and what it was leading her toward.

Outside, the roses hung heavy in the heat of high summer, their blossoms bent submissively before the slipping away of their days. Bees droned about them, ever busy. Passing from the glare of sunlight into the gloom of the crypt, Clio had to pause to let her eyes adjust. When they had done so, she moved slowly down the worn stone steps. By the time she reached the bottom, the air had cooled significantly. It brought relief to her heated skin and roused her from the weariness that threatened to overtake her.

She sat on one of the lower steps and looked around slowly. Aside from the evidence of her own digging in the dirt floor, there was nothing of note to see. No emanations of the past appeared to challenge her. Perhaps that was just as well. The present was proving daunting enough.

She rested her elbows on her knees and closed her eyes. It was very quiet in the crypt, so quiet it seemed she could—finally—hear her own thoughts.

Why had she done what she had in the cave, yielding to passion and impulse, as she had never come even close to doing before? Was it merely the shock of the struggle with McManus and Platt, and the realization of how very precarious life could be, that had prompted her to act so out of character? Or did she truly love Will Hollister, as she believed, and had simply seized the chance to fulfill that love?

Even if love was real, the thought of marriage was momentous, especially as she was just beginning to realize that it meant the loss of independence.

A deep sigh escaped her. The cherished daughter of loving parents, she had been allowed to find her own path to a very large degree ever since it became evident at a young age that she needed to do so. In the process, she had created a life for herself that, while not precisely exciting, was satisfying. Or at least it had been.

If she married Will, she would have to leave her beloved Akora. That itself was daunting, but to commit herself—more than she had already done—to a man who, whatever her feelings for him, was still largely a stranger? Could she truly do that? The very strength of his nature that drew her also hinted nothing would be as simple between them as she had assumed.

She wanted Will to be certain of his own feelings, but the plain truth was that she needed to be certain of her own as well.

After a few minutes, Clio stood, took a last look around the crypt, and climbed back up the stairs. The irony of her situation did not escape her. Just when the past no longer held quite the allure it had done, visions from it were warning her of danger and propelling her forward into an unknown future.

One that could not be postponed. It waited for her at the end of the long and winding road that led, two days later, to London.

THE COACHING INNS ARE MUCH IMPROVED FROM when I was a girl," Lady Constance said. They were approaching the city from the south along the Arundel Road. Off to the left, beyond the fields and farms that still encroached very close to the southern part of the city, Clio could make out the gleaming curve of the River Thames. As usual, it was clogged with all manner of boats, from tiny skiffs to barges, ferries, and the largest sloops able to pass beneath the bridges. The Thames remained the lifeline of London although the newer roads were taking on ever-greater importance. There were even some who said the "railroad" inaugurated the previous year to run between London and Greenwich would one day carry more freight than either the roads or the river.

"Then, the inns were to be avoided unless one was absolutely certain of what one would find," Lady Constance went on. Although she had permitted no indulgence of her age on a journey that might have tired a younger person, she looked very fit and in good humor. "Why, I remember one time I was traveling with my dear parents, going to Bath, I believe, when we took shelter from a frightful storm at an inn where we had never stayed before. The mice were the size of rats and as for the rats themselves . . . let us only say no cat was foolish enough to assault them."

"A memorable experience, no doubt," Clio said with a smile. Thanks to Lady Constance's good company, she had enjoyed the trip, but was glad to see it coming to an end. Or so she told herself. The part of her that would be happy to continue on and on, traveling from inn to inn without ever really getting anywhere was understandable enough, but cowardly.

"No doubt your family will be delighted by your return," Lady Constance said, "if a bit surprised."

"No doubt," Clio agreed, mulling over exactly what she would say to them. She had promised Will that she would not divulge anything about the threat to Queen Victoria, and that was a pledge she would keep without reservation. But her parents would require some explanation for her sudden reappearance.

Or so she thought. As it turned out, nothing was quite as she expected.

Drawing up in front of the gracious Mayfair mansion, set behind a high stone wall and wrought-iron gates, Clio was surprised to see wagons piled with crates, boxes, and barrels.

"What's all this, do you suppose?" Lady Constance asked. She had expressed a wish to greet Clio's parents, with whom she had been friends for years, before proceeding on to her own nearby residence.

"I have no idea," Clio said as Bolkum handed her down from the carriage. Above their heads fluttered the banner of Akora, emblazoned with the bull's head insignia of the house of Atreides. Guards, bare-chested above the traditional pleated white kilt worn by Akoran warriors, were on duty in front of the house. Seeing her, one of them turned and went inside, no doubt to report her arrival.

"Looks as though someone's departin'," Bolkum said as he also assisted Lady Constance. A groom appeared, to take the horses and carriage round to the stables where the animals would be given a good drink and allowed to rest.

More than merely someone, Clio thought, observing the quantity of goods rolling by. She knew that whenever her parents were in England, they took the opportunity to acquire new books, tools, weapons, and the like to take back with them to Akora. Anything that proved useful was then imported into the country, or improved upon and produced there.

The practice had served Akora well through the three thousand years of its history, assuring that it did not fall behind the rest of the world even while remaining largely apart from it. More recently, under the guidance of her father, Akora had emerged somewhat from its solitude. Even so, the Fortress Kingdom remained ever vigilant to danger from the outside. Its warriors, including those attending the family in England, were renowned for their training, discipline, and ferocity. Chief among them was the Vanax himself, Clio's father, the man who came down the broad steps of the house to greet her.

"Daughter, Lady Constance, welcome. Clio, did you receive your mother's note so quickly?"

Clio hugged her father, stepped back and looked at the tall man whose ebony hair was lightly sprinkled with silver. Unlike the guards, he was dressed as an English gentleman, suggesting he had either just come from or was on his way to a meeting. In his leisure time, Atreus preferred the far more comfortable Akoran mode of dress and could usually be found in a kilt or tunic.

"Mother's note?" Clio repeated. "No, I didn't receive anything."

Her father frowned slightly. "Then how did you come to be—?"

"Never mind about that," her mother said as she sped down the steps to embrace first Clio, then Lady Constance. Lady Brianna's hair was as red as her daughter's, her face yet unlined and her figure almost as slender as a young girl's. But her clear blue eyes held wisdom denied to many far older than she.

"It's enough that she is here. Clio, darling, I do hope Holyhood was wonderful. You must tell me all about it. Lady Constance, I am so glad to be able to see you before we leave."

"Leave?" Lady Constance inquired. She shot a quick glance in Clio's direction. "Oh, my, are you leaving?"

"It is time for us to return to Akora," Atreus said. "But I, too, am glad to have an opportunity to see you before we do so." He offered his arm to Lady Constance, who took it. Together they climbed the steps and entered the house.

Clio smothered a quick gasp when she saw what awaited her there. The vast, three-storied entry hall was empty of the fresh flowers generally arranged at the base of the statues set in alcoves throughout the hall. Double doors standing open to the state dining room revealed that the table long enough to sit sixty people and all the chairs around it were covered with dust cloths. Even as she watched, a parade of servants came down the winding staircase, carrying trunks and cases.

Turning to her mother, she said, "We are leaving? But why? I thought you meant to stay in England all summer." She tried to conceal her dismay, but doubted she succeeded entirely. Yet even as she spoke, she realized no one had actually said how long they would be staying. The trip to England, ostensibly to call on the new young Queen, had come as a surprise. Originally, her parents had intended only to go for the coronation, which would not be held for months yet. But once there, she had assumed they would stay longer.

"Events on Akora call us back," her father said quietly. He offered no further explanation but ushered them into the family parlor, a large and elegant room that was nonetheless considerably less formal than the house's state rooms.

"What a shame," Lady Constance said as she took a seat beside Brianna. "I have so enjoyed Clio's company."

"You're welcome to come with us, if you like," Brianna offered.

"Oh, thank you, dear. I have greatly enjoyed my visits to Akora and would love to go again. It's just that right now . . . well, there is much to do at Holyhood and elsewhere. I hope you understand?"

"Yes, of course. Now that Clio is here, we will be leaving in the next few days, but in the meantime, I hope we—"

"Mother, I'm not going."

"What is that?" Atreus asked. He was standing near the open windows looking out on the garden. His manner was surprised but not particularly concerned. "Of course you are going. Why would you remain here?"

"I'm sure she has a good reason, dear," Brianna said, but she looked at her daughter doubtfully.

"Yes, I do—" But what could she say, really? She had fallen in love—or at least in lust—with a man she had known for a handful of days, lain with him on a rock ledge in a cave, and turned down, or at least failed to accept, his proposal of marriage. She couldn't say any of that. These were her *parents,* for heaven's sake, and one of them was a highly trained warrior who thought sword-fighting was a good way to relax.

Or she could say, "I'm having visions of the past, and you know that when strange things like that begin happening to women in our family, something terrible is just around the corner." Oh, yes, that would assure her parents' willingness to leave her *alone* in London.

She was still fumbling for an answer when Lady Constance—dear, wonderful Lady Constance—said, "Clio promised to stay and help me. You see, ever since dear William passed away, there are things I've put off doing, and at my age—" She paused delicately. "Well, I just think I shouldn't delay too much longer and Clio"—she reached over and patted Clio's hand—"Clio so kindly offered to assist me."

To the end of her days, she would be indebted to Lady Constance. Breathing a bit easier than she had been moments before, Clio smiled at her parents. "I hope you understand?"

"Of course—" Brianna began, but she still looked uncertain. Atreus, however, seemed unperturbed. He left the windows and came over to the couches where the ladies were seated. Standing behind his wife, his hand resting on her shoulder, he faced Clio and Lady Constance.

"Is this your wish, then, Daughter, to remain in London?"

She looked into the eyes of the man she had never

sought to deceive in all her life, swallowed the lump in her throat, and nodded. "Yes, Father, very much so."

"We are closing up this house," Atreus said.

"Oh, Clio is more than welcome to stay with me," Lady Constance said quickly. "I assure you, she will be very well looked after."

Atreus smiled faintly. "I'm sure she will. How is your grandson, Lady Constance? I don't believe our paths have crossed since he was a child."

"Will is always very occupied, of course," Lady Constance replied, clearly startled by the question. All the same, she recovered quickly. "He has quite a head for business and always seems to be traveling to some place or other."

"Is he in London now?"

"Why, yes, I believe he is."

"He's a friend of our nephew, David Hawkforte, isn't he?" Brianna asked. She shared a glance with her husband that Clio could not decipher but which vaguely alarmed her all the same.

"Will has mentioned David, I believe," Lady Constance replied.

Brianna smiled. "How nice. Clio, dear, of course you may stay on to help Lady Constance with . . . whatever it is she needs to do. But, please, let us hear from you. Amelia is on her wedding trip in America and she still manages to write to the family from time to time."

"Of course I'll write," Clio said, prepared just then

to agree to anything. "And I'll do everything I can to help you get ready to leave. When are you going?"

"Soon enough," Atreus told her wryly. "There are one or two matters I have to see to before we sail." He did not specify what they were, but a short time later, he took his leave.

A serving woman brought in a tray of tea and sandwiches. The ladies lingered over them before Lady Constance departed for her own residence with assurances that Clio would follow within a day or two, as soon as she had assisted her mother and decided which of her own belongings she wished to send back to Akora or keep with her.

"More tea?" Brianna asked when they were alone.

"Yes, thank you." Clio straightened her shoulders and silently reminded herself that she was a grown woman. Her mother always would be her mother, but Brianna understood full well that Clio was no longer a child. Whether or not her father also grasped that was another matter.

"It didn't occur to me that you would wish to remain in England," Brianna said as she handed Clio her cup. "You were reluctant to leave Akora and come here, understandably enough considering the work you were doing at home."

For several months, Clio had been digging in the basement of one of the oldest houses in the Akoran capital of Ilius, not far from the palace where she lived with her family. Most recently, she thought she had discovered evidence that the house might have been, if only for a short time, the residence of the couple who were the founders of her family and, to a very large extent, of Akora itself.

News that her parents were going to England and expected her to come with them had hit hard. She had argued to stay on Akora and continue working, but her father, unaccountably, had refused. She supposed it did seem strange that she was not leaping at the chance to return.

"I do hope to continue that excavation," she said, realizing that was both true and one more complication. "But at the moment, I think it better for me to stay here."

"To help Lady Constance?"

"I have the greatest affection for her."

"As do I," Brianna said serenely and offered her daughter the tray of sandwiches.

THE VANAX OF AKORA RODE TO WHITEHALL WHERE he met by arrangement with Lord Melbourne, the Prime Minister. The two were old acquaintances and sometimes allies who understood each other very well. They were both smiling when Atreus departed.

He went next to St. James Street and the venerable Palladian residence housing White's, the oldest and most prestigious of the gentlemen's clubs lining St.

James. His arrival caused a flurry of excitement manifested in true club fashion by a rustling of newspapers in the ground floor reading room and the clearing of several throats.

Atreus was not a member and generally nonmembers were not permitted past the entry hall. But he was something better—royalty—and he was not to be denied.

"Certainly, Your Highness; of course, Your Highness," the head porter said when informed of his requirements. "Right through there, Your Highness."

At the door of the snooker room, Atreus paused and took an appreciative breath. He was known to indulge in a good cigar from time to time, and if there was one thing White's could be relied upon for, it was an absence of cheap tobacco. A pleasant blue haze hung over the snooker tables but did not prevent him from seeing the two men in the far corner of the room. He went directly to them.

The younger of the pair greeted him. "Uncle," David Hawkforte said, "this is a surprise." The tall, dark-haired young man gestured to the green felt table. "Care for a game?"

"Thank you, no," Atreus replied. He looked to his nephew's companion. "Hollister, I presume?"

CHAPTER XII

SLOWLY WILL LOWERED THE CUE HE WAS HOLDing. Face-to-face with Clio's father, he did what any superbly trained, quick-thinking man would do, looked around for an escape route. None made itself apparent, and besides, honor must be served.

"Sir," he said, inclining his head while keeping his eyes locked on Atreus, the better to anticipate any move he might make. The Vanax had to be in his fifties but he looked like he could take down most men decades younger. On the other hand, he did not look like the sort who would be perfectly fine with what had gone on at Holyhood.

How in hell could he possibly know? Will had left there three days before, reaching London the following morning. Unless Clio had dispatched a letter to her parents immediately, and chosen to tell them what had happened, he failed to understand why this encounter was taking place. Or had he misinterpreted the situation? The man who led an island nation renowned for its military prowess appeared to be unarmed. Certainly, he gave no indication of intending Will's imminent demise.

"Melbourne said I might find you here," Atreus said. He appeared amused but watchful.

"Did he?" Will asked. "Is there something I can do for you, sir?"

David, ever resourceful, took the opportunity to wave over a waiter and order three brandies. While he did so, Atreus said, "The Prime Minister tells me you were in Scotland recently."

Following a lead to Umbra's identity, which had turned into a blind alley. Will leaned against the table, doing his damnedest to appear no more than politely responsive. "I have business interests there."

"We have mills on Akora. We're thinking of bringing in some of the newer technology. I'd like to know what you think of it."

The Vanax of Akora—Clio's father—had sought him out to discuss the finer points of power looms? Royalty had its prerogatives—and its eccentricities—but this still struck Will as odd. Even so, he supposed he should be grateful the encounter was turning out to be so prosaic.

They adjourned, with their brandies, to the terrace overlooking the back garden. There, Will found himself drawn out about virtually every detail of the operation of a mill, including the sources for raw materials, the preferred forms of energy, and the treatment of workers. Atreus asked frequent and precise questions. Before long, the discussion turned to finances. Will was as circumspect as any man about such matters, but he realized after a while that he was revealing a fair amount of his own financial situation to Atreus and to the increasingly amused David, who sipped his brandy and listened to them both.

At length, the Vanax of Akora appeared to be satisfied. He rose and nodded to his nephew. To Will, he said, "Come to dinner." Lest there be any misunderstanding, he added, "This evening."

When he was gone, shown out by the obsequious head porter, Will leaned back in his chair, sighed deeply and muttered, "But he doesn't rule, he just serves."

David laughed. "I don't know where you heard that but it is true, on some level. It's just that my uncle's approach to serving his people is to make sure that everything works out exactly the way he thinks it should."

"I gather he's quite good at it."

"He should be." David hesitated, then said quietly,

"Do you know anything about how the Vanax of Akora is chosen?"

Will shook his head. "I presumed the position was hereditary."

"It isn't. There's a . . . ritual, I suppose you'd call it. I don't know the details, almost no one does, but apparently any man who seeks to become Vanax and is not suitable to the position, doesn't survive the ritual."

"Are you serious?"

"Completely. At any rate, Atreus did survive. He's been Vanax for over thirty years. In that time, he's led Akora from only the most cautious and secretive contact with the outside world to where it is today. He's taken a hell of a lot of risks, but they've paid off." David paused for a moment, then looked at Will directly. "One thing my uncle's never taken any chances with is his family."

"I have no idea what you're talking about." It was a lie, but under the circumstances, Will thought it justified. Besides, if you couldn't lie to your friends, who could you lie to?

"Don't you?" David asked. "I wrote to Clio, suggesting that if she was bored with London, she should come to Hawkforte. She wrote back to thank me, but said she was accompanying your grandmother to Holyhood where you've just been."

There was a reason why he had never involved himself in the intrigues of *amour*, so popular among some.

They were absolutely impossible to keep from unraveling.

"David . . ."

"Will, we've been friends for years. You've watched my back; I've watched yours, and we're both still alive to tell the tale, although not to anyone who shouldn't know. Hell, I even like you. But if you hurt Clio . . . what can I say? Don't let me find you."

Fair enough, and exactly what he'd likely say if their positions were reversed. The problem was that they weren't. David was as close as he'd ever had to a brother and David had just threatened to kill him, or words to that effect. Hell.

"I don't suppose it's occurred to you that she could hurt me?"

The younger man looked at him for a long moment. Slowly his expression changed. It went from being the normal look of a man who might have to do something he'd really rather not have to do, to profound gratitude for having escaped similar circumstances. Quietly he said, "Like that, is it? You poor bastard."

He raised a hand, summoning the waiter and another round of brandy.

By the time he reached his London house, Will was wondering if perhaps he'd had too much to drink. Three brandies—or was it four?—on an empty stomach might not have been the best idea. Still, he had several hours yet before he was expected for dinner, plenty of time for a good, hot soak and a pot of coffee.

Walking into the elegant house only a few blocks from the Atreides' residence, he was surprised to notice the lamps lit in the drawing room. He never used that room, as the servants well knew. His grandmother liked it, but she was at Holyhood.

He took the stairs two at a time, rang for a servant, and when his valet arrived, requested a bath. And coffee. Definitely coffee.

"Will milord be going out this evening?" the valet asked with the dignity of the long-aggrieved. His name was Mather and never mind that he had only been in the job a few months, he had come to understand why the Earl of Hollister could not keep a valet. The position of valet required an appreciation for the paramount importance of fashion. Generally, even the most style-impaired employer could be made to understand that the cut of his cravat really did matter. But not his lordship. He was far more likely to take his cravat off and, Mather secretly suspected, based on what he had observed of the Earl of Hollister, turn it into a weapon of some sort. That really did not bear thinking about.

"Out," Will said, "yes, out, going to dinner. Probably talk about mills again . . . or something."

"As you say, milord. Your bath will be prepared directly." With a hint of hope, the valet added, "If I might suggest, his lordship's hair could do with a bit of a trim."

"Fine, fine . . . Blather, isn't it?"

The valet winced. "Mather, sir, I'm Mather. If you'll just give me a moment, I'll see to that coffee."

YOUR HAIR LOOKS LOVELY, DEAR," BRIANNA SAID as she finished brushing the smooth, red-gold strands that reached halfway down Clio's back and curved under gently. "I'm so glad you don't do that awful crimping and curling the young women here seem to like."

"We both know I have your hair," Clio said with a smile. She met her mother's eyes in the dressing table mirror. "And I thank you very much for it."

Brianna laughed and patted her shoulder. Softly she said, "I'm going to miss you."

Clio took the silver-backed brush from her and set it down on the marble top of the table. Still looking at her mother, she said, "We've been apart before, when you made trips to England with Father and I stayed on Akora."

"Yes, but that was different. Then I knew that you were safe at home with everyone to look after you."

"I will be safe here, Mother, truly." At least she hoped it was true. There were dangers to be faced, yet she could not help but believe that together she and Will would surmount them.

Together, which brought her back to the fact that he had no intention of letting her help him.

"Mother . . . when you and Father met, did you simply realize that you were meant to be together?"

Brianna considered her reply. Carefully she said, "When your father and I met for the first time, he was near death because of an attempt on his life."

"I meant after that—"

"Yes, I know you did. When we met again, it was here in England where I had come seeking information about my original parents. They were long dead, as you know, but Lord William, Lady Constance's husband, was my mother's cousin. He and Lady Constance offered me a home with them."

"You mean, you might have remained here in England?" Clio had never known this about her mother. She was struck by the possibilities. Had Brianna made that choice, Clio herself would never have been born.

"Yes, I might have," Brianna said. "But your father came and he was quite determined that we should wed."

"Was he?" Perhaps it was a family tradition, men determined on matrimony. "How did you feel about that?"

"Oh, I was wildly in love with him, but there were . . . challenges. At any rate, we overcame them and here we are. Now, why do you ask?"

"No reason in particular. I was just curious."

"Hmmm, well, in that case, I'm going to dress for dinner. I'll see you downstairs." Her mother dropped a quick kiss on her cheek and turned to go. At the bedroom door, she stopped and looked back at Clio. "Why don't you wear the sapphire silk? It looks marvelous on you."

BLATHER—NO, MATHER—HAD DONE A DECENT enough job. Moreover, he'd done it without a lot of fuss. Will's hair was neatly trimmed, he was freshly shaven, his clothes felt all right even though the shirt had been starched, and best yet, his head was clear. He had a strong sense that last part would be particularly important when dealing with the Vanax of Akora.

As he approached the Akoran residence, on foot as the night was pleasant and the distance short, he reflected on his earlier conversation with Atreus. Either the man played a very deep game, or he had no notion of Will's relationship with his daughter. The question, then, was whether or not to enlighten him.

There was a case to be made that such was the honorable course. Also a case that it was damn close to suicide. Near the wrought-iron gates that framed the gravel path leading up to the mansion, Will decided he'd gauge the situation, including how many weapons appeared readily to hand, before making his decision.

A kilted warrior opened the front door and, upon being told Will's name, stood aside to admit him. Aside from the man's appearance—bare-chested, wearing only the kilt and with a short sword at his waist—the entry to the house could have graced that of any residence in which great wealth and power were matched by restrained good taste. That is, except for the fact that the furniture in adjacent rooms appeared to be covered with dust cloths and there was a general air of vacancy everywhere Will looked.

He needed only a moment to realize the cause: The Akorans were leaving. When had that decision been taken and why? And more to the point, what did it mean for Clio and for him?

He was pondering that when his host appeared. The Vanax of Akora was still dressed in English clothes, although, like Will, he had a penchant for informality and comfort. His suit of charcoal-gray wool was well tailored but not extravagantly so, and he did without the fashionably high shirt collar that many men wore despite it leaving their necks perpetually chafed.

Looking relaxed and in good humor, Atreus greeted Will. "Please forgive the disorder; we're in the process of packing."

"So I see. Are you leaving England, Your Highness?"

"For the moment, but we'll be back for the coronation. Ah, there you are, my dear." Turning, Atreus greeted the stunningly beautiful woman who had just entered the hall.

The Vanax made the introductions as Will bowed over the Lady Brianna's hand. He was struck by how much she resembled Clio, or more correctly, the other way around. There were distinct differences in their features, but their brilliantly blue eyes and glorious red hair marked them as mother and daughter. Brianna's smile even reminded Will of Clio's.

"How nice to meet you, or should I say, to meet you again. I don't suppose you remember our frog-hunting expedition?"

"Alas, Your Highness, I do not and I beg your pardon for so remiss a memory."

"Quite all right, considering that you were six years old at the time. I have never had the opportunity to give you my condolences on the death of your grandfather. Please accept them now. He was a dear friend."

"Thank you. I know he was very fond of you. I regret I have not called while you have been in England. Business matters have kept me occupied."

"The Earl of Hollister has interests in mills in Scotland," Atreus informed his wife. "We were talking about them earlier today."

"Were you, dearest?" Brianna cast her husband a look Will could not decipher. "How nice," she said. "We always find such interesting things to take back with us, but I do hope my husband is not planning to import an entire mill."

The gentlemen were chuckling over this little bit of feminine diversion when Will's glance happened to be drawn to a movement at the top of the stairs. He broke off abruptly and stared at the vision who had appeared there.

She had to be a vision, didn't she? After all, the real Clio was still at Holyhood where he had bid her to remain.

She was not walking down the steps of her parents' London home, clad in a gown of shimmering sapphire silk that emphasized her narrow waist and the high, full curve of her breasts.

She paused when she caught sight of him, laid a hand delicately just above her heart and appeared to pale. Her mouth—that exquisite mouth he couldn't seem to stop thinking about—formed a small expression of dismay.

Also shock, and just possibly horror.

"Clio—?" he said before he could catch himself.

She reached the bottom of the stairs, looked from him to her parents, who were observing them both, and returned her attention to him.

"Will . . . I had no notion you were here." Her voice was low and tight, her tone suggested the discovery did not fill her with unalloyed delight.

"Nor I you," he said and cast a look of heightened wariness in the direction of the Vanax, who merely smiled.

"I wasn't aware the two of you were acquainted," Atreus said smoothly.

"Did you meet at Holyhood?" Brianna inquired, the very picture of innocence.

"Yes," Clio replied, still staring at Will. She could not seem to draw her eyes away from him. What was he doing here? How could he possibly have appeared like this? And how on earth was she supposed to face him and her parents at the same time?

"Dear Lady Constance," Brianna said. "She's always so good about bringing people together."

"It wasn't like that, Mother," Clio said at once, well aware of the older woman's matchmaking reputation. "Lady Constance wasn't even expecting Will . . . that is, the Earl of Hollister, to arrive at Holyhood."

"Wasn't she?" Atreus inquired. "What took you to Holyhood?" he asked Will. Without waiting for a reply, the Vanax said, "But let's not talk in the hall. May I offer you a drink before dinner?"

"Thank you, sir." Anything but brandy, and even then, Will had no intention of imbibing except with the greatest moderation. All his instincts were on high alert as he considered that both he and Clio had been lured into an encounter neither had anticipated. Clearly, the Vanax and his consort merited very close watching.

Yet for all that, dinner was unexpectedly pleasant. Atreus and Brianna were both gracious and extremely well-informed. They effortlessly maintained the conversation despite the tendency of the two other participants to lapse into silence and stare at each other. At length, the talk turned to the new Queen and the prospects for her reign.

"I believe she will surprise everyone," Brianna asserted. "Everyone speaks of how young she is and how malleable, but I think she has a mind of her own."

"Then let us hope she hones it," Atreus said. "England faces great challenges."

"Better to face them with Victoria than with Augustus Frederick, don't you think, Father?" Clio inquired.

They were in the family dining room, a far smaller and less formal chamber than that used for diplomatic dinners. The menu was a surprise to Will, being lighter, fresher, and altogether more appealing than the meals he was accustomed to encountering when dining among the nobility. The main course was a simple one of salmon, which tasted as though it had been grilled over an open fire, accompanied by crisp green beans and rice, the latter new to him except when served in a sweet pudding he had hated as a child and never touched since.

"I'm sure the Duke of Sussex has many strengths," Atreus replied. "Whether he would be the best man to lead England at this time is another matter."

Seated beside Will, Brianna said, "Nicely put, dear, but I rather think the best man for the times is a woman."

"The British monarch doesn't actually have all that much power, does he . . . or she?" Clio asked.

"That depends a great deal on who happens to occupy the throne," Will said. He looked at her across the damask-covered table, observing how the light of the tall, white candles in their silver holders revealed the purity of her features. Her gown left her shoulders bare. In the firelight, her skin had the sheen of alabaster.

With difficulty, he dragged his mind back to the matter at hand. "A popular monarch can have a great deal of influence, which can be translated into power. For that matter, in a time of rapid change and confusion, a monarch who is not particularly popular may nonetheless seize the moment and make use of his—or her—high office to advance personal objectives."

"Is that something Augustus Frederick would do?" Clio asked.

"But the Duke of Sussex is not going to be king," Brianna said. "Victoria will marry, have children, and the succession will pass to them."

"That is certainly to be hoped," Will agreed and turned his attention to the tray of grapes and cheese that was brought in just then. He was beginning to relax, thinking that dinner had turned out well after all, when Atreus leaned back in his chair, swirled the ruby-red wine in his glass and said, "I suppose we should discuss the reason I asked you to come by tonight."

CHAPTER XIII

"STAYING?" WILL REPEATED. HE WANTED TO BElieve he had heard Atreus wrong, but by all appearance, the Vanax of Akora had said exactly what it sounded like he had. "Clio, that is, Her Highness is staying in England?"

"Lady Constance has been kind enough to invite me," she informed him with a note of challenge.

"How very good of my grandmother." One more person he needed to be vastly more careful of. "Did you arrange all this before you came up from Holyhood?"

"On the way," Clio said. "We came together."

Rather than admit that he was so poorly informed

as to the doings in his own household that he had not known his grandmother was present there, Will said, "I was under the impression, Your Highness, that you did not care for London."

"But it is such an exciting place," she replied. Did he imagine it or were her teeth clenched? "So much happens in London . . . or could happen."

"That is certainly true and so much of it might turn out to be unpleasant or even dangerous."

"Dangerous?" Atreus interjected. "The city has been peaceful of late."

"Yes, it has," Will said, "but that isn't necessarily good. It might mean various rivalries, hostilities, and so on are becoming pent up, likely to explode, as it were."

"Do you really think so?" Brianna inquired, looking concerned.

"His lordship exaggerates," Clio said tartly. "Besides, I wouldn't dream of disappointing Lady Constance."

"Your care for my grandmother is to your credit, but—"

"It does seem like an excellent opportunity for Clio to become better acquainted with England," Brianna said.

"However," Atreus countered, "if you do not feel able to properly assure my daughter's safety, Hollister, Clio will return with us to Akora."

Clio's hand clenched beside her plate. A knife lay

inches away. She did not actually reach for it, but Will could have sworn her fingers moved in its direction. "Father, please, there is no need—"

"Of course I will assure her safety, Your Highness." How could he not if he was to make any claim later to becoming her husband? Whether he knew it or not—and Will was not about to assume anything about the extent of Atreus's knowledge—the Vanax had neatly trapped him. Either Clio was safe in his care or she was not. If she was not, there was no possibility of any future for them. If Atreus played chess, and Will thought that highly likely, he had just scored a checkmate.

"You will?" she asked, staring at him. He could tell she was trying to decipher his swift reversal.

"Certainly. You will be entirely secure in my grandmother's company." Even if he had to send them both back to Holyhood and make damn sure they stayed there.

"Well, then," Atreus said, "that's settled. We'll be leaving the usual contingent of guards here at the house, but otherwise we intend to sail in three days."

"So soon," Brianna murmured.

Atreus leaned across the table and covered her hand with his. "We must get home, my dear." To Will, he said, "My nephew, Gavin Hawkforte, David's elder brother, is on Akora seeing to a matter for me. I'm eager to discover how he's doing."

"Before we go, we must pay our respects to the

Queen," Brianna said. She looked to her daughter. "Come with us to Buckingham Palace tomorrow. I know you are acquainted with Victoria, but I would like you to know her a little better before we leave."

"Ideally, you could spend some time in her company while you are here," Atreus said. "Take her measure, as it were."

Clio's smile stopped just short of being triumphant. "What an excellent idea, Father, and I'm sure his lordship could not possibly have any objection. Where could I be more secure than with the Queen herself?"

They both played chess, Will decided. Atreus had probably taught her. Like as not, they'd had father-daughter matches late into the Akoran evenings.

By mutual agreement, the ladies did not leave the gentlemen to their cigars but remained with them, chatting as night fell over the city. At length, Will made to take his leave, but before doing so, he came to a decision. He truly liked the Vanax and his wife, and respected them. They gave every evidence of being decent, forthright people. Moreover, he had a healthy respect for their power and for the importance of the relationship between England and Akora.

That being the case, he straightened from his bow over Clio's hand and looked to her father. "Sir, if you wouldn't mind, might we have a private word before I go?"

Will had not yet released Clio's fingers, which clenched fiercely around his as he spoke. She was on the verge of objecting when she stopped herself. How could she, really? What possible reason could she offer for not wanting her father and the Earl of Hollister to speak together alone?

The swift and scathing look she shot Will did not deter him. To the contrary, he merely smiled, bid her goodnight, and followed Atreus into his study. The heavy oak doors closed behind them.

"Mother—"

Brianna shrugged. She looked at her daughter with sympathy and very womanly understanding. "Go to bed, dear." When Clio would have objected, she added, "There's really nothing else to be done."

To bed, then, but certainly not to sleep. She lay, looking up at the canopy, her ears straining for any sound. When she finally heard what she thought was the door to her father's study opening and then the front door opening and closing, Clio jumped from the bed. She hurried into her robe and slippers, grabbed a candle, and sped from the room. But she was too late. By the time she got downstairs, she was informed by the guard stationed in the entry hall that the Vanax had retired for the night.

Of course, she could go after him, knock on her parents' door, and plead to be told what had transpired. At fourteen, she probably would have done so. At twenty-four, she would not.

Returning to bed, she spent several fruitful hours

contemplating all the horrible things she could do to Will Hollister, before finally dozing off.

Early the following morning, but not so early that her father had not already departed the house, Clio sought out her mother. Brianna was in her sitting room, still wearing her ivory silk-and-lace peignoir, and enjoying her morning tea. Seeing her daughter, she held up a hand.

"I don't know," Brianna said before she could be asked.

"But you must," Clio exclaimed as she took the seat beside her mother. She had dressed for the visit to Buckingham Palace in one of her favorite gowns, a bodice of daffodil-yellow silk trimmed with ivory lace and a skirt of dark, spring green intricately embroidered along the hem with a garden of tiny flowers. She wore only one petticoat and that of starched muslin without padding, although she rather liked the fuller look skirts were taking on. In her experience, days at the palace tended to be long. She meant to be comfortable.

But first she had to find out what had happened the night before.

"Your father said nothing," Brianna insisted. "He did not wish to speak of the matter."

"But he tells you everything . . . doesn't he?"

Her mother looked at her chidingly. "I have never presumed so, any more than I tell him everything. Even in the closest relationships, people are entitled to some privacy. However, Atreus did make it clear that he had no intention of discussing whatever was said between him and the Earl of Hollister."

Taken aback, Clio asked, "Well, then, how did he seem?"

The corners of Brianna's mouth curved in a private smile. "Very much himself." More seriously, she said, "I'm sorry, darling, but as much as I, too, would like to know what went on between them, I don't have a glimmer." Her look turned shrewd as she added, "Perhaps you do."

Perhaps she did, but she was going to take her mother's advice and maintain a little privacy. A bit lamely, she said, "I'm sure we'll find out eventually."

"I'm sure we will," Brianna agreed. "Now, dear, help me decide what to wear."

They left the house an hour or so later and proceeded by open carriage to Buckingham Palace. Clio was eager to see the royal residence, the object of an extravagant renovation by the great architect John Nash on behalf of profligate King George IV, which had more than doubled the size of the original structure. Until just a few weeks before, Victoria had lived at the far smaller Kensington Palace, where she was born and raised. Her decision to remove to Buckingham Palace had come as a surprise to the entire Court and raised speculation that she was seeking a clear break with the childhood spent under the scrutiny of her domineering mother.

Whether that was true or not, it was undeniable that Victoria was the first monarch to make the palace her home. Approaching the vast, three-sided structure, they passed beneath Marble Arch, commemorating the British victory over Napoleon. As the arch rose above them, Brianna leaned over and said, "Do you know there's talk of moving it?"

It took a moment for Clio to understand what her mother meant. "Moving the arch? But why . . . and how?"

Brianna shrugged. "As to the how, I cannot say, although the British are ingenious at such things and I suppose they'll devise a means. As to why, can you imagine that so immense a palace has almost no bedrooms?"

The palace was huge, although not in comparison to the palace of Ilius, the royal city of Akora. But then, that palace had been under construction for more than three thousand years, with rooms, corridors, reception halls and the like carefully maintained and added on to but never demolished. The result was what some regarded as a labyrinth, although Clio, who had lived there all her life, could find her way unerringly to any part of it.

Even so, Buckingham Palace was certainly so large that it should have boasted dozens of bedrooms, and every other amenity anyone could possibly desire.

"Not sufficient for a family," Brianna said, "which,

of course, is what everyone is hoping Victoria will have very soon."

"She isn't even betrothed yet, much less married."

"Rumor has it Melbourne intends to do something about that rather quickly. Ah, good, here we are." Alighting from the carriage with the help of the Akoran guard who had accompanied them, Brianna took her daughter's arm. "Your father is meeting us. He's sure to be about here somewhere."

She ignored the eager stares of the nobility and privileged commoners who were milling about and drew Clio up the grand staircase and down a corridor to the Queen's reception room. It was a large, high-ceilinged room ornately but not, Clio thought, comfortably furnished. When she said as much to her mother, Brianna laughed.

"Your aunt Joanna was so amused the first time she came here. She recognized the furniture as having been made for Carlton House, that late, unlamented folly of King George IV's that was torn down only a few years after being completed."

"To be replaced by this more recent and still lamented folly?"

"Exactly. Oh, well, it seems to suit Her Majesty."

If the smile on the face of the young woman who stood beneath a canopy of gold on a small dais at the far end of the room was any indication, this was true. Clio had met Victoria several times, but only once since the death of the late king, her uncle. It was impossible to ignore her youth or her diminutive size—she was only eighteen and scarcely five feet tall. But she held herself very well, and despite her rather conventional prettiness, Clio thought she had the look of a woman who could surprise people.

Near her stood a tall, slender man with aquiline features and silvered hair that framed his face in seemingly artless curls. The overall impression was saved from femininity by the presence of a strong, cleft chin and impressive sideburns. Viscount Melbourne, England's Prime Minister, was in close conversation with the Vanax of Akora who, seeing his wife and daughter, excused himself and went to greet them.

"Father," Clio said a bit warily. She had no notion of what he might be thinking and that unsettled her deeply.

He kissed her cheek, took Brianna's hand and said, "The Queen is eager to see you both."

So it appeared, for she greeted them warmly and spoke with particular enthusiasm to Clio, one of the very few people she could address as a near-equal. "I am so glad to hear you will be remaining in England, Your Highness. I hope we will have the opportunity to become much better acquainted."

Beside her, Melbourne smiled.

"I shall be delighted, Your Majesty," Clio said and found, a bit to her surprise, that she meant it.

They joined the Queen for luncheon, as did the Prime Minister. Of Victoria's mother, the Duchess of

Kent, who had been such a controlling presence in the life of the princess, there was no sign. It was Melbourne who sat at the Queen's left, Atreus being on her right as precedent required, and it did not escape Clio's notice that between the young monarch and the elderly Prime Minister there seemed to be both trust and true affection.

A short time later, as she left Buckingham Palace, Clio caught sight of a tall, well-built man speaking to several other people near the columned entrance. Sir Morgan Kearns did not see her, for which she was grateful, but his presence dampened her pleasure in the day, reminding her as it did of the danger facing Victoria and the urgent need to discover the identity of Umbra before he could strike again.

She tried, without great success, to put that concern from her mind over the next several days as she helped her mother prepare to leave London. While Atreus attended last-minute conferences with political and business leaders, Brianna continued the seemingly endless effort to ready the household for its return to Akora.

Well over a hundred people were traveling, a full complement of guards and retainers, but they were nothing compared to the three entire cargo ships filled with everything from books, paintings, and fabrics to a full-sized and functioning locomotive identical to that used to propel the London-Greenwich railroad.

"What your father wants with this, I can't imagine," Brianna said as she stood on the dock at Southwark, observing the locomotive being loaded onto the ship that would carry it to Akora. When it had descended fully into the hold, she checked it off on the very long list she consulted. Horses from Ireland went on board next. Brianna checked them off as well. Such close attention to detail could have been delegated to one of the several Akoran commanders in charge of the ships, but Brianna took her responsibilities as consort seriously and preferred to see to such matters herself.

Even so, she confessed that she was tired when she and Clio returned to the Mayfair mansion. "I'm going to have a bit of a rest, dear," Brianna said. "If I don't, I shall be positively foul company this evening."

Her mother was never anything of the sort, but the day, coming as it had after a largely sleepless night, had left Clio weary as well. Even so, she hadn't been able to sleep during the day since childhood. If she tried to do so now, she'd just toss and turn.

Instead, she chose a book from the library and went outside to sit in the garden. The day was warm by English standards, pleasantly cool by Akoran. She deliberately picked a bench in the sun, heedless of what that would do to her complexion. Personally, she liked a few freckles, which were all she ever got, and thought it silly that they were considered unfashionable.

The book, Jane Austen's *Persuasion,* was a favorite of Clio's. She had plucked it from the shelf for no other reason, but reading it again now, she was struck by its significance to her own situation. The heroine had spent years regretting not marrying the man she loved. Happily, within the pages of the novel, she was given a second chance, but in real life, there were no assurances of any such thing.

She was mulling over whether she had made a terrible mistake not accepting Will's proposal, when a wave of dizziness moved over her. Slowly, she lowered the book and raised her head. Perhaps she had strained her eyes.

The light in the garden seemed suddenly too bright. She blinked against it and opened her eyes again, to discover she was no longer alone.

People were strolling through the garden. Not Akoran warriors or retainers who would have had some reason to be there, but people in English garb, walking among the flower beds and fountains, chatting together.

What was this? Had she fallen asleep after all or was she seeing another vision of the past?

Slowly she rose, leaving the book open on the bench. Scarcely breathing, she forced herself to look very closely at every detail of the scene before her.

The garden was in bloom, the people were dressed as though for summer, the ladies with their parasols to protect themselves from the sun. When would such a gathering have taken place? Her parents entertained when they were in England, as was necessary in their position, but their preference was for state dinners, not garden parties. Why would they have—

A young man strolled by her. His expression declared he was in good cheer, but he wore a black mourning band around his upper left arm.

Since the death of the late king, formal social life in London had been suspended. Even so, there were still informal gatherings. Hadn't her mother written something to her about having hosted a "little" get-together that Clio would miss because she was at Holyhood? If that was truly what she was seeing, her visions had come almost a thousand years from the distant past to the very near present.

Her head throbbed. She put a hand to her brow and struggled to concentrate. Could she recognize anyone? But the scene before her was wavering, the people becoming indistinct. She struggled to hold on, not to let go of it, desperate for some hint, some clue as to why this was happening to her.

The ground beneath her feet buckled. Clio lost her balance and fell.

CHAPTER XIV

CLIO!" WILL SPRINTED DOWN THE GRAVEL PATH to where Clio lay beside a bench. Gathering her into his arms, he turned her over gently. She was very pale, even her lips seemed drained of color, and she did not move.

Cursing, he carried her over to a nearby fountain. Setting her beside it, he tore off his cravat, wet it, and wiped her face with the cool water. He did not breathe again until her eyelids fluttered.

"Will?" She reached out a hand and pressed her palm to his cheek. "Are you real?"

Despite himself, he smiled. "As real as it's possible

to be." Helping her to sit on the side of the fountain, he kept an arm around her waist. "What happened?"

"I don't know exactly. . . . I got dizzy. . . . There were people in the garden."

The garden was empty and he had seen no one leave it. Grimly he asked, "You had another vision?"

"I think so, yes. Oh, Will, I don't understand what's happening! At first I was seeing events from a thousand years ago. If I'm correct about what I saw just now, it was within the last few weeks. Whatever is causing this, it's coming closer."

His arm tightened around her. He had come to the house, hoping to have a private word with her. His intent was to make one more try to convince Clio to return to Akora with her parents instead of deliberately putting herself in the path of danger by being close to the Queen.

Now he was reminded that he did not have the luxury of considering only his private desires; he was called to a higher duty. With the greatest reluctance, he said, "Have you seen anything that could have any possible bearing on the threat to the Queen?"

She shook her head. "I don't think so. But that doesn't mean I won't see something that does have significance." She turned in his arms, looking at him. "Will, you must understand, I have to stay here."

He sighed deeply and drew her closer. Holding her, he said, "I do understand." The admission was wrung from him and he quickly added, "I just don't like it. I wish there was another way."

"But you agree there isn't?"

"I agree . . . that if you do 'see' anything you think bears on the Queen's safety, you must tell me about it at once."

A slight frown appeared between her brows. "Tell you?"

He nodded. "Tell me and trust me to take care of it."

Men, they were ever the same. Her father, her uncles, her brother, they all had the instinct to protect and cosset women, which was not to say that was necessarily bad. All except her twin had reason to know the true capabilities of the gentler sex, having lived through tumultuous times when the courage—and actions—of the women they loved, proved every bit as vital as their own. She had to wonder if one day Andreas might not experience something similar.

But for now she wished Will could see her in a different light. "If wishes were horses—"

"What was that?" he asked.

"Never mind." She pushed lightly against his chest, trying not to notice how hard and strong he felt beneath her hand. "Let me up, please."

He began to, then stopped. Instead, he bent her slightly, holding her just above the edge of the fountain, and smiled down at her. "In a moment."

"Now," she insisted and pushed again, but, truth be

told, the effort was halfhearted. She was caught, staring at his mouth, remembering how it felt against her own.

Remembering and being reminded, for he lowered his head just then and kissed her, not a gentle or coaxing kiss, but the kiss of a man claiming a woman as his own. Instantly her body leaped in response. She clung to him, returning his kiss in full measure, utterly forgetful of where they were.

Breathing hard, Will raised his head and looked down at her. "You are a contrary woman."

She willed the rapid beat of her heart to slow, and when it did not, said anyway, "No, I am not. I have made no secret that I desire you."

Under other circumstances, the look that crossed his face would have prompted her to laugh out loud. As it was, she was hard-pressed not to do so. "Is something wrong?" she asked innocently.

He started to shake his head, stopped and said, "I'm not accustomed to such frankness from a woman."

"I despise coyness."

"There might be some middle ground," he suggested. He was smiling again and looked, whether he knew it or not, well pleased.

She shrugged. "There might." Straightening in his arms, she drew a little apart from him and glanced around the garden. It was empty again, except for the birds darting about. The people—whoever and whyever they had been there—were gone.

Her mind, ever agile, moved on. "What did you talk of with my father?"

"I wondered when you'd get to that." Will stood but Clio remained where she was, her skirt spread out over the cool stone rim of the fountain. Behind her, the water splashed in diamond droplets that caught the sun filtering through the heavy branches of the trees. Her head was tilted slightly to one side as she looked at him.

Did she realize how tempting she was, he wondered? He had known beautiful women and respected the power they could wield even as he thought himself immune to their wiles. With Clio, he was no longer so certain.

Therefore he said, "My conversation with Atreus was private."

He thought she might try to persuade him to tell her what had been discussed, and was prepared to deal with that. But instead, she simply stood and said, "Very well. If you have come to see my father again, he is not home."

"I came to see you." When she looked at him questioningly, he said, "I thought I'd make one more try to convince you to leave with your parents."

"Then why haven't you?"

Was he less truthful than she? He did not wish to think so. Certainly he was not open to the possibility that he was less courageous. "Because I am willing to admit the chance, however slim, that what is happening to you—this 'gift' of which you speak—might help protect the Queen."

He braced himself, expecting . . . something? Hurt that he would use her in such a way. Resentment that he seemingly put the safety of the Queen above her own. Any of the myriad responses he thought she might have.

But not her sudden smile as she leaped up and came to him. "Why, Will, I do believe you are making progress."

He flexed a little in the legs, the way a man will when he's facing an opponent who has just surprised him. "Do you?"

"You seem to recognize that I might be of use."

"And that's . . . good?" Wanting to keep her safe was wrong, but wanting to use her was fine?

"It's not bad, which I perceive is what you expected me to think. I can actually help in this matter. I *will* help."

"By staying close to the Queen and thereby endangering yourself?" He could not deny the fear this provoked or the anger that came hard on its heels.

"Myself," she emphasized. "My own self. It is for me to make such choices, not for you to tell me what I may or may not do."

"It is for me to protect you," he insisted. "I have that right." Never had he thought in such terms, but he could not do otherwise. She had awakened something in him, something ancient and primal, at the core of what he was as a man. It would not be resisted. Surely she would realize that.

"No," she said very clearly, though the effort cost her. Her throat was suddenly clenched, her chest heavy. From passionate kiss to sudden confrontation, the speed of change between them left her floundering. Yet she was very clear in what she thought. "No, you do not have that right, not now and not ever. Lying with you did not give it to you and marriage would not do so either."

"What are you saying?"

"That it is too easy for protection to become a prison. If you were an Akoran man, you would understand this. You would realize that however noble your instincts, trying to order what a woman can and cannot do, is harmful to her. But you are not Akoran, you are—" She broke off, horrified by what she had been about to say.

"I am what, Clio?" He stood before her, his face hard and his eyes suddenly hooded, concealing his emotions.

"I was going to say you are *xenos,* but I don't mean that. I truly don't think in such a way."

"But you would be correct to say that. I am a stranger."

How could he be, when she knew the scent and touch of him in the dark, the power of his body driving into hers, the sound of his voice when he cried her name at the peak of pleasure? Knew that and so much more, but not, perhaps, enough.

"We come from different cultures," she allowed. "It is to be expected that we would see things differently."

"You are telling me that your father, your brother, any man of Akora would stand by and allow a woman he cared for to go into danger?"

"I am not saying he would do so easily, but he would understand that women have much to contribute. Throughout our history, it is the combined strength of men and women—not the strength of men alone—that has benefited our people. Together, we have always been able to do far more than we can do separately."

He studied her for a long moment before he said, "That is what you want, isn't it? A partnership?" The very notion was odd to him. He had never thought in such terms and did not believe he could do so now. Men and women had their separate spheres; they overlapped in places but still remained as they had always been—separate.

"I might not have put that name to it, but it is good enough. Yes, that is what I want. It's what I've seen around me in the most loving couples and I am not willing to settle for anything less."

"And if that means settling for nothing?"

She glanced over at the bench and the book lying there. Its heroine had deeply regretted her choices. But

Anne Elliot was not an Akoran woman and Clio Atreides most definitely was.

She went to him and laid her hand on his chest in a gesture at once reassuring and just a little placating. Tilting her chin back, she looked up at him. Her voice soft and low, she said, "Perhaps I have more faith in you than you do in yourself, Will."

Before he could respond, indeed, while yet his mind grappled with that, she was gone in a swirl of silk, leaving behind her the scent of jasmine drifting on the summer air.

TWO DAYS LATER, CLIO STOOD ON THE DOCK AT Southwark. She brought with her a heavy heart and a pinned-on smile. Behind her were the private warehouses her family maintained, lining a road down which very few non-Akorans ever came, even in these more open days. Ahead, occupying all the available quays, were the half-dozen vessels that together would form the convoy bearing the Vanax and his consort home. The gray water of the Thames lapped against their hulls as sunlight glinted off the curving prows carved into the fierce heads of bulls, their horns gilded and their eyes blood-red.

There was the usual mad scramble that preceded any sailing. With the tide about to turn, fresh food was still being loaded for the voyage. A boy hurried by with a handcart balanced high with melons, just as Brianna said, "Now, Clio, dear, you know how to contact our banker should you require funds, and of course the guards remaining at the house will be available at a moment's notice to assist you, should there be any need. Your father wanted to send several of them over to Lady Constance's with you, but I assured him that would not be necessary. However, if you have the slightest inkling that I could be wrong, you must not hesitate to—"

"Mother, I'm sure everything will be fine." She spoke far more confidently than she felt, for as the moment for her parents' departure neared, she was struck by how truly she would miss them. Even so, she knew without a shadow of doubt that what she was going to do was both right and necessary. She only had to get through the next half hour or so without revealing her conflicted feelings.

"I'm sure it will be, too," Brianna declared firmly. Her smile wobbled. "Let us hear from you."

"I will," she promised and embraced her mother. They were wiping away tears when her father came upon them. He sighed deeply and held out his arms. They both went into them and were comforted.

"We have to board," Atreus said after a few minutes. His voice was unusually husky. "Kassandra and Royce have already done so."

Clio's aunt and uncle had come from Hawkforte the

previous day and were traveling to Akora with her parents. Her other aunt and uncle, Joanna and Alex, were in America where they were helping Andreas establish the Akoran embassy.

David was along to see his parents off, as well as to bid farewell to Atreus and Brianna. He came to them now and smiled gently at Clio.

"It will be all right, cuz, you'll see."

"I'm sure it will," she said, but was glad of his support all the same. Of Will, there was no sign. Not that she had expected him to be there. Most likely he was hunting McManus and Platt, or meeting with Melbourne, or looking after the Queen, all perfectly legitimate and important things for him to be doing.

She wished he was here.

If wishes were horses—

A final embrace from her parents, the last admonitions to have a good time and stay safe, and they were gone up the gangplank. Clio waved while the plank was pulled on board and the lines were thrown. She waved as the sails were raised and caught the wind. She continued waving as the lead vessel inched away from the dock and kept right on doing so as it moved out onto the Thames. She waved and waved until her arm throbbed and she couldn't see anymore because of her tears.

When she turned away finally, Will was there.

He had taken David's place beside her and he was holding out a white linen handkerchief.

"Sorry," he said. "My meeting with Melbourne ran late. Did they get off all right?"

She blew her nose rather loudly, bestowed upon him a smile that stole his breath, and said, "Why, of course they did. There was no problem at all."

Pocketing his handkerchief—she could not possibly return it in its present condition—she blinked away the last of her tears and took the arm he offered. "I don't usually get so emotional," she said.

"Oh, no, of course not."

"I mean it; I don't." Not for a moment did she mistake his silence for agreement. Still, just then it was far and away enough that he had come.

"Are you any closer to identifying Umbra?" she asked as they walked toward the carriage.

Will shook his head. "Unfortunately not. We have men throughout London looking for McManus and Platt, but so far there is no sign of them. Without them to lead us, we have no way of finding Umbra."

"And the Queen, what of her? Has she been told?"

"The Prime Minister believes that is not advisable."

"That is quite a decision for him to make, since it is her life that is at risk."

"She's eighteen years old, Clio. Until a few weeks ago, she never even slept in a room by herself. Now suddenly she is the monarch of a rapidly expanding empire and the whole world is watching her. Melbourne believes that is enough for her to cope with."

"But if she knew, she could agree to take precautions."

"Her schedule is carefully controlled, and since we are all officially in mourning for the late King, no one expects her to be out and about much. If someone is going to kill her, that person is going to have to get very close to her."

He handed her up into the carriage as he spoke, but did not follow. Bolkum twisted around in the driver's seat and gave her a smile. Clio returned it before she said to Will, "I saw the crowd at Buckingham Palace. How difficult do you think it would be for someone to get close?"

"Very. Did you notice how many people were actually in the receiving room and how many sat down to luncheon with the Queen?"

"Only a few, in both places," Clio acknowledged. "But I am still concerned that there were so many within a few rooms of her."

"The situation is far from ideal," Will admitted. "But for the moment, it is the best that we can do. No one, Melbourne included, wants this to become public. The knowledge that the Queen is vulnerable could spark public unrest."

The unrest that, Clio knew, was always bubbling just beneath the surface. England was experiencing a time of extraordinary change as "factories" spread across the country and drastically altered people's lives within a single generation. For some, that change brought improvements, but for others it did not. They found themselves robbed of their traditional livelihoods, sometimes forced from their lands and plunged into dire poverty from which there seemed to be no release.

The restraints that kept society functioning were challenged as they rarely had been. In that situation, any sudden and dramatic event that disrupted the existing order could prove catastrophic.

"Whoever is doing this," she said quietly, "is a fool."

Will nodded. "If the goal is to put Augustus Frederick on the throne, he may find that he has inherited not a realm but instead a revolution."

"Augustus Frederick," Bolkum snorted. "One more empty-headed fool. Seen their kind before. Never come to any good."

"Let us hope this one comes to nothing at all," Will said. He nodded to the older man. "Kindly see Princess Clio to my grandmother's residence."

Bolkum was taking up the reins when Clio said, "Will, is that not also your residence?"

"Yes, generally it is."

David came up behind him just then and grinned when he heard what Will was saying. He put an arm around his shoulders as he told Clio, "Will's going to be staying with me for awhile. With the seniors heading for Akora, the house here will feel awfully empty. I'll be glad of the company."

"I have the dreadful suspicion that I've run you out of your own home," Clio said to Will. "It never occurred to me that could happen. After all, Lady Constance is on hand as chaperone."

"And a very good one, I'm sure she is," David said. "But Will and I have a lot of work to do, I think you know about what, and this way we can stay up all night, lob ideas off each other, do whatever's needed."

Clio sensed her father's hand in all this but did not say so. It had not escaped her notice that if Will was off with David, he would not be close at hand to keep an eye on her.

And that, she told herself, was all to the good. Far off in the distance, she could still make out the sails of the Akoran ships. Very soon, they would vanish from sight.

For the first time in her life, she would be left to her own resources. Even as she knew the situation was perilous, she could not contain a spurt of excitement.

CHAPTER XV

THE SENSE OF BEING ON THE EDGE OF MOMENTOUS events remained with Clio when she woke the following morning in her rooms at the Hollister residence. The sitting room and bedroom were at the back of the house, overlooking the garden. They were graciously furnished in the gilded style of Louis XV, the bed carved in swirling curves of white and gold, with the armoire and dressing table of similar design.

Clio took little notice of them as she sped through her toilette and hurried downstairs. Lady Constance had gone to call on old friends nearby, which left Clio eating breakfast alone when a footman arrived bearing a silver tray holding a single letter. The envelope was addressed to Clio in a feminine hand and bore, on the reverse side, a blob of red wax embossed with the seal of the Queen.

Opening the letter, Clio scanned it quickly and was delighted by its contents. She was invited to call upon Victoria at "her pleasure" but the young monarch added ingenuously, "I do hope it will be very soon, as I am eager to enlarge upon our acquaintance already so pleasantly begun."

That was more than sufficient for Clio. She made short work of breakfast and was soon on her way to Buckingham Palace. Passing beneath the Marble Arch once again, she spared a thought for how on earth the enormous structure could be moved, but quickly enough other, more immediate matters diverted her.

The same crowd she had seen the day before appeared to be on hand, with perhaps a few variations. Barely had she stepped from her carriage when Sir Morgan Kearns broke off his conversation with several other men and approached her.

"Your Highness, what a delight," he said, bowing gracefully. "I had heard of your parents' departure and assumed you had gone with them."

"Obviously not," she said, and by dint of pretending a need to hold up her skirts, avoided giving him her hand. No doubt Sir Morgan was accounted handsome by many and perhaps even considered congenial, but she disliked the boldness of his gaze, suggesting, as it seemed to, that he believed his attentions would be welcome. Perhaps they were, by the likes of Lady Catherine Mawcomber, but Clio found the very thought repellant.

"Do excuse me," she said, brushing past him. It was not a cut, precisely, for she had acknowledged him, but it was close enough to outright unfriendliness that Sir Morgan could not possibly mistake her intent. The Princess of Akora did not care to know him. From the corner of her eye, she saw the swift look of anger that passed over his features before being replaced by an empty smile.

Having never attempted to gain the slightest advantage from her family connection—that being quite literally a foreign notion on Akora—Clio was nonetheless relieved when the majordomo recognized her. She was swept through the crowd with admirable efficiency and escorted to the entrance of the Queen's apartment.

The Prime Minister was just leaving. Seeing her, Melbourne inclined his silvered head, dismissed the man who was with him, and smiled. He had, Clio thought, a startlingly sweet smile that truly did reach his eyes.

"Your Highness," he began.

"Please," Clio interrupted impulsively, "would you do me the kindness of addressing me by my given name?" When he hesitated, she continued, "You see, we don't use titles very much on Akora and every time someone refers to me by one here, I have to stop myself from looking over my shoulder to discover who is being addressed. It's really quite disconcerting, always twitching about, as it were."

Melbourne laughed. He looked startled by the sound, giving Clio the impression that he didn't laugh all that often, but he rallied quickly. "I would be delighted, my dear, and please call me William. Far too few people do these days."

She held out her hand, pleased to give it to him. "It shall be my pleasure, William. I trust the Queen is well?"

The seemingly innocuous question—for who did not inquire about the health of the Queen?—caused the Prime Minister to raise his brows. With a glance around their immediate vicinity, he lowered his voice before replying.

"Our mutual friend informs me that the present situation is known to you."

By which cryptic reference she divined that Will had told Melbourne she had learned of the plot against the Queen.

"He attempted to keep it from me," she said loyally.

"To his credit, but done is done. I must say—Clio—while I admire your desire to help, I am deeply concerned about your safety. Frankly, having our sovereign at risk is bad enough without confronting the possibility that the beloved daughter of a cherished ally might also be endangered."

"We both know—William—that your concern could have been alleviated by sharing it with my parents who, in possession of such information, I am quite certain would not have left me in England."

"That did occur to me," the Prime Minister said frankly, "as it did to Hollister. We discussed the matter."

"And concluded—?"

"That you might be able to help."

She could scarcely believe him. "Will said that?"

Melbourne—who it was said was a secret romantic—smiled again. "It was torn from him. I practically had to use tongs."

Deflated, Clio sighed. "That sounds more in character."

"He is concerned for you, as he has every right to be."

"He is accustomed to working alone or," she corrected, "with perhaps the help of my cousin David. Now he must accept that womanhood is no bar to capability."

"As we now have a female monarch—long may she reign—perhaps we must all absorb that fact. At any rate, please assure me you will have due regard for your own safety. I have the highest respect for your parents and would never wish to bring them sad tidings."

Unspoken between them was the acknowledgment that, personal tragedy aside, the impact on relations between their two nations would be catastrophic.

"And I would never knowingly place myself at needless risk," Clio assured him. She thought that sounded rather good, but it didn't impress the canny Prime Minister.

"Oh, dear, that's exactly the sort of statement, all hedged round with qualifiers, that I make in Commons when I don't want to be pinned down to anything."

Clio felt just a twinge of guilt, but she was amused all the same. "When I was a little girl, I used to sit behind my father's chair when he had Council meetings or addressed assemblages of our citizens. I was always busy playing with things I'd found, usually dug up, but perhaps I unknowingly absorbed his manner of speech."

Melbourne directed a telling look in her direction. "I daresay you absorbed a great deal more than that. Will has no notion what he's taken on."

She drew back just a little. "Taken on?" Just how much had Will told the Prime Minister? Surely not all *that* much?

"A poor choice of words," he allowed. "Forgive me, my dear, I'm quite inept at such matters. At any rate, I know the Queen is eager for your presence."

They chatted a few more minutes before Melbourne opened the door for her and stood aside. As she entered the Queen's private sitting room, he said softly, "We both want the same outcome to all this, but please do not place yourself at risk."

His words lingered with her as she went forward to greet Victoria, who held out her hand at the sight of her and quickly drew her into a conversation revealing the Queen's keen interest in all matters Akoran.

For an eighteen-year-old woman—girl, really—who until recently had never been allowed a moment alone, Victoria proved to have an agile mind and insatiable curiosity.

"I understand the present geography of Akora resulted from a volcanic explosion more than three thousand years ago," she said as they sat over a pot of tea. A footman hovered some distance away, out of hearing range, but otherwise they were alone.

"It was an immense explosion," Clio said. "What had been one island was ripped apart into two, with the Inland Sea lying between them."

"And Akora is beyond the Pillars of Hercules?" The thought appeared to thrill the Queen, who was said to be well read in Latin but regrettably deficient in Greek.

"As the western edge of the Mediterranean was known to the ancients," Clio said. "Our location out in the Atlantic is responsible in large part for our ability to maintain our separateness from the rest of the world for so long."

"I, for one, am glad you are not so separate now," Victoria said. She had a round, pretty face framed in dark brown hair that was gathered in coils behind her head. Her hands were rather plump but her movements, when she poured more tea for them both, were graceful.

"Akora seems a terribly romantic place," she confessed. "Not at all like England."

"Unless you are Akoran, in which case England seems terribly exotic."

"Does it really?" Victoria asked. "How extraordinary. Romantic England . . ." She tried the notion out but shook her head. "It defies comprehension."

"This is only my second trip to England," Clio said. "I was very small when I came before and remember little of it. But this time, as we approached the mouth of the Thames, a fog bank rolled in. I was on deck and I could see the little tendrils of fog creeping over the bull's head prow of our vessel until it was entirely hidden. Crewmen on each of the ships in our convoy began to ring the bells so that the navigators would know how close each vessel was to the others. The bells tolling and the slap of waves against the hulls were the only sounds. The fog smelled of the sea but also of land. Far, far above it, I could just make out the dim circle of the sun."

"Were you afraid?" Victoria asked, hanging on the picture Clio painted. "Did you worry that you might strike rocks?"

"The thought did not occur to me, but perhaps it should have. Instead, all I could think of was what lay beyond the fog. *England,* a name out of legend and mystery. A place of round tables and knights, fair ladies and great daring from which people have ventured out all over the world, even to plain old Akora."

The Queen laughed. "Good heavens, I never thought of it in such a way." More seriously, she added, "And yet I do think England is a truly wonderful place and I want to do my absolute best for it."

"I'm sure you will. You do, after all, have the able assistance of Lord Melbourne."

"I am intensely grateful for it," the Queen said with all sincerity. "He appears to be the wisest of men and is already my dear friend. Although," her voice dropped a notch, "he does seem very insistent that I should marry and soon."

"Are you not inclined to do so?"

"No . . . not precisely. As a woman, I know full well that I need the guidance of a man."

She paused, seeking Clio's reaction, but got only, "Well . . . if that is how you feel—"

"But that's right, don't you think? Women are meant to be wives and mothers. Our proper sphere is the home. Isn't that how it is on Akora?"

"Not entirely," Clio said, choosing her words. "Generally speaking, we find that partnerships between men and women work best."

Assuming, of course, that the man in question wasn't too stubborn and stuck in his outdated ways to see the value of a woman's insights, not to mention her courage, persistence, and—

"What an intriguing notion," Victoria said. "I do

face the quandary of finding a husband who will accept that I am Queen *regnant,* not Queen consort, and who will be able to assist me without attempting to usurp my position." She frowned at the thought. "That would be very unpleasant personally, in addition to causing profound political difficulties."

"Do you have anyone in mind?" Clio asked.

"No . . ." Victoria smiled suddenly, looking very much her eighteen years. "But I confess, I shall not mind looking!"

They laughed over that, but quickly enough the young princess grew more serious. "It is *very* important for me to marry wisely. The succession—" She broke off, understandably reluctant to contemplate what would occur in the event of her own early death.

Mindful that she trod on very sensitive ground, Clio said, "May I confess? I do not understand the British succession at all. It is hereditary, I believe, yet it does not always pass to the eldest son."

"It should in the normal course of events," Victoria said. "However, it has not recently." With the air of one well schooled in an intricate subject, she explained, "The late King, my uncle, had no children, therefore the throne passed to the line of his next eldest brother, my father. Sadly, my father was not alive to inherit and so the throne has passed to me, as his only child."

"And while you have no children to inherit, the

next eldest brother, Augustus Frederick, Duke of Sussex, would inherit?"

"Not precisely. The Duke of Sussex is next in line for the British throne until I have a child, that is true, but he isn't my next eldest uncle. That would be Uncle Ernest—"

Was it Clio's imagination, or did the young Queen flinch at the mention of that name?

"Uncle Ernest—?"Clio prompted. The tips of her ears warmed a bit. Here was something, whatever it might be.

"It gets a bit complicated," Victoria said apologetically. "You see, my family has connections to the principality of Hanover in Germany. For many years, the ruler of Great Britain and Ireland and the ruler of Hanover have been one and the same. However, unlike Britain, Hanover is under Salic law, which means no woman can ever inherit that throne."

"So when your uncle, the late King, died—"

"The thrones had to be divided. I became Queen of Great Britain and Ireland. My oldest surviving uncle—that would be Uncle Ernest—became King of Hanover."

"And he is there now?"

"I certainly hope so!" Catching herself, Victoria flushed prettily. "What I meant was, I certainly expect so."

As Clio continued to ponder the convoluted twists and turns of the British succession, and what they might mean to the hunt for Umbra, the two went on to speak of other matters. The young Queen quickly revealed herself to be well read, curious, and genuinely intent on understanding the world better.

"I do so wish to do good," Victoria said at one point, a bit plaintively.

It made Clio like her, although she would have done so under any circumstance. There was nothing about Victoria to dislike. She seemed a genuinely unpretentious, good-hearted young woman presented with responsibilities that would have challenged many far older than she. Yet she made no complaint, indicating only a heartfelt desire to fulfill her duties well.

And this was the person whom Umbra—whoever Umbra might be—wanted to kill. The very thought angered Clio and raised all her protective instincts. She was still steaming over it when, having concluded her pleasant visit with the Queen, she prepared to leave the palace.

And go where . . . do what? As much as she enjoyed Lady Constance's company, returning to the Hollister house held little appeal. She wished to be useful, most particularly in some way that would advance the cause of thwarting Umbra.

Heaven forbid that Will should be on hand or that he should allow her to assist him. For all his acknowledgment, so Melbourne claimed, that she could be helpful, he showed no inclination whatsoever to avail himself of her assistance.

That left her to her own devices and she promptly put them to use. Sir Morgan Kearns was still loitering near the entrance to the palace as she approached. She supposed it was the done thing these days to be seen there, considering how very many people were doing so. Ignoring them, despite various attempts to gain her attention, she put aside her instinctive dislike of the man and approached him.

His look of surprise was comical, understandably enough given her earlier dismissal. She smiled ingenuously and this time offered her hand.

"Do forgive my haste upon arriving, Sir Morgan. I was anxious for Her Majesty's company."

Shocked though he was by her sudden reversal, Sir Morgan rallied quickly. The tall, dark-haired man bent over her hand and said smoothly, "There is nothing to forgive, Your Highness. I trust you found Her Majesty well?"

"Extremely, but now I must determine what to do with the remainder of my day. Unfortunately, I know so little of London—"

She dangled it before him, the improbable but nonetheless ultimate carrot that he, Sir Morgan Kearns, would be seen in the company of no less than the Princess of Akora, escorting her around the city.

"If I might be so bold, Your Highness," bold Sir Morgan offered, "I should be delighted to show you our fair city."

"How kind of you." She gestured to her carriage,

waiting nearby. Peering down from the driver's seat, Bolkum scowled but mercifully said nothing as Sir Morgan assisted her up and took his place beside her.

It was, to be fair, a lovely day. Rare for summer, the city did not stink. Clio credited that to the westerly breeze and offered silent thanks for it.

As the carriage moved away from the palace, Sir Morgan appeared still overcome by his great good luck. "What would you like to do?" he inquired. "Shopping . . . art galleries, perhaps . . . what would please you?"

He seemed genuinely to wish that she be pleased, but her own motivation was quite different. She wanted to learn much more about Sir Morgan, the better to gauge what involvement, if any, he might have with Umbra. To that end, she said, "I would prefer that you decide. Show me whatever it is you regard as the most impressive sight in London today."

He looked at her for a moment as though he assumed she was joking, saw that she was not and turned thoughtful. "Well . . . then, let me see . . ." After a moment, he gave directions to Bolkum, who snorted under his breath and slapped the reins.

A short time later, as they sat staring at a vast building under construction, Sir Morgan seemed to experience a twinge of doubt as to the wisdom of his selection. "I suppose you find this a bit odd," he said tentatively.

"That depends. What is it?" The building, or so

much of it as was complete, was two stories in height, made of a cream-hued stone, and topped with a red-tile roof. What appeared to be an adjacent bell tower was as yet unfinished. The overall effect could have graced Venice or Florence, but it did well enough beside the Thames, adjacent to London Bridge.

"It will be the London terminus for the London-to-Greenwich Railway," Sir Morgan said.

"The railway that began operation last year? The one passengers can ride on, not just freight?"

"Yes, that's the one. I myself have ridden on it." Hesitantly, he said, "Several times, actually. I find the experience exhilarating."

"Do you?" She had wondered if he might have depths beyond the idle search for pleasure, but never had she imagined this. "I cannot conceive what it must be like to travel at so great a speed. How fast does it go?"

"It has been clocked at twenty-two miles per hour," Sir Morgan informed her with the pardonable pride of a man who has submitted himself to the rigors of technology. "But naturally, it doesn't travel at that speed on a normal basis. Fifteen miles per hour would be more typical. The entire track is laid on a viaduct comprised of nine hundred seventy-eight arches in all. As you undoubtedly realize, construction has been quite an undertaking."

"I would think so—"

"I was privileged to see the plans before work began, and while I will admit they appeared daunting, I became an investor. Now, of course, I am very pleased with the results, the financial reward being only one among them."

"I can see that you would be—"

"It's really the notion of *progress,* you see, people moving about as they've never done before, being linked in all sorts of new ways. It never occurred to me that anything could be quite so gripping."

"Fascinating."

"I'm *so* glad you think so. Do you know, the best estimates are that at the present rate, within only a few years, the railway will have made more than one hundred thousand trips between London and Greenwich? Can you imagine that, one hundred thousand!"

"Astonishing . . . absolutely astonishing."

"And only the beginning. While it is true that most of the railways under construction right now are intended to carry freight, there will be more meant solely for passengers. Why, one day I believe people who live miles away from London—*miles*—will journey into the heart of the city each and every day to work or merely to amuse themselves. And they will do all that by railway."

"Will they? That's quite astounding." But not remotely as astounding as the far more amazing discovery that Sir Morgan Kearns did indeed have a passion, however it had nothing whatsoever to do with either

Lady Catherine Mawcomber or political intrigue. Sir Morgan Kearns was fascinated—utterly and completely fascinated—by railways. His features were suddenly animated. Moreover, he looked delighted at the opportunity to share his enthusiasm.

"Please don't think me presumptuous," he said, "but when you said I might decide where we would go, I wondered if it was at all possible you could find this interesting. I cannot tell you how pleased I am that you do."

"But how could I not?" Clio said, not untruthfully. She did find the idea of the railway exciting, just not quite as enthralling as Sir Morgan did. "It is an historic achievement."

"It is indeed." He consulted his pocket watch. With the smile of a man who has contrived a marvel, he said, "If you would care for a closer look, the train is due to arrive in just a few minutes."

"Is it? Here?" Now this was interesting. "Of course I would love to see it."

Assisted down from the carriage, Clio gave her skirts a twitch to straighten them and addressed Bolkum. "Kindly remain here. I daresay, the railway might frighten the horses."

"Daresay," Bolkum muttered. He looked disinclined to venture anywhere near the thing himself.

"Quite a few people find it intimidating," Sir Morgan confided as they walked toward the high, arched passageway that gave access to the tracks. "But I assure you, there is nothing to be afraid of. It is rather noisy and the locomotive itself gives off plumes of steam, but all that is perfectly normal."

"I'll keep that in mind," Clio said as they made their way around the piles of construction material and nearer, but not too near, to the edge of the tracks. Other people were gathering there. A general air of excitement pervaded, which mounted as the distant sound of metal grating on metal could be heard.

"Here it comes," Sir Morgan said, a bit unnecessarily. He joined the rest in straining for a look.

Moments later, an object unlike any Clio had ever imagined, came into view. From the bed of what appeared to be a wagon, rose a tall black metal stack, belching steam. It was connected to a large red tank outfitted with an impressive series of gears and axles, and equipped with an enormous coal scuttle. This, she gathered, must be the locomotive similar to the one she had seen being loaded into the hold of the Akoran ship. Two men hovered over it, one pulling on a large lever that activated a brake. Behind the locomotive was another, even larger tank, carried on its own wagon and constructed of wood. It appeared to hold water. And behind that—

Clio did not know whether to laugh or gasp. The locomotive pulled a series of what appeared to be carriages, painted variously in red or white as was the entire train, and with their wheels resting directly on the tracks themselves. They seemed identical to the larger carriages found careening down the turnpikes sprouting all over England, but instead of being drawn by horses, they were attached to the locomotive. Passengers hung out the windows while their cases, boxes, and trunks were secured outside on the roof, just as they would be on normal carriages.

Lastly came the most startling sight of all, an entirely open carriage riding on a flat wooden bed that was hooked to the rest of the train. Several ladies and gentlemen occupied it, the ladies carefully swathed in hats and veils to protect their faces from the rigors of so great a rate of speed. In the rear seat, perched above them, was a footman. Barely had the train screeched to a halt than he jumped down, carrying with him folding steps that he set beneath the carriage. Other railway workers were doing the same along the length of the train. The doors were flung open and the excited passengers disembarked, to be greeted by those who had turned out to welcome them.

There was much laughter and good cheer, as well as here and there a look of palpable relief at having survived so daring an experience.

"When the terminus is completed," Sir Morgan explained, "the train will come directly into it, of course. A station is under construction at the other end of the line, in Greenwich, but work on it has barely begun."

"This is extraordinary," Clio said and meant it. The implications of what she was seeing were just beginning to set in. "Does it run in all weather?"

"On inclement days the open carriage is covered over, but the closed carriages remain in use. Service did have to be suspended for a time last winter because of the condition of the tracks, but efforts are under way to assure that that does not happen again, except in the case of truly dire weather."

"It's safe, even in heavy rain?"

"Most definitely. In fact, it's a good deal safer under those conditions than a carriage being driven on a road that is not yet macadamed. Mud can be very slippery."

"I see . . . no wonder my father took a locomotive back with him."

"Do you think railways might come to Akora?" Sir Morgan asked excitedly.

Clio did not wish to disappoint him but she answered honestly. "Of our two large islands, Kallimos, where the royal city of Ilius is located, is likely much too hilly to make a railway practical. Leios, on the other hand, is very flat. However, the people there are countryfolk devoted to the rearing of horses. I doubt very much they would appreciate a railway."

"The countryfolk here don't appreciate them, either. There was no end of difficulty securing rights of way for the viaduct. However, no one can stand in the path of progress."

Clio suspected people would continue to try but she did not say so. Having revised her opinion of Sir Morgan for the better, she agreed when he suggested they examine the train more closely while it was being prepared for the return trip later that day to Greenwich. They spent a pleasant hour doing so, as he answered all her questions with clear delight at having found so receptive an audience.

They had left the station and were chatting amicably en route to Sir Morgan's residence, where he would take his leave of her, when the carriage turned onto Regent Street. In late afternoon, the thoroughfare was busy with shoppers, office workers, and deliverymen, as well as the peddlers and pickpockets kept at bay by the uniformed police. The latter seemed, at least to Clio's eye, to be out in greater force than usual.

Wondering whether her impression was true and if it was a result of the heightened security around the Queen, she did not notice the man who emerged from one of the offices along Regent Street.

Nor did she observe the quick flash of surprise followed hard by anger that overtook Will when he saw who shared the carriage with her.

CHAPTER XVI

"WHAT WERE YOU THINKING OF?" WILL DEmanded. He stood in the center of the drawing room, doing his damnedest to hold on to his temper and not succeeding terribly well.

An hour had passed since he had seen Clio in the company of Sir Morgan Kearns. An hour of waiting for her to return to the Hollister residence, worrying about her, and fighting the impulse to go after her and beat Kearns to a pulp.

All the while not calling attention to himself or rousing in anyone's mind the possibility that something might be afoot.

"Discretion," Melbourne had said so often that Will was heartily sick of the word. "Discretion at all times. If any hint gets about that there is a plot against the Queen, it is impossible to know what might occur."

No, Will thought, it was not. The most immediate response would likely be that the Queen's determination to achieve independence from her acutely protective and domineering mother would lessen drastically. She would be drawn back into the Duchess of Kent's sphere, with the result that Melbourne's influence would be severely diminished.

That was to be avoided, not merely for Melbourne's sake, but for the country's.

And so he waited until the drawing room door opened and Clio stepped in, shutting the door behind her. Upon hearing his voice, she stopped cold, took a quick breath and answered with complete composure.

"I was attempting to determine if Sir Morgan Kearns might possibly be Umbra or, failing that, might know Umbra's identity."

Will sought to equal her calm and found he could not. A pulse twitched in his jaw. To make matters worse, he could not stop looking at her. She was so damned lovely and he remembered so damned well what she felt like beneath him, above him, all around him.

"You thought it wise to go off alone with a man who might be Umbra?"

"We were not alone. We were in the middle of

London, in plain sight of hundreds of people, and Bolkum was with us."

How could any man who looked so . . . supremely, amazingly magnificent that her heart tripped over itself at the mere sight of him, much less the memory of being taken by him to the very heights of ecstasy . . . how could that man be so incredibly *obtuse*?

"I see . . . and where precisely did you go?"

"To view the terminus of the London-to-Greenwich Railway, and to see the train itself as it arrived." At his look of disbelief, she smiled. "Sir Morgan Kearns is a fanatical devotee of anything and everything to do with trains. Would you like to know precisely how many arches there are on the London-to-Greenwich viaduct? I can tell you. How fast the train travels or how many trips it is expected to make within the next few years? I shall be happy to enlighten you, as Sir Morgan has enlightened me."

"He went on like that about a train?" Will did not hide his skepticism.

"He is enthralled by it. It is far and away the most exciting thing in his life."

"So he led you to believe."

That gave her pause, but not for long. "He did not lead me to anything. Besides, if we cannot eliminate even one of those who were at Holyhood, we are not a single step closer to identifying Umbra."

"We are one step closer."

"And how is that?"

"Lady Barbara is dead."

She stared at him in shock. "Lady Barbara Devereux? But how?"

"She fell from a window at the back of the Devereux residence into the garden. A maid found her. Her neck was broken."

"And Lord Devereux—?"

"Was at his club, in the presence of several dozen witnesses."

"When did this happen?"

"This morning, while you were with the Queen."

"Well, then, Sir Morgan could not have had anything to do with it. He was at the palace when I arrived and I encountered him again when I left."

"The Devereux residence is scarcely ten minutes' walk from the palace. How long were you with the Queen?"

"Several hours," Clio acknowledged.

"Long enough for a man to leave, kill a woman, and return."

Which would mean that she shared her carriage with a man who had just committed a brutal murder. Had chatted and laughed with him, had even thought how surprisingly pleasant he was, if in an eccentric sort of way. It did not bear considering.

"Couldn't Lady Barbara's death have been an accident?" she asked.

"It could have been," Will acknowledged. "But she is one of a small group of people that may very well include Umbra, who knows I am hunting him and must therefore conclude that Melbourne is aware of the plot to kill the Queen. He may be seeking to eliminate anyone who can tie him to that plot."

"But it is Lady Catherine who is reputed to be Sir Morgan's mistress, is it not? Lady Barbara is merely an acquaintance."

"So rumor has it. At the very least, if I am right, we can say with certainty that Lady Barbara was not Umbra."

"You considered 'he' might be a woman?" That surprised her; she would not have expected him to do so.

"Of course. It would be foolish to overlook any possibility, although I did think it unlikely."

"Why?"

"Because I doubt Platt or McManus would obey a woman, and my contact with Toffler assured me he would not have done so."

Reluctantly Clio nodded. "Very well, Lady Barbara was not Umbra, but was in all likelihood killed by him. That eliminates her husband."

"And leaves the Mawcombers, Lord Reginald and Lady Catherine."

"You said Umbra is not likely to be a woman."

Will shrugged. "I could be wrong. However, I don't believe it's either of them. I think it's Kearns."

The man who had prattled on so raptly about trains and seemed to have no other concern in the world? Could the same man plot regicide? Clio could not conceive of it and yet the possibility could not be dismissed. "Then arrest him," she said.

"On what charges? We have no evidence."

"You said Toffler's quarters were searched surreptitiously, leading to discovery of the letter signed by Umbra. Wouldn't it be possible to do the same with Sir Morgan's residence and also to acquire a sample of his handwriting?" When he did not reply at once, Clio asked, "Or is it that a man of Sir Morgan's standing has more protection under your laws than does someone of Toffler's ilk?"

"It's already been done," Will admitted. "Kearns' handwriting does not match that of the letter signed by Umbra."

"Handwriting can be disguised," she reminded him.

"That is so, but nothing at all incriminating was found, therefore we have no reason to detain Sir Morgan."

No, Clio reflected, they did not. And she had no reason to think him guilty . . . except that Will believed he was. Though she saw no particular reason to tell him so, she could not dismiss his concerns. They lingered in her mind.

But were pushed aside when he said, "The Prime Minister has invited us to supper."

"Has he? This evening?" An evening with Will, even if not alone, was an unexpected pleasure.

He nodded. "Do you know much about Viscount Melbourne?"

"I know what everyone knows—his late wife was Caroline Lamb, who had a scandalous affair with the poet Byron. She died years ago and Melbourne has never remarried." She thought for a moment, trying to recall what she had heard over the years. "I believe their only child also died."

"He adored the boy and mourns him still. A few years ago, Melbourne was accused of alienating the affections of another man's wife."

Clio did not mistake the meaning of that, however delicately it might be phrased. "Good Lord, had he?"

"No, the husband was attempting to blackmail Melbourne. When the Prime Minister refused to pay, and no evidence of the charges could be produced, they were withdrawn."

"I see—" In fact, she did not. What was the purpose of recalling old and very private business?

When she asked as much, Will said, "The point is, that very few men in political life—including entirely innocent men—could have survived such a scandal, much less done so after having had a scandalous wife. That Melbourne did so speaks to the great respect he is accorded."

"Including from you?"

"Yes, including from me. I have disagreed with him on various issues—his opposition to reform, for example. But I would never doubt that his intent is to serve England and the Queen to the best of his considerable abilities."

"However—?"

In the steady glow of the oil lamps, his smile softened the hard contours of his face, if only momentarily. "Did I speak of any reservations?"

"No, but I heard them all the same. Something about Melbourne gives you pause."

"Not precisely. His only weakness, if it can be called that, is that he is a sentimental man, a romantic, if you will. Having never known true love, he believes in it deeply."

"Rather than deny its existence?"

"I don't think he could do so and live."

Clio turned away and found herself gazing at a small but powerfully evocative landscape painting on the wall near where she stood. It depicted a windmill beside a canal, a prosaic enough subject, but the work was filled with vibrant light that seemed to pour out of it.

"Is that a Rembrandt?" she asked.

Will came to stand beside her. Looking not at the painting but at her, he said, "It is one of his earlier works, I believe."

She met his gaze. "Do you also share Melbourne's belief in the existence of true love?"

He did not answer at once but merely continued looking at her. Beneath his scrutiny, her skin warmed. She fought the impulse to lower her eyes and finally lost.

He laughed, very softly. "I think I might be persuaded to believe in it," he said, before taking her hand and raising it gently to his lips.

"WHAT WILL YOU WEAR?" LADY CONSTANCE INquired eagerly. She had returned from visiting her friends to the news that Clio was dining with the Prime Minister—and just as excitedly from the good lady's point of view—with her grandson.

"I haven't decided yet," Clio said. They were ensconced in her sitting room. Every evening gown she had brought with her had been removed from the wardrobe in the adjacent bedroom and spread out on every available surface for their inspection. She was surprised by how many of them there were.

"I thought I sent most of these back to Akora," Clio said, staring at the piles of silk, lace, and satin, much of it embroidered with pearls and precious gems.

"You did," Lady Constance replied. "But at the last moment, your mother and I agreed they should come here instead."

"I should be grateful, I know, but all it means is that I cannot imagine which is best to wear this evening."

"That depends." If eyes really could twinkle, Lady Constance's did just then.

Fingering an overskirt of gauze so thin it seemed to disappear against her skin, Clio asked, "On what?"

"On whether you want my grandson's attention to be on the Prime Minister or on you."

Clio waged a brief—very brief—struggle with her nobler self. Fortunately, it yielded quietly. "This one, I think," she said and lifted a gown of gossamer silk, woven of gold and silver threads so that sun and moon alike seemed to shine within it.

An hour later, she met Will at the bottom of the double stairs, which curved in the shape of butterfly's wings as they rose from the marble entry hall to the floors above. He was in evening dress, which should have had a taming effect, but only seemed to emphasize the wild beauty of his form. She was thinking about that, and of how startled he would be by any such description, when she realized he was staring at her.

As well he might. The gown was lower cut than any she usually wore and emphasized the femininity of her form. Such were the gown's underpinnings that her breasts were pushed rather high, swelling above the bodice, while the slimness of her waist was exaggerated.

In deference to the gown—and the occasion—she had deigned to don a corset, one of those instruments of torture she usually avoided at all cost. Truth be told, it was a pretty confection that merely refined her curves rather than abused them.

"That is a lovely gown," Will said. He cleared his throat. "And you . . . you make it even lovelier."

So heated was the atmosphere between them, that she took refuge in gentle humor. "Good heavens, is that a compliment?"

The footman offered her wrap, a transparent web of golden lace. Will took it and draped it over her bare shoulders. He bent his head slightly, very close to her ear. "Have I been remiss in compliments?"

A shiver ran through her. She was suddenly, startlingly conscious that her nipples were hard, and was glad that the stiff fabric of the corset concealed them. Even so, she was vividly aware of the pressure of that garment against them as she turned and, as lightly as she could manage under the circumstances, said, "That depends on whether compliments require words. You have been . . . complimentary in other ways."

As when he drove into her, his hard face riven with pleasure, and called her name at the peak of his release. That was the sort of compliment to warm a woman on the coldest night of eternity.

All things considered, it might not be a good idea to remind him of that just then. For a fraction of a moment, Clio entertained the notion that they would disappoint the Prime Minister.

Reason returned, if only barely, when the footman opened the door, calling their attention to the carriage that awaited them.

CHAPTER XVII

DINNER WITH THE PRIME MINISTER WAS, CLIO decided, interesting. It was *interesting* to behave with utmost propriety when she was feeling entirely improper. It was *interesting* to pretend an appetite for the admittedly excellent food and wine when her desires were of an entirely different sort. Most particularly, it was *interesting* to watch the entrancing Earl of Hollister cope with the same dilemma.

They dined in Melbourne's private apartment in Buckingham Palace. He had moved into it only a fortnight before, at the entreaty of the Queen. "The arrangement is entirely temporary," he informed them shortly after their arrival. "In the present unsettled period"—thus did he refer obliquely to the possibility of regicide—"I prefer to remain close to Her Majesty."

"An excellent idea," Clio said. She took little notice of the room except to see that the furniture was of dark wood and very substantial, as though to discourage anyone who might think of rearranging it. Melbourne, like as not, would have no inclination to do so. He appeared to have put no personal imprint of any sort on his surroundings, except perhaps for the small, framed portrait of the Queen on a side table.

Yet he was, for all that, a man who made his mark in conversation, possessed of a quick, darting mind and a seemingly endless fount of stories that were genuinely engaging.

"My memory dooms me," he said when they had progressed as far as the lemon ice that cleansed their palates between the fish and meat courses. "It appears to have recorded virtually everything I have experienced or witnessed since I was thirteen months old."

Clio might have doubted him, however silently, but he went on to relate tales of the great and near-great he had met over the course of his almost sixty years. His conversation skirted the ribald, for he seemed to enjoy testing propriety, but never did it succumb to the least degree of viciousness.

At length and inevitably, the talk turned to more serious matters.

"I spoke with Lord Devereux," Melbourne said, "after receiving the dreadful news of his wife's death. He is most distraught."

"I had the impression they lived their lives largely apart," Will said.

"No doubt they did," Melbourne agreed. "Such has been the style for so long now." He cast a glance in the direction of the Queen's portrait. "I suspect that will be changing before long."

Pressing the tips of his fingers together, he peered over them at Clio. "Her Majesty said you gave her some very good advice on the subject of marriage."

"I did?" She was genuinely surprised, not to mention disconcerted to have the matter come up in Will's presence. He of the marriage proposal so charmingly made and still looming over her.

"She said you told her marriage should be a partnership between a man and a woman."

"I am not certain I put it in so many words."

"Yet that is what you believe?"

"It is what I have seen," she replied carefully, "in the marriages of many of those closest to me."

"Then you have been most fortunate," Melbourne said. "At any rate, it does appear that Lady Barbara was the victim of foul play. There were indications of a struggle in the room from which she fell. Whatever his feelings for her, or lack thereof, Lord Devereux displays the expected degree of revulsion against such violation."

"Was anyone seen going in or out of the room?" Will asked.

The Prime Minister shook his head. "Unfortunately not. At that hour, all the servants were busy below stairs. They are all accounted for, by the way."

"Clio and I have discussed the likelihood that Umbra killed her," Will said.

"For what purpose?" Melbourne inquired with no suggestion that he disagreed.

"To conceal his identity," Clio replied. "If Umbra is, as Will and I both think, one of the circle that came down to Holyhood, Lady Barbara might have seen or heard something that doomed her."

"That would seem to indicate that the culprit is either Lord Reginald Devereux or Sir Morgan Kearns," their host said.

"What about Lord Mawcomber?" Clio asked.

"Lord and Lady Mawcomber are not in London," the Prime Minister replied. "They have gone to Bath."

The waiters returned to place before them medallions of beef in peppercorn sauce. When they were alone again, Will said, "Clio spent some time in Sir Morgan's company earlier today. She is not inclined to think him guilty."

"Nor do I presume he is innocent," she hastened to say. "It is only that he seems so . . . content with simple things, as though he could not possibly bestir himself to intrigue beyond the bedchamber and, frankly, even that surprises me."

"Fascinating," Melbourne murmured. "On what do you base this?"

Before she could reply, Will said, "He likes trains."

"He does what?" Melbourne inquired.

"Trains," Will repeated with a grin. "Apparently, Kearns is fascinated by them. He took Clio to see the London-to-Greenwich Railway."

Their host looked askance at the mere idea. "The railway? That horrible, noisy thing? Why on earth would Kearns want anything to do with that?"

"He is infatuated with the notion of progress," Clio said. On an afterthought, she added, "He also mentioned he's made quite a lot of money from it."

Will and Melbourne both looked at her in surprise. "Made money from it?" Will asked. "The London-to-Greenwich? In five years perhaps, and then only if it isn't supplanted by something better. The construction costs were astronomical, far outstripping even the highest estimates."

"I was asked to become involved in that," Melbourne said. "Can't imagine how anyone would think I'd be interested in something of that sort, but have to say, good thing I wasn't."

"Kearns has not made money from his investment?" Clio asked.

"Couldn't possibly have," Will informed her, not without a certain note of satisfaction. "The line is popular, certainly, but the best estimates now are that it will have to carry upwards of ten million passengers before the investors see a shilling."

"Then Kearns lied," she said slowly.

"How astonishing," Will murmured, and pretended not to notice when she scowled at him.

"We are keeping an eye on Sir Morgan," Melbourne said, "but it is difficult in the congestion of London, particularly when the watchers cannot draw attention to themselves."

"Surely," Clio ventured, "with the Queen herself at risk, any amount of scrutiny is justified if it stops Umbra, whoever he may be."

"You might think so," Melbourne said, "but I must ask myself who is behind Umbra, whoever he may be. What is his motive? Is he a political fanatic acting out of brute conviction? Or does he work on someone else's behalf?"

"On behalf of Augustus Frederick?" Clio suggested. She was not English, and therefore more willing to entertain the notion that one member of the royal family might be seeking to gain the throne by killing another. Moreover, she was only a generation removed from a period in her country's history that had seen an attempt to kill Akora's own leader, her father.

A quick look she could not decipher passed between Melbourne and Will. The Prime Minister said, "While it is true that Her Majesty's uncle, the Duke of Sussex, is next in line for the throne, there is no evidence whatsoever linking him to this matter."

"It is to be hoped that no such evidence is found," Will interjected. "If a royal is involved, the knowledge of that would shake the monarchy to its foundations, not to mention what it would do to England as a whole."

Melbourne agreed. "We live in precarious times. People are seeing their way of life threatened and transformed. To make them further doubt the institutions that maintain society . . . I shudder to think where that would lead."

Clio allowed herself a sip of wine as she pondered her response. In the intimacy of the room, it would be very easy to lapse into confidences. She had to remember that, charming though Melbourne was, he would use any advantage for England's welfare.

Slowly, she said, "The view from Akora, as I understand it, is that much of Europe will be swept by revolution in the coming years. The social strains and—to be frank—the ineptitude of most European governments make that inevitable."

To her surprise, the Prime Minister chuckled. "The view from London is identical, dear lady. However, we intend to make absolutely certain that England is the exception, the literal island of calm in the sea of chaos. And—to be frank—chaos can present opportunity, which we will seize." He paused a moment, then added, "But most particularly, we do not intend to be drawn into foreign conflicts that would distract us from our larger goals."

Clio thought that a rather cryptic remark, since she had no idea what foreign conflicts he might mean. However, not for a moment did she doubt that England, under the leadership of men such as Melbourne—and of Will—would achieve great things. Assuming, of course, that it could remain above what promised to be a deadly fray.

"So you will leave Sir Morgan at large?" she asked.

"We will keep him under close scrutiny," Will said. "But we have to recognize that he may elude us, in which case we must be prepared for him to strike."

Clio had her own thoughts about what those preparations should include, but she chose to keep them to herself for the time being. The meal was almost concluded, they were lingering over coffee, when she said, "Would you gentlemen be good enough to explain something to me?"

The Prime Minister looked at her benignly, while Will betrayed a hint of wariness. Give the man credit, he was learning.

"What would that be, my dear?" Melbourne asked.

She paused, smiled, tilted her head just a little to one side and asked softly, "If Victoria dies, why is the Duke of Sussex next in line instead of her Uncle Ernest, who is already King of Hanover?"

As the men stared at her, she added sweetly, "After

all, Ernest is the elder, isn't he? Surely, he should take precedence."

It fell to Will to say, "I wasn't aware you were so well versed in the matter of the succession."

"That is also what Her Majesty and I discussed today."

"She didn't mention it—" Melbourne began, only to sigh deeply. "As she would not. It is a sensitive matter. Suffice to say that with the death of the late King, the thrones of Great Britain and Ireland on the one hand, and of the principality of Hanover on the other, which have been united for several hundred years, are now sundered for all time."

She raised a brow delicately. "Ernest could never inherit the British throne?"

"Never," both men said in unison. Will added, "His character is such that his departure from this realm was a great relief. Parliament would never permit his return in any position of authority."

"I see—" She looked from one to the other, realizing for the first time how truly well they worked together. They were so different in many respects—Melbourne a man for the drawing room, while Will looked so much more at home with a sword in his hand—and yet they saw eye-to-eye when it truly mattered. The avoidance of foreign conflicts, for example, including that which would flow inevitably from the murder of a queen.

"Just one more question," she began and hid a smile as they braced themselves.

Into the silence that descended, Clio asked, "Is the King of Hanover aware that any dreams he fosters of becoming King of Great Britain and Ireland are doomed to failure? Or does he believe they have a chance of success?"

IT WAS LATE WHEN THEY LEFT THE PALACE. THE night air was cool and there was a hint of rain in the offing. The top remained down on the phaeton. Will handed Clio up and climbed into the driver's seat beside her.

"Did you enjoy yourself?" he asked as he slapped the reins lightly.

"It was a lovely dinner," Clio said.

"I'm glad you thought so." He cast her a cautious glance, similar to those she had been receiving from him ever since revealing her knowledge of "Uncle Ernest."

They rode in silence, broken only by the crack of the horses' hooves against the cobblestones, until Will said quietly, "We would prefer for the matter of the King of Hanover to remain entirely private."

The matter of a foreign monarch possibly plotting to usurp the British throne through an act of regicide? Yes, she supposed they—being Melbourne, Will, and likely her cousin David as well—would greatly prefer that. Moreover, she thought it the wisest possible course of action, assuming they were able to stop him.

"What would it mean if he succeeded?" she asked softly.

Will did not hesitate. His answer was succinct and to the point: "War, that is all it could mean. War with Hanover and with anyone who got the notion that Britain was weakened and therefore vulnerable."

"With Germany, possibly, given its close ties to Hanover?"

He nodded. "Almost certainly, but let's not overlook France. I suppose if I tried, I could figure out how many wars there have been between Britain and France down through the centuries. Off the top of my head, I can't tell you, only that there have been a great many."

"A huge war, then?" A war that might possibly engulf Akora.

"We have interests all over the world," Will said, "as do Germany and France. A war that begins on the continent of Europe no longer necessarily will remain there. 'World war' is a bizarre thought, but it is not out of the question."

The very idea sent a chill of horror through her. She leaned a little closer to him and sighed deeply.

It was close to midnight; the streets of London were empty of most traffic. She was surprised, after a few minutes, to realize that another carriage was a short distance behind them.

Even so, she thought little of it until Will suddenly

pulled on the reins, sharply turning the phaeton onto a narrower street. Clio sat up straighter and held on to the side of the seat.

"What are you—?" Before she could finish the question, she heard hooves galloping over the pavement to their rear. A glance over her shoulder revealed a dark, enclosed landau bearing down on them. Only the driver was visible, but he was hunched in his seat and so muffled in a cape that she could make out nothing of him.

"Get your head down," Will ordered as he spurred their horses on. They reached the other end of the street and emerged onto a broader avenue. Crouched on the seat, Clio saw the landau follow. The driver was either very determined or very reckless. She heard the crack of the whip as he forced his team to an even faster pace. They came around a curve and for a moment, the two right wheels of the landau seemed to rise slightly from the ground. Clio held her breath, thinking the carriage might turn over, but an instant later, it righted itself and continued after them, closing very quickly.

"How are you with horses?" Will asked matter-of-factly. He might have been inquiring if she liked roses or preferred tulips.

"Well enough, I suppose. Why—?"

"Here, take the reins." When she would have demurred, he said, "Just keep them steady. We're coming up on the Strand; it's a straight run, no turns."

With the reins pressed into her hands, she could hardly refuse. The muscles of her arms tightened as they took the force of the powerful horses surging forward. She caught her breath and focused hard on maintaining control, but almost lost it when, out of the corner of her eye, she saw Will draw a pistol from the inside of his jacket.

He was priming it to fire when a shot rang out behind them, echoing harshly against the stone walls of the buildings lining the road. At the sound, the horses bolted. For a heart-stopping instant, Clio thought the reins would be wrenched from her grip. She managed to hold on to them, but only just, as the phaeton careened wildly out onto the Strand.

Beside her, Will rose in the seat, calmly took aim, and returned fire.

CHAPTER XVIII

THE NEXT FEW MINUTES—SHE DID NOT THINK it was more than that—passed in a blur for Clio. She fought desperately to control the fear-maddened horses as Will reloaded and fired again. Shots continued coming from the landau where, she now realized, there had to be more than one man.

Mercifully, the broad avenue of the Strand was empty. She caught a glimpse of vessels bobbing gently on the high tide of the Thames. They passed by in an instant and she saw the pylons of London Bridge up ahead, not far from where she had been earlier in the day with Sir Morgan.

Was he in the carriage? Was he one of those firing at them? Another shot and she slapped the reins hard, driving the horses on. Above her, Will flinched suddenly. She looked up to see blood staining his right arm.

"My God—" she cried.

"It's nothing, keep going!"

She obeyed, but only because there was no alternative. The landau was the heavier carriage by far and not built for racing, but it was pulled by four horses instead of the phaeton's two. It might not catch them, but it could come close enough to deliver a fatal shot.

She had no idea how many bullets Will might have left or how long he could keep firing with an injured right arm. But she did know that the Strand did not go on forever. If she recalled, it curved around St. James's Park, into the vicinity of where the palace of Westminster had stood until its destruction by fire only a few years before. In its place was a vast empty space, seemingly a hole in the very fabric of London.

Beyond it lay Whitehall and the government offices. An embankment ran alongside them, giving access directly to the river. With another shot echoing in her ears, and the landau seemingly closer, she urged the horses on.

At home on Akora, her brother and cousins drove chariots. She had tried her hand at them a time or two, but nothing had prepared her for what she thought to do now. It would be risky in the extreme, but there was also a chance it would work.

"Sit down!" she yelled to Will.

"What?" About to fire again, he looked down at her in surprise.

"Sit down! There's a curve coming up. If we can take it and they can't—" She didn't have to finish, he realized at once what she intended and nodded quickly. Taking his seat again, he also took the reins from her.

She let them go without hesitation. He was the stronger and more adept, therefore more likely to make the maneuver successfully. It was her idea, but his was likely to be the better execution.

An apt choice of word, as it turned out, for as the curve loomed in front of them, Will deliberately took it hard, steering the horses directly toward the river. The landau followed. Dark water lay directly in front of them when, at the last possible moment, he pulled up violently, sheering their horses off toward the right.

The driver of the landau attempted the same maneuver but failed. Panicked by the sight of the water hurtling toward them, the horses reared. The body of the landau was torn loose from the rest of the rig and sent hurtling into the river. It splintered as it struck. Clio had a glimpse of two bodies being thrown far out into the depths of the Thames before both vanished from sight. The horses, freed of any control, raced on, vanishing in the direction of the park.

"Wait here," Will ordered. He returned the reins to her and jumped down from the phaeton. Quickly, he soothed the horses, who responded to his touch and voice. When they were calmed, he stood at the water's edge, scanning the river carefully in search of survivors.

"There were two of them," she said when he returned to the carriage. "Do you think either could have lived?"

Will shook his head. "I'm fairly sure I shot the driver. He was already losing control before his horses panicked. The other was thrown out of the landau and likely died when he hit the water."

"Do you have any idea who they were?"

"My guess is Platt and McManus."

She had surmised as much for herself, but suddenly it did not matter. Whoever they were, there were far more pressing concerns. "Your arm—?"

"It's a flesh wound, nothing more. But look, we have to get off the street. The night watch patrols regularly and could be by here at any moment."

"David's house—?" She was thinking of sparing Lady Constance the shock of being awakened by the arrival of her wounded grandson.

But Will surprised her; he shook his head. "No, turn at the next right, up there."

She did as he said and shortly found that they had entered a pleasant street lined with colonnaded buildings some three stories in height. At so late an hour, only the gas lamps along the pavement were lit, casting a pale glow over their surroundings.

"Keep going," Will urged. "There, you see that lane between the buildings off to your right? Take it."

When she did, she discovered they had entered a mews hidden away behind the taller buildings. Clio drew the phaeton to a halt as Will jumped down. Despite his injured arm, he insisted on helping her to do the same.

"Let's get the horses untacked," he said. It was only then that she realized the mews housed stables. Their arrival had caused just enough of a stir to prompt a few whinnies. These died away quickly as they took the horses into adjacent stalls and got them settled.

By the time they were done, the right sleeve of Will's jacket was encrusted with blood.

"That's enough," Clio said firmly. "The horses are seen to and now you must be as well. Sit down." She gestured to a nearby pile of straw.

Instead of doing so, he grinned and said, "That was quite a ride."

"It was, now sit down." Did the man have a block of wood between his ears? He'd been shot, for heaven's sake. The wound needed tending and to do that, she had to find soap, more water—cold would have to do—and better light.

"I don't know about you," he said, "but after an experience like that, I wouldn't mind a bit of a rest."

"Good, then—" Before she could tell him yet again

to sit down, he grabbed her hand and led her away from the stables. "Where are we going?" Clio demanded. She was almost tripping over the hem of her gown; she'd left her wrap in the phaeton, and she couldn't seem to do anything except notice how wonderful he looked.

"In there," he said and cocked his head toward the stone building. Near the lane where they had entered, was a back door. Will took a key from his pocket, put it in the lock and turned it.

The door opened.

"What is this place?" Clio asked as they stepped into a cool, marbled hall.

"An apartment building," he replied. "Do you know what that is?"

"A building of apartments in which people live, rather than in houses?" she asked with a hint of asperity.

"You have those on Akora?"

"Of course we do. Heavens, the Romans had them."

Will lit one of the lamps left out on a small table near the back door, likely for late arrivals. He held it out with his good arm, revealing a hall that ran through to the street. Halfway down either side of the hall were double doors.

A sudden possibility occurred to her. "Do you have a friend living here?"

"Not precisely. Clio . . . I love my grandmother dearly, but—"

Understanding dawned and with it came a smile. "But there are times when a man wants his privacy?"

He looked relieved. "Exactly, and tonight it proves especially useful."

She could not possibly have agreed more. The apartment was on the ground floor, through the double doors on the right. Will opened them with another key and stood aside for her to enter. Inside, Clio discovered a spacious entry hall and beyond it a high-ceilinged room that managed to be both comfortable and elegant.

It was also unrelentingly masculine. The furniture was of dark wood and leather. There were books everywhere, as well as a faint and not unpleasant aroma of cigar smoke.

Will set the lamp down and went over to open the high windows fronting on the street. She followed him and laid a hand gently on his uninjured arm.

"Please, let me help you take off your jacket and then you must sit down." It was the last time she intended telling him that before she pushed him down.

"It really is only a flesh wound," he said even as he obliged her. The jacket was stuck to his shirt and to the skin below, but he did not flinch as they eased it off. Clio dropped it onto a nearby chair and peered at the tear in his shirt. "This has to come off, as well," she said, reaching for his cravat.

"There's much to be said for a bold woman." He spoke lightly but she wasn't fooled. His gaze had narrowed, probably with pain, and his high-boned cheeks looked flushed. Unless, of course, there was another reason. . . . He was, after all, a very strong man and she had every reason to know that his passion ran deep and fierce.

The shirt followed his jacket, revealing not only the broad sweep of his chest but also the jagged tear the bullet had made in his right arm. Clio swallowed hard at the sight of it but managed to keep her composure.

"Where can I heat some water?" she asked.

"The kitchen is through there," he said, indicating a door leading toward the back of the apartment. When she turned in that direction, he went with her.

"We might as well take care of this in there," he said. "You won't have to carry any water and there are plenty of lamps."

"We really should summon a doctor. I think you require stitches."

"A doctor will mean questions I do not care to answer."

There was no arguing with that and so she did not try. It was enough that he sat still while she lit several lamps, got the stove going, and put on water to boil. She had just finished doing that when she realized he was staring at her.

"Is something wrong?" Clio asked.

He shrugged broad, bare shoulders. "I didn't expect a princess to be so adept in the kitchen."

"I'm not in the least adept. Now my cousin Amelia,

she's a marvel, cooks like a dream. I can boil water, but just barely."

His look was heated and made her feel the same. "Fortunately, that's all we need right now," Will said.

"Actually, I could do with a brandy." Especially if she was going to do any stitching. She wasn't adept at that, either.

"Make it two," he said and pointed toward the butler's pantry behind the kitchen.

Two brandies later, when the water was boiling, Clio eyed the wound again. "You were lucky. Another inch or so and it would have splintered the bone."

"You can tell that? That must mean you've had some training with this sort of thing." He sounded tentatively hopeful.

"I have a great-aunt who is Akora's most skilled healer."

He had just begun to look relieved when she added, "I really wish I'd spent more time with her."

"But you spent some time?"

"Hmmm . . . does that hurt?" She touched the skin around the wound lightly.

"No . . ."

"Tell me the truth."

"A little."

"That's better. Have another brandy."

Will shook his head. "I don't think so."

"Then perhaps I should."

"I'd rather you didn't."

"Oh . . . all right. I suppose there's not much point in putting it off any longer."

"You really could just bandage it and I could see a doctor later."

"No, that's not a good idea. There's more chance of infection if you do that. Would you know where I could find a needle and thread?"

"In one of the drawers, perhaps."

She did, after a little searching, and tossed both into the boiling water. "What are you doing that for?" Will asked.

"My great-aunt always does it. Look, before we get started, could you help me out of this dress? I can't move around comfortably in it." And she was far beyond any concern for modesty, especially with this man who drew her so powerfully. The sight of him shot, wounded, at risk of his life had reminded her—again—of how fleeting life could be and how very wise it was to seize it when the opportunity came.

Besides, once she started stitching, he'd be glad to have his mind elsewhere.

Wounded or not, Will sprang to assist. The gown of gold and silver pooled at Clio's feet before she folded it neatly over a kitchen chair.

Thoroughly distracted, he stared at her. She was wearing a confection of a corset that ended at the top of her thighs, her modesty preserved by a scrap of lace. Her long, tapered legs were enclosed in silk stockings that ended halfway up her thighs, calling attention to the velvety expanse between them and the corset. She still had her shoes on, but as he watched, she lifted one foot, set it on a chair, and undid the strap, kicking off the shoe. The other followed before he remembered to breathe again.

She straightened, looked at him and smiled. "Do you want something to bite on?"

"What?"

"When I'm stitching your wound?"

"Oh, no . . ." He continued staring at her. "I didn't think you usually wore a corset."

"I don't," she said as she used tongs to remove the thread and needle from the boiling water. Doing so, she remembered what Melbourne had said about Will's admission of her usefulness having to be pulled from him with the same implement.

"I realize it's a shocking lapse on my part," she continued as she carefully threaded the needle. "Corsets seem *de rigueur* here in England, but on Akora they're unheard of."

"What made you decide to—" He broke off, as though having forgotten what he meant to ask.

"Wear one? Oh, it was the dress; I just thought it would look better with rather than without. And besides, this really isn't much of a corset, is it?"

She was being shameless, but it was working. Even as she pulled a chair up beside him and bent to look more closely at the wound, he seemed to have no thought for what she was about to do.

Unfortunately, she had far too much thought, to the extent that as she pressed the jagged edges of the wound together and prepared to make the first stitch, the world swam in front of her eyes.

"Clio—?" Will took hold of her elbow, steadying her. "Are you all right?"

"Fine, I'm fine." Never mind that she wasn't, she would just have to do what had to be done.

Grimacing, she applied the needle. Will's muscles tightened beneath her hand, but he made no sound and did not move in the slightest. For that, she was profoundly grateful.

By the time she was done, sweat beaded on her forehead and she was nauseous.

"It's all right," he said quickly the moment she finished the last stitch and turned away to the sink, hanging her head over it. Nothing actually happened, but for several unpleasant moments, she thought it would.

"You did wonderfully well," Will said, holding her against him. Her head rested on his bare chest and both of his arms were strong around her. "It's all over. Just put it out of your mind."

"I should be saying that to you. You're the one who was hurt . . . really almost killed!"

"I was not almost killed," he corrected tenderly. "To the contrary, the bullet practically missed."

She raised her head, meeting his gaze. "Oh, Will, I just don't think I can stand that again. It was the second time, after all."

"This will be finished soon, really."

"Not soon enough," she said, and to her horror, realized her lower lip was trembling.

Will had a solution for that and he applied it swiftly. She was still lost in his kiss when he lifted her, heedless of any injury he might do to his arm, and carried her from the kitchen.

CHAPTER XIX

"THIS IS SHAMELESS," WILL SAID AS HE LOWERED Clio onto the bed. The room was in darkness. Making his way across it, he'd bumped into the wardrobe and scarcely noticed. Her arms were around his neck, drawing him down.

"I don't care," she said. "I haven't been able to think of anything but you, want anything but you—"

His body, already scarcely under control, took a happy lurch in the direction of complete anarchy.

"But wait," she cried out suddenly, causing his heart to plummet. Scrambling up against the pillows, she said, "What about your wound?"

His wound? What wound? Vaguely, he recalled being shot. That must be what she was talking about.

"Sweetheart," he coaxed, "forget about that. It's nothing . . . less than nothing." Nothing was more than nothing except satisfying the raging desire that blocked out all rational thought and made him forget everything except—

His conscience fought its way out of the deep, dark hole he'd tried to shove it into and elbowed its way back to the fore.

She hadn't agreed to marry him.

All things in their own time and that was definitely for later.

He left her just long enough to yank the curtains closed across the windows and light a lamp beside the bed. "This time," he said as he made short work of his boots, "I want to see you."

She was sitting up against the pillows, her red-gold hair in disarray and her eyes very wide. Her breasts swelled above the lacy rim of the corset. She watched, enthralled, as he stripped away the rest of his clothes.

Naked, he came to her, joining her on the big bed. Her hands stroked over his shoulders, down his broad back, savoring the startling size and strength of him. So different from herself, so astonishing . . . she could not touch him enough, could not be close enough to him. He completed her in some essential way she had never understood before, for all that she had grown up in the sensual atmosphere of Akora.

All the same, her upbringing served her well. She turned in his arms, her hands gripping the edge of the headboard. "Would you mind?" Over her shoulder, she smiled at him. "This corset is becoming so uncomfortable."

She expected him to undo the laces for her, but he did not. Instead, he wrapped an arm beneath her and lifted her so that she was on her knees, facing away from him.

"Is it?" he murmured against her heated skin. "Just keep it on a little while longer."

She might have protested but his fingers were moving over her thighs, stroking the tender inner skin lightly, brushing against the scrap of lace shielding her womanhood.

"Will—" It was getting very hard to breathe, for reasons that had nothing whatsoever to do with the corset.

"Just a little longer," he repeated and slid one stocking down her leg, over her bent knee and off. His mouth retraced the path, his tongue lapping behind her knee. When she jerked suddenly, he said, "Don't move. Hold onto the headboard."

She obeyed, but only because the excitement thrumming through her made it impossible to do otherwise. With exquisite care, he removed her other stocking, rolling it slowly down her leg, and ran his hand over her from ankle to hip in a gesture that was shockingly, tantalizingly possessive.

"You have the softest skin," he murmured.

"Hmmm . . . Will—"

"Soon, be patient." He found the edges of the little *cache sexe* between her thighs, secured only by thin straps over her hips, and removed it. She was left only in the silk and lace corset that pushed her breasts high and made it impossible for her to draw a truly deep breath such as she needed right—

"*Now,* please, Will—"

"No," he said very clearly, and eased a finger into her. She cried out, her hands grasping the headboard, as wave after wave of pleasure crashed through her. The sensation was stunning but only served to heighten her arousal, stopping tantalizingly short of release.

The corset left the bottom part of her buttocks bare. They brushed Will's powerful chest as he continued the sweet torment. When she truly believed she could not bear it any longer, she tried to straighten but he would not allow it. Instead, he pressed a hand between her shoulder blades, at the same time lifting her hips higher and drawing her legs farther apart. Slowly he thrust into her, waiting until she adjusted to him, then drove again and again, hard and deep.

Her response was instant and overwhelming; she climaxed, crying out his name and holding onto the headboard so fiercely that it shook. At the last, Will curved his body completely over hers, his teeth grazing the soft skin at the base of her neck as the power of his own release overwhelmed him.

THE CORSET WAS DIGGING INTO HER WAIST. CLIO opened her eyes, wondered for a moment where she was, then remembered. She lay sprawled on the bed in a posture that could only be described as indecent. Slowly, she drew her legs together and looked over at the man beside her.

Will was lying on his side, one arm bent at the elbow and his head resting in the palm of his hand. He was smiling at her.

"Why aren't you asleep?" she asked, even as she was swept by self-consciousness. A glance down at herself confirmed that her breasts had nudged above the edge of the corset, her nipples peeking out amid the lace trimming. The nest of red-gold hair between her thighs was damply curled and clearly visible between her legs. Worse yet, they were lying on top of the covers. She couldn't even reach for a sheet.

"I suppose I should be," he allowed. "But the view proved much too entrancing."

"Yes, well—" She looked around for something, anything to draw over herself, but stopped when Will burst out laughing.

"You are a most contradictory woman," he said.

"Just because I lost control of myself—"

"Most delightfully. Here, let me help you out of that thing." Turning her over, he made swift work of unlacing her corset.

For a scant moment, she contemplated how he had gained such expertise, then dismissed the thought. There was no reason for her to begrudge that which she benefited from so thoroughly.

Clio breathed a sigh of relief when she was finally freed. The corset had left marks below her breasts. Will soothed them most effectively. She sighed again and curled into his arms. They lay together, bathed in the soft breeze that fluttered through the curtains.

Sleep beckoned but she fought it. The moment was too precious to let slip away in unconsciousness. Even so, her eyelids were growing heavy when a sudden thought occurred to her. Looking at him over her shoulders, she said, "Will—?"

"Hmmm." His eyes were closed. He did not look as though he planned to open them again anytime soon.

All those years combing through the vast library beneath the palace of Akora or scampering about in the dirt, digging up remnants of the past. All those years of paying only the scantest attention to the education every Akoran woman was supposed to receive. It was amazing what she'd absorbed while being such a negligent student.

Her bottom was nestled between his thighs. She wiggled it just the tiniest bit.

Instantly alert, Will said, "I thought you were tired." He sounded pleased that she was not.

"I was but then I wondered, since you have this place, why did you plan to stay at David's?"

He was silent for a moment before admitting, "I didn't until your father . . . suggested it."

"Father did? When?"

"When we had that little chat. I told him I'd asked you to marry me."

"You did *what*?"

"Well, of course I did. Atreus was leaving for Akora. How could I know when I'd have another chance to ask for his approval?"

"But you did tell him I hadn't accepted?"

She felt his smile against the curve of her shoulder. "I told him you were making me suffer."

"Oh, Will, for heaven's sake, I was doing nothing of the sort."

"He said your mother did the same to him."

"She did not! Mother?" Clio was dumbfounded. "I had no idea. Are you sure he said that?"

"Absolutely, along with a few other things, including that he thought for the sake of propriety I should move in with David until you made up your mind."

"Oh . . ."

"You have made up your mind?" When she didn't reply, he turned her over onto her back and looked down at her sternly. "You know, Clio, having to deal with a life-and-death struggle to protect my Queen is bad enough, but I really wouldn't want to think that you'd had your way with me under false pretenses."

"Had my way—?" He couldn't possibly mean that as it sounded . . . could he?

Will sighed deeply and moved away from her. He sat on the edge of the bed, affording her a view of his back. It was an enthralling view and might have distracted her had she not been so concerned about his feelings.

"Will—" She scooted up on her knees and reached out a hand tentatively.

"First in the cave," he said without looking at her, "and now here? It's hard for me to say this, Clio, but I'm beginning to feel you're just . . . toying with me."

"Toying?" Could he possibly be serious? She couldn't see his face but his voice sounded suspiciously husky.

Very suspiciously as she realized a moment later when Will burst out laughing, grabbed hold of her and pulled her onto his lap. Ignoring her glare, he said, "God, you're fun to tease. You have to marry me, Clio. I've never met a woman who was lover, friend, and partner all at once. Don't expect me to go back to living without you."

"Oh, Will—"

"I know I'm asking you to give up a lot. Akora has been your home all your life, but we could visit there often, and England has much to recommend it. You already like Holyhood and besides—" He broke off suddenly. "Did you hear that?"

Still basking in the pleasure of his proposal, Clio shook her head. "Hear what?"

Will didn't answer. He was already off the bed, pulling on his trousers as he moved toward the bedroom door. "Wait here, don't move."

She reached for a corner of the counterpane, dragging it over herself as she stood. It was all very well to be told to let him go into danger unaccompanied, but she wasn't about to do so, not with the likes of Umbra still on the loose.

Will cracked the door open and glanced out. She saw his shoulders stiffen.

"What is it—?" Clio murmured.

"Not what," Will said dryly. "Who." He looked back, saw she was decently covered, and stepped out of the room.

From the other side of the door, Clio heard him say, "How is it I forgot that I gave you a spare key to this place, David?"

"You really need to work on your memory," her cousin replied. He was sitting in an armchair in the living room, facing the bedroom door. To a casual eye, David Hawkforte looked entirely at ease and relaxed. Clio wasn't fooled for an instant. She knew him well enough to realize that he was furiously angry.

Besides, he was fingering a knife he'd taken from a leather sheath at his ankle. "I did tell you," David said, "that if you . . . overstepped with Clio, it would be wise not to let me find you."

"What you actually said," Will reminded him, "was that if I ever *hurt* Clio, not to let you find me. I haven't hurt her."

"Is that so?"

"It most certainly is so," Clio declared. She brushed past Will wrapped in the counterpane, kicking the portion of it that formed a train out of her way. Her head was high and pride lit her eyes. Every inch the princess, she said, "Kindly put that knife away without delay."

David looked from her to the half-naked man beside her and shrugged. " 'Fraid I can't do that, cuz. Family honor and all."

A little spurt of fear darted through her. Her cousin was an eminently civilized man. Surely, he wouldn't—?

She stepped in front of Will, who was lounging back against the frame of the bedroom door, looking amused.

"David," she said softly, "whatever the customs are here in England, you know perfectly well that on Akora, it isn't unusual for couples to . . . anticipate their wedding night. Heavens, if you're honest, you'll admit it's a family tradition. Your own parents—"

"No need to go into all that, cuz. The fact is, for there to be a wedding night—anticipated or otherwise—there has to be a wedding." He leveled a hard look at her. "Is there going to be?"

"Well, of course there is! You couldn't possibly think that Will and I wouldn't be married."

David was rising out of the chair, grinning, even as Will spun her around, took both her hands in his and said, "Darling, you've made me the happiest man in the world."

That was rather nice, as was the kiss they shared while her cousin affected to find something fascinating in the books filling the shelves along one wall. When they were done, Clio stepped back a little and glanced at both men. A little furrow formed between her brows.

"You two didn't contrive this—?" But how could they possibly have done so? She and Will had only come to the apartment after being attacked. Unless, of course, he'd intended to get her there under some pretext anyway, and had arranged with his good friend ahead of time to take advantage of the situation.

If he had, she would never know, for both men appeared the very picture of studied innocence.

"Oh, never mind," Clio said. "David, we must tell you what has happened."

By the time they finished doing so, they were all seated in the kitchen, drinking coffee Will had made. Clio was back in her gown, while he had donned a fresh shirt along with the trousers. It was almost dawn.

"Two bodies washed up against the pylons of London Bridge a few hours ago," David said after he had absorbed the details of their wild ride beside the

Thames. "Your guess that it was Platt and McManus who attacked you was right."

"Then they are both dead?" Will asked.

"Definitely," David said. "Which would leave only Umbra himself."

"With Toffler, Platt, and McManus all gone to their rewards," Clio said, "perhaps Umbra will give up any plans he still has to attack the Queen. After all, he can't have very much hope of success if he has to act alone."

"He may," Will said, "or he may lie low until he believes we think the danger is passed and then strike." Turning to David, he asked, "Have you learned anything more of use?"

David nodded. To Clio, he explained, "We've been investigating everyone who appeared at Holyhood after Will let Toffler know that he had to meet Umbra face-to-face before revealing the Queen's schedule. Mawcomber and Devereux are both in severe financial difficulties. They live far beyond their incomes and gamble to try to make up the shortfall, which has only led them into even direr straits. Mawcomber is in danger of losing his family's estate to creditors, and Devereux isn't likely to be sailing around on his yacht very much longer."

"Then it could be either one of them," Clio said.

"It could be," her cousin agreed, "but then there's Kearns." He paused long enough to take a sip of his coffee. Setting the cup down, David said, "A year ago,

Sir Morgan Kearns was buried in debt, his situation made even worse by his ill-advised investment in the London-to-Greenwich Railway. Today his circumstances are vastly improved. He doesn't owe a farthing and is in the process of buying himself not one but two residences, a town house here in London and a country estate in Kent." He paused, then said, "My information is that he expects to conclude both sales within the month."

"Tell me Kearns has not had some distant relative die and leave him a fortune," Will said as he poured more coffee. Clio covered her cup. She had already had more than enough stimulation for one evening.

"All of Sir Morgan's family," David said, "such as he has, appear to be hale and hearty."

"Then someone is paying him to assassinate the Queen," Clio said. The full horror of precisely what that meant, struck her hard. Regicide was far more than the murder of an individual; it struck at the very heart of a nation and its people.

"So it appears," Will said. "But without evidence, we can only watch him and hope to prevent whatever he plans to do."

Clio got up, took her cup over to the sink and washed it. The prosaic action soothed her and at the same time it gave her a chance to think. When she turned back to the table, both men were watching her.

"There is another choice," she said.

Will was shaking his head before she finished. "Absolutely not, it's out of the question."

"What is?" David asked, more encouragingly.

"Sir Morgan Kearns has sought my friendship," Clio said. "I assumed he did so because of my position, and in a way, I was right. I have become friendly with the Queen. It is a reasonable assumption that I would be privy to her schedule."

"No," Will said again. He came over to where she stood and touched the back of his fingers to her cheek in a gentle caress. "Clio, I will not put you at risk."

As deeply touched as she was by this, she said, "There would be no risk or very little." Before Will could object further, she went on, "All that needs to be done is to lure Sir Morgan out, to make him believe he has an opportunity to strike at the Queen. The act of doing so will incriminate him and give you everything you need to make certain he will never again be a threat to anyone."

"How do you intend to make him believe that such an opportunity exists?"

"Quite simply," Clio said and told them.

CHAPTER XX

"I WON'T REMIND YOU HOW MANY YEARS I'VE SERVED your family," Bolkum said. He stood stiffly in the center of the drawing room. They were all gathered in the London residence of the Hawkfortes, not far from the house Will shared with his grandmother and even closer to the residence of the Atreides.

"I don't actually know how many," David told him cheerfully. His mood in general was greatly improved since learning that his cousin and his best friend intended to marry. "You and Mulridge seem to have been at Hawkforte forever. At any rate, you must know we wouldn't ask if there was any alternative."

"You're daft to ask," Bolkum shot back. He stroked his lush black beard protectively. "Short I may be, although among some I'm considered a fair height, but to suggest that I could ever be mistaken for a woman—"

"At a distance," Clio said swiftly. "In a cloak and veil, and obscured by bushes. Sir Morgan will never get a good look at you. We only wish to create the impression that his quarry is present."

"His quarry being the Queen?" Bolkum demanded. "You think I can pass for an eighteen-year-old *girl*?" Now that he'd had a chance to think about it a bit longer, he seemed torn between outrage and hilarity. "Would Sir Morgan be blind, by any chance?"

"He is not," Will said. "Nor, all evidence to the contrary, do I believe he is a fool. However, as reluctant as I am to accede to this plan, the fact is, there is no one else we can turn to."

"No one else who can play the Queen?" Bolkum asked, trying to contain a grin.

"Who could we trust?" Clio inquired as she went to him and laid a hand gently on his arm. "This is a matter requiring the greatest discretion. Not only is a young woman's life at risk, so, too, is the future of this country."

"Aye," Bolkum said slowly. "I've seen it at risk before and I've seen what you of Hawkforte"—he looked to David—"and of Holyhood and Akora have done to keep things on an even course. I could tell you stories . . ."

"You always say that," David remarked. "But you never get around to telling them."

"Ah, well, there's reason enough for that. Never mind now, you lot really believe I can fool Sir Morgan?"

"He has sought such an opportunity for months," Will said. "With any luck, he will convince himself that his chance is finally at hand."

Bolkum did not look entirely convinced, but he did ask, "Just how do you intend to get him there?"

"With this," Clio said and handed him the note she had just penned:

> *My dear Sir Morgan— I write to thank you for acquainting me with that marvel of progress, the London–Greenwich Railway, and to share with you some exciting news. Upon returning from our excursion, I informed a certain lady of what I had seen. It will not surprise you that, although this lady was aware of the railway, she was not fully informed as to its true significance. After a brief discussion, this lady indicated most enthusiastically that she would very much like to experience a ride on the London–Greenwich Railway for herself.*

"Her Majesty said that?" Bolkum asked, looking up from his perusal of the letter.

"Her Majesty has no awareness whatsoever of anything transpiring here," Will informed him. "Read on."

As this lady is presently in mourning for her late uncle—

Bolkum looked up again. "That's clever, he'll think you mean the late King." He resumed reading.

—you will understand that she must be circumspect in regard to her public appearances. Therefore, kindly call at the Atreides residence today at four o'clock. I and the lady, whom I am sure you will understand prefers not to be named, will await you.

"Not to be named *or* seen," Bolkum muttered as he returned the letter. He patted his beard, frowned and, with palpable reluctance, said, "I suppose you'd better send it, then." Before any of them could react, he warned, "Just make sure we're all clear, no one ever says a word about this, an' I mean *ever.* I don't care how long after the fact it is, it will never be long enough for me to be hearin' about how I dressed up as a woman. This gets buried deep, all right?"

They all agreed, assuring him that whatever took place in the coming hours would never be known beyond their own small circle. Bolkum was, at length, satisfied with that and went with them to the residence of the Atreides shortly after midday.

Only a handful of Akoran guards were present. Will and David took them aside, explaining to them what needed to be done and swearing them to secrecy. Meanwhile, Clio shepherded Bolkum upstairs.

"We'll just try on a few capes," she told him.

And practice how to hold himself, how to walk, how to keep his head sufficiently covered by the hood of the cape so that his features, including his truly impressive beard, could not be seen.

"If you could just tuck the beard into your shirt," Clio suggested tactfully, an hour or so later when she believed she was on the verge of tearing her hair out. Bolkum did not walk, he lumbered. He did not merely stand, he held himself with the erect bearing of a soldier. Moreover, he found the hood a great nuisance and the cape itself even worse.

"A beard does better when it has the air," Bolkum informed her solemnly.

"It will only be for a few minutes."

He obliged, if grudgingly. A short time later, they descended into the main hall where Will and David awaited them. Both men kept their faces rigorously blank as they beheld Bolkum, his short, stout form enveloped in the black cape that Clio had found buried in the depths of a wardrobe and quickly hemmed so that his feet would not tangle in it.

"I still say this isn't going to work," Bolkum informed them.

"It has to," Will said. "The letter has been delivered. Lord Melbourne has agreed to keep Her Majesty occupied and out of sight. The people we have watching Sir Morgan tell us he is on his way here now."

Clio's stomach did a slow flip but she ignored it. "We'd better all get into position, then," she said and led the way out to the garden.

Very shortly thereafter, she was in the small family drawing room when one of the Akoran guards informed her that Sir Morgan Kearns had arrived.

"Sir Morgan," Clio exclaimed as she came forward to greet him. "I am so pleased you received my note."

"Dear lady," he bent over her hand. His eyes, when he raised them, were narrowed. "I trust I did not misunderstand it?"

"I am quite certain that you did not." She turned to the guard on duty in the hall. "Thank you, Cleios, you may withdraw."

When the guard had done so, Sir Morgan said, "The house is under guard, even now with your parents away and you not actually in residence here?"

"Only a handful of guards remain," she assured him. With a silent prayer that she would be forgiven for besmirching the honor of the men who served her father to the death, she said, "This is considered quite desirable duty. They spend their time out back in the stables, gambling and consuming wine."

"I see . . . then we are alone?"

"Not entirely," she said with a little smile that she hoped looked suitably arch. The truth was that she was dreadfully nervous and fighting to conceal it. In straightening from his bow over her hand, Sir Morgan had inadvertently allowed his jacket to bulge open just enough for her to glimpse the gun in a leather sling beneath it. The effort to pretend that she had not seen it—and did not know what he intended to do in the next few minutes—strained her powers of subterfuge to the utmost.

So, too, did the certain knowledge that he could not possibly intend to leave her alive as a witness to his terrible crime.

She and Will had not spoken of that, but she knew it was uppermost in his mind. All the same, there was nothing to be done except to proceed.

"The lady I mentioned is in the garden," she said, indicating the double doors leading out to it.

"Then let us not keep her waiting."

They entered the garden. At its center, a fountain in the shape of a dolphin splashed softly. Clio had always loved the fountain. The sight of it comforted her as she took a deep breath and willed herself to calm.

"You understand," she said, "we must be very discreet?"

Sir Morgan's right hand slid beneath the front of his jacket. "Dear lady, I would not dream of being anything less."

"I have sent the servants away and told the guards to remain in the stables."

"Excellent, then there should not be any problem."

Gravel crunched beneath her foot as she stepped out onto the path. "Are we to use your carriage?"

Sir Morgan was scanning the garden and heard her only belatedly. "What? Oh, no, regrettably mine is in need of repair. I presumed you would have one available—"

"Yes, of course, that is no problem. An enclosed carriage, I think. You understand, the lady is veiled?"

"Yes, yes, certainly. Where is she?"

"Over there," Clio said and pointed to the far end of the garden near a cluster of tall bayberry bushes. The bushes and the area adjacent to them were shadowed by a willow tree and further obscured by the nearby wall. It was just possible to make out the short, very erect shape swaddled in the black cape.

Sir Morgan's hand rested within his jacket. A nerve in his right upper eyelid twitched. "That is . . . the lady?"

Clio nodded. Her mouth was very dry, but she managed to speak normally. "She is looking forward to meeting you."

"I'm sure she is," Sir Morgan said. He reached out with his free hand and before Clio could recognize his intent, seized hard hold of her.

"Sir Morgan—!"

"Be quiet! Say nothing to alarm her or you will die."

"Die? Why, whatever do you—?"

"I said to be quiet!" Sir Morgan hissed. He pushed Clio ahead of him as together they approached the "Queen."

"I don't understand—" Making a token effort to struggle, Clio ignored the fear racing through her and strove to keep him sufficiently diverted so that he would not glimpse what else was happening in the garden.

Or at least what else she most fervently hoped was happening. Will and David were there somewhere, she was sure, but for the life of her, she could not catch a glimpse of them.

And it would be her life—hers and Bolkum's—if anything went wrong at this very late moment.

She took a breath and let it out slowly. Sir Morgan was not making the mistake Platt and McManus had made; he would not fire without a clear and certain shot. To do that, they had to get closer still.

"Call to her," he demanded, squeezing her arm. "Get her over here."

"I couldn't possibly, she is the Queen."

"For God's sake—"

"Why are you doing this? I don't understand. You must be mad."

"Mad?" His face darkened and the hand within his jacket shook, but only a little. "You have no idea what it is like, none," Sir Morgan hissed. "You were born to privilege, as was she. You've lived all your life with everything you could desire. You've never had to work—"

"Do you work?" She knew the answer full well but still wanted to hear him say it.

Yet he surprised her, saying quite seriously, "Of course, I do. I work as every gentleman does, to advance myself. But it's all gone wrong. My father had his living from our manor, as did his father before him, but that's not possible any longer. Everything is changing, and how is a man to know what to do?"

Clio had no response to his oddly plaintive question, but she was certain of one thing. "Killing the Queen will not prevent change."

"How ignorant you are! She is Melbourne's tool and he . . . he has no notion of how much harm he is doing this country. It will take a strong hand and a determined one to see England through these times."

"The Duke of Sussex—?" She dangled the name, hoping against hope that Sir Morgan would say something, anything to reveal who might be the goad she was certain had to lie behind him. But he ignored the question and gripped her arm so tightly she winced in pain.

"Call to her!"

"I will not!"

"Then, by God, you will die before her!"

He let go of her suddenly and shoved her so hard that Clio staggered a few feet from him and almost lost her balance. She was perilously close to sprawling onto the lawn, straight in the path of the gun he pulled from beneath his jacket, when there was a blur of motion.

Will came seemingly out of nowhere but really from around the corner of the house. Heedless of the gun, he hurtled directly at Sir Morgan, colliding with him just as the other man attempted to pull the trigger.

They struggled, locked together, grappling for the weapon. Sir Morgan was both tall and fit, but Will had the honed strength of a warrior and was fighting to save both the woman and the country he loved. He slammed his fists into the other man again and again without mercy, crunching bone and spraying blood. Sir Morgan reeled back, tried to stay upright and failed. He fell in a heap beside the fountain. The gun landed some distance from him, just within his reach.

Clio ran to Will and was in his arms, clinging to him, when a shot rang out.

CHAPTER XXI

"WHY?" WILL DEMANDED. AN HOUR HAD PASSED since Sir Morgan's arrival at the house, his attack on Clio, and his death. The body had been removed, no trace of the struggle in the garden remained. Bolkum was restored to his normal self. He had joined the others in the drawing room, where Will addressed David.

David, who, unaccountably for one whose bravery could not be questioned, had hung back when Will launched himself at Kearns. David, who had waited for the moment when he would have a clear shot at the man who, had he lived, might have been persuaded to tell them who really lay behind the plot against Victoria.

"There was never any possibility of putting Kearns on trial," he said in response to Will's question. He was still pale, but overall he looked very much the cousin she had always known, a handsome, intelligent young man with a profound love for Hawkforte and for England.

"A trial, by its very nature, would be public," he continued, "which means that what happened here would become known to all, with all the repercussions that would bring."

"You arranged this with Melbourne," Will said. He was staring at his friend, as though seeing a part of the man he had not known existed. There was no rejection in his eyes, not precisely, but there was surprise and caution.

"We spoke of it after this plan was devised," David acknowledged. "The Prime Minister believed your attention would be on Clio, as it was quite rightly. That left me."

To bear the weight of an act that could be seen as murder.

There was silence for a moment, before Clio said quietly, "Sir Morgan had dropped his gun, but it was still within his reach when you fired at him."

David shot her a grateful look, though his manner remained tense and somber. "That is what I will tell myself for the next fifty or however many years remain to me. I did not shoot him in cold blood . . . exactly."

On impulse, Clio went to David and put her arms around him. He hugged her back silently.

Watching them, Will sighed deeply. "Surely, Melbourne wanted to know whatever Kearns might have said?"

David released Clio and stepped back a little. He ran a hand through his dark hair as he nodded. "Ideally he would have liked to know, but under the circumstances, we agreed Kearns could not be left alive, and this was the only way I could see to it. . . . and still live with myself."

Will hesitated only a moment longer before going to David and putting his hand on his shoulder. Looking him in the eye, he said to him quietly, "Never mind about Melbourne; I'll deal with him. Without your help, Clio or I could have been killed."

David looked at him gratefully. Bolkum snorted just then, came over and patted both men on their backs. He had to reach up to do so, but the "pats" he delivered made them stagger.

"Don't be tearin' yourself up about it, lad," Bolkum said. "Kearns was a bad one, seen his kind before, more times than I care to tell. Believe me, they never come to a good end."

That said, Bolkum took himself off. David left a short time later, to see to the disposition of Sir Morgan's remains.

"It will appear he was the victim of a random attack," David said before he went. "In a city where gunshots are reported late at night near Whitehall, and mysterious carriages are seen careening along the Thames, such an event is regrettably believable."

With a faint, sad smile, he departed, leaving Will and Clio alone in the drawing room. At once, Will went to her and held her for several minutes. Neither spoke. It was enough they were both safe and together.

At length, she sniffed—she absolutely was not going to cry—and asked, "Do you think David will be all right?"

"In time, but he's an honorable man who took on a task he will view, at least in a part of his mind, as dishonorable. He will not come to terms with that easily."

"I wonder if Melbourne considered that when he asked it of him?"

Will shrugged. "I doubt it. The Prime Minister is a decent enough man, so far as that goes, but he is not above using others to achieve his ends."

"Victoria must never know of this. She is so young and so idealistic that her faith in him would be shaken to the core, just when she truly does need to depend on him."

"There is another reason for her not to know," Will said. "Without the information Kearns might have provided, we can't be certain what was really behind this. From what I overheard him saying to you, his motives weren't clear."

"No, they weren't," Clio agreed. "Money was a factor and there was something about needing a strong hand, but it was all jumbled."

"Never mind." He cupped her face in his strong hands and smiled. "Don't be worrying about all this. I have to go see Melbourne but I won't be long, and then—"

Despite everything they had just been through, Clio's spirit lightened. She was with the man she loved and would love for all time. Beside that, all the troubles of the world seemed to fade and every challenge appeared conquerable.

"And then?" she asked softly.

"And then there's the little matter of you making an honest man of me."

"Oh, that—" Her heart speeded up as she saw the fire in his eyes.

He bent his head, kissing her first gently and then with passion that left no doubt where the encounter would lead if they did not end it swiftly.

Her hands on his shoulders, meaning to push him away but not quite managing it, Clio said, "Go to Melbourne. The sooner that is done, the better."

He went but not at once, and by the time he left, her hair was in great disorder and her lips were slightly swollen. She was smiling but her mood turned more somber almost the moment the door closed behind

Will. She waited until she was certain he had gone, then went out into the garden.

All appeared exactly as it should be. Robins and finches darted among the bushes, bees buzzed among the peonies and roses whose fragrances perfumed the air, and the fountains sparkled brightly. The thought that a man had died there only a few hours before seemed inconceivable, yet it was not that which occupied Clio's mind when she sat down on the bench, folded her hands and gazed at the garden.

What she was about to attempt might seem insane, yet she felt she had no choice. Since the first vision of the past had come to her in the crypt at Holyhood, she had believed there had to be a purpose to such a "gift." Further, she believed it must have to do with the peril faced by England, a danger that might spread even as far as Akora.

The visions had been coming closer in time, bringing her to a point she thought must have occurred only a few weeks before, right here in the garden of her parents' home. But why? What was she meant to see?

Whatever it might be, the fact remained that as the minutes passed and she remained in the garden, she saw nothing the least untoward. The present seemed to wrap around her as securely as a swaddling blanket, holding her confined and contained.

And yet . . . she had slipped such boundaries before, drifted free of time and seen the past as though it still existed somewhere in the vastness of Creation.

Somehow, she must do so again.

But the more she concentrated, the more mired she felt. At length, and in desperation, she went back inside, found the very same book she had been reading just before the first vision in the garden—Jane Austen's *Persuasion*—and returned to the bench, this time with the book in hand.

She opened it and forced herself to read, holding out little hope that the ploy would work, yet not knowing what else to do. But the story of Anne Eliot and her Captain Wentworth proved captivating even under such stressful circumstances. Without her even being conscious of it, Clio's awareness of the garden faded away.

Only to return some indeterminable time later when a woman walked past her.

The woman was a bit plump, her dark hair was arranged in ringlets framing her face, and she was dead. Or at least, she was from Clio's perspective. The woman was Lady Barbara Devereux and she had no business being in the garden when she had been pushed out a window and broken her neck only two days before.

Yet there she was. Staring at her, Clio closed the book. Her heart pounded wildly, she felt cold all over and bile rose in the back of her throat. Slowly and with great difficulty, she forced herself to stand.

Lady Barbara was about to enter the house. As though in a dream, Clio followed, her mind reeling from the implications of what she was doing. She was moving through past and present all at once, as though within her and for only a tiny fragment of time, they overlapped.

Was it possible she could misstep and become caught in a place where time itself had no clear meaning? How would she ever find her way out, back to Will, and the future they could build together?

She had no answers but she did keep going. To turn back now was unthinkable. This was what she had sought, hoped for, and it must be seen through to whatever end awaited her.

Lady Barbara had disappeared into the house. Clio stepped through the doors from the garden and looked around. Very vaguely, she was aware of other people—guests and servants—but they seemed far less distinct than Lady Barbara herself. The faintest of them could almost be mistaken for the flickers of light and movement that occur sometimes out of the corner of the eye and have no clear explanation.

The doors stood open to the drawing room. She stepped inside, finding it without dust covers, the vases filled with fresh flowers, their petals fluttering lightly in a breeze that had come and gone weeks before.

There were two men in the room. One was Sir Morgan Kearns. At the first sight of him, Clio pressed her lips tightly together, to keep from crying out. Lady

Barbara was bad enough, but she had seen Sir Morgan die only a few hours before.

He gave no evidence of his imminent mortality as he spoke with a second man Clio did not recognize. He was slightly shorter than Sir Morgan, white-haired, with a luxuriant white mustache and sideburns. His bearing was very erect, in keeping with the uniform he wore.

Clio had no knowledge of uniforms. They didn't exist on Akora, except for the pleated white kilts warriors customarily wore, and she had never had any reason to take note of European uniforms. However, she took close enough note of this one, observing the scarlet tunic above white breeches, the gold epaulettes on the shoulders, and the dark blue sash across the man's chest.

She noted, too, the envelope he was handing to Sir Morgan, one emblazoned with a wax seal similar to but far from identical to the seal on the envelope Clio had received from the Queen.

Both men glanced in her direction just then and frowned. For a stomach-wrenching moment, she thought they could actually see her. But they were looking at Lady Barbara, who smiled in surprise at discovering them and said something Clio could not hear.

Nor could she still see Lady Barbara very well. That lady seemed to be dissolving out of the world she no longer inhabited, as did Sir Morgan and the other man. The room itself was shifting slightly, the angle of the light changing, the flowers vanishing and the whole room appearing as though time had lurched forward to suddenly catch up with itself.

"Something wrong, lass?" Bolkum asked. He was standing directly behind Clio, looking at her closely. "I thought you were in the garden."

"I was . . . Bolkum, quickly, help me find a piece of paper."

Kind—and wise—man that he was, Bolkum did not question her but quickly took paper and pen from a drawer, handing them to her.

Perched on the edge of one of the couches, leaning on a book Bolkum also provided, Clio took a deep breath and swiftly, before the image could fade from her memory, sketched the design she had seen on the wax seal of the letter being given to Sir Morgan by the man in uniform. She was not, in her estimate, an artist; however, she had ample experience sketching the small, often intricate items she found in her diggings. When she was done, she looked up to find Bolkum studying her.

"Time's a funny thing, isn't it?" he remarked with a smile.

What was that he'd said? He couldn't possibly know what had been happening to her. "Excuse me—?"

"I said 'time's a funny thing.' It seems like it either hangs heavy or there's not enough of it. But in fact, it's like a great, grand river carryin' us along."

"I suppose it could be like that—"

"Did you ever wonder about the first people who figured out how to build a bridge over a river?"

"I found the site of an old bridge on Akora, not far from the palace." She had spent a happy summer exploring it when she was thirteen, but had no idea why she was talking about that now.

"Ah, then, you have thought about it. Must have been a marvelous thing, bein' able to get up above the river, get a look at it in one direction or the other without just bein' swept along by it."

"One direction or—?" A thought was forming far in the back of Clio's mind. A thought almost too outrageous to be entertained . . . and yet— "Bolkum, how old are you?"

His smile widened until it seemed to take up the whole of his face. "Oh, very old, lass, very old indeed. I could tell you stories—"

She reached out and clasped his gnarled—and rather hairy—hand. "How I wish you would."

He hesitated and she saw the temptation in him, the ancient and compelling lure of the tale to be spun, the wonder to be revealed. "Well . . . now, I can't say I've ever done that. Used to know a storyteller, though, best I've ever met. He was a marvel."

"What was his name?"

Bolkum chuckled. "His name was Dragon, and he had a brother named Wolf and a friend called Hawk. Can you believe that?"

"These were men, who had such names?"

"Oh, yes, lass, they were men indeed. Men of a sort you wouldn't have any trouble recognizin'."

"And you could tell me stories of them?"

The very old "man" who was no stranger to bridges, what crossed over them and what lurked beneath, looked at her and came to a decision. If there was one thing he had observed in his very long life, it was that there came a time for all things under the sun and then some. "I could. If I'm right thinkin', I'll be able to find you at Holyhood?"

Clio stood, holding the sketch she had made. She looked around the perfectly ordinary room in the perfectly ordinary day, through which time moved perfectly properly, carrying her along to the future she was only now truly believing would be hers.

"Yes," she said with a smile that matched Bolkum's own. "At Holyhood. Find me there."

"I'll do so, lass," he called, but she was gone, hurrying out into the summer day.

CHAPTER XXII

"HOW DO YOU KNOW THIS?" MELBOURNE asked. Clio and Will were meeting with the Prime Minister in his private apartment. Clio had been escorted there shortly after her arrival at Buckingham Palace.

Informed that the Prime Minister was in conference with the Earl of Hollister, she had asked that the earl be advised of her presence and her urgent desire to speak with him. Scant minutes later, she was showing Will the sketch she had made and describing the man who handed the letter to Sir Morgan.

Now, without hesitation, she informed Melbourne, "Sir Morgan told me."

It was not, strictly speaking, the truth. Sir Morgan had died without telling anyone anything of particular use. But his actions weeks before his death, in the drawing room of her parents' house had, in a way he could not possibly have imagined, been vastly more revealing.

Melbourne glanced at Will. "You said nothing of this."

"Will didn't hear him," Clio said quickly, "and I was so distraught after everything happened—" She paused for a moment, her silence a pointed reminder that she knew of the use to which Melbourne had put her cousin, and would not forget it. "Will had to leave to come here before I was sufficiently recovered to tell him."

"I see," Melbourne said slowly. He sat down behind his desk and regarded them both. "Very well, kindly tell me exactly what Sir Morgan said."

"Several weeks ago, my parents hosted an informal gathering at their residence here in London," Clio said. "Sir Morgan was in attendance, as was the *aide-de-camp* of the King of Hanover. I'm sure if you wanted to, you could confirm that with my parents. However, it would hardly be discreet to do so. You see, during that gathering, the aide gave Sir Morgan a letter from the King of Hanover."

She glanced at Will as she spoke. He had identified

the seal from her sketch and recognized the white-mustachioed man from her description. Between the two, neither of them had any doubt of what had occurred.

"Do we know the contents of the letter?" Melbourne asked.

"No, we don't," Clio acknowledged.

"However," Will interjected, "we also have no innocent explanation for the King of Hanover, who has been denied the throne of Great Britain and Ireland, being in private correspondence with a man plotting the murder of the Queen. It is my surmise that Sir Morgan and the King's *aide-de-camp* used the cover of that gathering at the Akoran residence to pass a final communication from the King to Sir Morgan, confirming the arrangements for the assassination."

Melbourne sighed deeply but he did not dispute Will. It fell to Clio to ask what had been troubling her for some time. The daughter of a king—or as close to one as Akora had—she had to know: "Is the King of Hanover truly capable of such a horrendous act?"

Both men looked at her in surprise. "Dear lady," Melbourne said, "let us just say that His Majesty has earned himself a reputation of such nature that it is virtually impossible to imagine anything he would *not* do. The small matter of murdering his niece—and anyone else who got in his way—would hardly give him pause, especially when the prize is a crown he believes should be his, in any case."

When she had taken a moment to digest this, Clio asked, "What will you do now?"

Melbourne settled back in his chair, steepled his fingers and shrugged. "Nothing."

Will and Clio exchanged a glance. "Nothing?" Will repeated.

"Nothing that I will be seen to do. If we are to avoid war, there must be no hint of this. However, I will send my own emissary to the Court of Hanover. It will be made clear to His Majesty that for the remainder of his life—whatever may be left of it—he will be carefully watched. He will be left with no doubt that before there could be any possibility of the crown of Great Britain and Ireland joining that of unhappy Hanover on his wretched head, he would follow the likes of Sir Morgan into a well-deserved grave."

"You would commit regicide to prevent regicide?" Clio asked quietly.

Melbourne smiled as he stood and came around to the other side of the desk where they were seated. "There is no moral equivalency whatsoever between the King of Hanover and Her Majesty, Queen Victoria. One represents the worst aspects of the hereditary system and the very dregs of humanity; the other is living proof that on occasion, something of rare goodness can emerge from the most unlikely sources."

"I see," Clio said and she thought she truly did but she had no opportunity to contemplate the matter further, for just then, the door opened and Victoria herself walked in. The Queen looked very young and just a little shy.

"I do hope I am not interrupting," she said as Will rose. Both he and Melbourne bowed to her.

"Not at all," Melbourne assured her gently. "We were just—" He broke off, abruptly aware that he was without a plausible explanation for why the three of them should be together in close conversation.

"Discussing our happy news," Clio said as she went to the Queen. With a glance over her shoulder at Will, who was watching her with a faintly sardonic smile, she said, "Lord Melbourne tells me it is good manners, when a peer of the realm weds, to request the sovereign's permission."

As Victoria's eyes grew very wide and the beginnings of a delighted smile curved her mouth, Will stepped forward. "Your Majesty, I do request that permission and also that you will do us the great honor of being present at our marriage."

"I would not miss it for all the world," Victoria exclaimed. Her romantic spirit was clearly moved. She could not have been happier for them or more eager to know all the details.

"You have not known each other very long, have you? And yet you are quite certain of this? Yes, of course, you must be. Did you realize immediately? Was it the *coup de foudre,* as the French say, the thunderbolt that heralds love? Oh, whatever it was, it must have been terribly romantic!"

Clio thought back to the night she had pursued Will into the confrontation with Platt and McManus, then escaped with him to the tide-flooded cave and the rock ledge. She grinned as he said solemnly, "Extremely romantic, Your Majesty."

Victoria sighed with pleasure. "I thought as much. But tell me, when is the wedding to be?"

Will and Clio exchanged a glance. He was a peer of the realm, she a princess of Akora. In the ordinary course of events, the celebration of their marriage would require months of planning, complex arrangements and logistics surpassed only by those of a major military campaign.

But there was nothing remotely ordinary about the events that had led them to this moment, and everything quite extraordinary about their feelings for each other.

"Next week," Will said without hesitation.

"At Holyhood," Clio declared just as firmly.

"Next week?" The Queen stared at them in astonishment. "Is that possible?"

"I'm sure if any two people can make that happen," Melbourne said, "they stand before us right now."

"That's wonderful," Victoria declared, "but"—she looked to Clio—"if it is to be next week, your family will not be able to attend."

"They will understand," Clio assured her and knew it was true. "Besides, I'm sure Will wants to visit Akora. We can celebrate our marriage again there."

But first, it was Holyhood's turn to welcome the happy couple and Lady Constance's great joy to see them wed.

CLIO AWOKE TO THE SOUND OF RAIN DRUMMING against the windows of her room at Holyhood. Her first thought was that it could not possibly be raining. It was, after all, her *wedding day.* But raining it was, as she sipped tea, bathed, donned a simple morning gown, and went to pay her respects to the Queen, who had arrived the previous afternoon. Melbourne accompanied Her Majesty. Clio thought it remarkable how well he fitted into a household that was, for the moment, otherwise entirely female.

Will had gone to stay at Hawkforte with David, but they would be returning several hours before the ceremony. In the meantime, there was a tremendous amount still to be done. That was just as well, for it prevented Clio from thinking overly much about the fact that her family would not see her wed.

But they would, she reassured herself, when she and Will reached Akora. She was looking forward to showing him her home and already had his promise that they would visit often. She was also tremendously excited about beginning a new life in England.

The two sentiments threatened to clash as she sped through the day, chatting with the Queen, helping

Lady Constance, and cheered by Faith, Hope, and Charity who arrived to assist her.

The rain finally let up and the clouds parted. A weak ray of sunshine undertook the seemingly impossible task of drying out the lawns before the crowds assembled. Seeing Clio staring out at the still-sodden grass, Lady Constance declared, "You've done quite enough. Now what you need is a good cosseting. Girls, she should get off her feet and have a nice cup of tea."

Both helped but her nerves were frayed when, too soon, the time came to dress.

"Will is here," Lady Constance declared, sticking her head in just as Clio's gown was brought from the wardrobe. "He looks anxious."

"His lordship looks wonderful," Faith insisted. "He's in with Her Majesty right now and I heard them laughing."

"How nice—" Was that her voice, that weak, thready thing? That really would not do. "I think I'd better have another cup of tea."

Everything speeded up after that. She had chosen to leave her hair down, crowned only with flowers that Will had sent. The tiny roses went perfectly with her wedding dress. After brief indecision, she had chosen to be wed in a gown in the Akoran style. Made of blue silk that matched her eyes, the deceptively simple tunic left her arms bare, emphasized her slim waist and fell gracefully in pleats to her feet. With it, she carried a bouquet that matched the wreath of flowers in her hair.

She was almost ready, indeed thought she was, when Lady Constance said, "My dear, there has never been a lovelier bride. You certainly need no adornment, but it would give me the greatest pleasure if you would wear these."

The pearls she drew from a Moroccan leather case were the largest and most beautiful that Clio had ever seen. As she exclaimed over them, Lady Constance said, "They have been in the family for generations. My dear William gave them to me on our wedding day. It is my great pleasure to give them to you."

Clio would have demurred, really overwhelmed by the gift, but Lady Constance insisted. She fastened the pearls around Clio's neck herself.

David was waiting for her when she stepped out of her room. Her cousin looked very fit in black trousers and frock coat with a pearl-gray vest beneath. He smiled when he saw her and held out his hand.

"Damn if you don't do us proud, cuz."

"As do you, David," she said and kissed him on the cheek. Shadows still lingered in his eyes and she hoped they would pass with time.

"Ready, then?" he asked, tucking her arm into the crook of his.

She took a breath and let it out slowly. "As ready as I can be."

Arm in arm, they went down the stairs, through the

marble entry hall, and out onto the rolling lawns stretching down to the sea. As they stepped outside, a great cheer went up from the assembled throng.

The sun was slanting westward, its golden rays transforming the tiny droplets of water still clinging to the grass and leaves into glittering jewels. The air was fresh with the perfume of the garden.

The path to Holyhood's small chapel was lined with well-wishers. She saw Mister Badger, grinning broadly, as was Mister Smallworthe and a very stout woman she assumed to be Missus Smallworthe, Doctor Culpepper who held a small girl on his shoulder so that she could see better, and so very many more. All of Holyhood had turned out, it seemed, as well as Lady Constance's and Will's friends from all over.

Every seat in the chapel was taken and all rose as Clio entered. Down at the very front, she caught sight of the Queen and Melbourne, both looking completely relaxed and at ease. Beside them sat Lady Constance, who was both smiling and weeping all at the same time.

And then, Clio saw nothing other than Will. He stood, tall and almost unbearably handsome, just below the simple altar. His garments were similar to David's but he wore on the fold of his cravat a brooch of silver and diamonds twining in a serpentine design. On another man, it could have appeared foppish. On Will, it looked splendidly barbaric and entirely suited to him.

She went to him on David's arm, her cousin taking her hand in his before placing it gently in Will's hand. Her husband-to-be's touch was warm, gentle, and strong, a benediction all its own and a very private sort of homecoming.

Together, they stood before God and all those gathered, and spoke their vows in voices at once calm, steadfast, and rich with the significance of the moment. When the priest pronounced them husband and wife, the assembled guests did not contain themselves but broke with decorum and raised a cheer. Even in her dazzled state, Clio could not help but notice that the Queen joined in unreservedly and even poked Melbourne with her elbow as the couple went by, asking if he didn't think they looked absolutely splendid.

Outside, a sunset of pure, unbridled extravagance bedecked the western sky. Torches were set up all around the tables laden with food and forming a circle around the area cleared for dancing.

Will led her into that firelit circle as the fiddle player struck a tune. This was—for all the high nobility of its chief participants—a country wedding and it was into a country dance that he swept her. Round and round the circle they went, his strong hand at her waist, as all around them the people clapped in time and her own heart beat wildly.

There was a moment, in the midst of that dance, when everything seemed to slow. Then there was only Will, his eyes filled with love and laughter, holding her. Clio, who had come to appreciate that time was very different from what she had once thought, knew that moment for what it was—a gift as rare and precious as each of the glowing pearls around her throat. Even as the moment lingered, she wrapped it in memory, tucking it away safely so that she could always find her way back to the circle and the dance, to Will's arms and the knowledge of perfect love.

"Hurrah!" the young Queen shouted and so did all the others. "Hurrah! Hurrah!"

Melbourne bowed and offered his hand to Victoria, who took it with delight and joined the dance. Other couples flowed into the circle and their laughter rose to the heavens, where the first stars were just beginning to appear.

The stars had become a sea and the sun had long since set when Clio discovered what all the secret preparations at the far end of the great lawns had been about.

The crowd cried out in amazement as a ribbon of light soared into the sky, quickly followed by another and another, the trio exploding in a burst of bright red and gold sparkles that fell gently back toward earth. More fireworks followed, each seemingly bigger and more elaborate than the last. Roman rockets blazed across the sky, entire giant chrysanthemums of fire exploded above them, great wheels of light spun and on and on until the heavens themselves appeared transformed. Right at the last, an immense fountain of fire exploded directly above Holyhood, pouring down through the velvety night.

While yet that fountain had everyone entranced, Will scooped Clio up in his arms. He laughed at her surprise as he strode swiftly away from the crowd, past where it was said the ancient gates of Holyhood once stood. Through them he took her and on, down to the shingle beach where, she saw to her amazement, a ship rocked gently on the water, awaiting them.

CHAPTER XXIII

DAVID HAS OFFERED HAWKFORTE FOR OUR honeymoon," Will said when they had boarded the single-masted sailing ship. Around them, the dark water reflected the remnants of the fireworks that were still falling to earth. Off in the distance, they could hear the muted sounds of merriment at the celebration of their wedding. But for them, the time had come for a far more private celebration.

"Where will he be?" Clio asked as she went into her husband's arms.

"He says he has business elsewhere."

They looked at each other, sharing the silent thought that it was likely David who would carry Melbourne's message to the King of Hanover. David, Shield of England, who would make clear the fate awaiting any would-be usurper of the throne.

"When he comes back," Clio said, "we must do something very nice for David."

"Or find someone very nice for him," Will suggested with the air of a man who, having discovered the marvels of true love, wished to spread the glad tidings.

"We should confer with Lady Constance," Clio said, nibbling at his lower lip.

"And with the Queen, who shows matchmaking tendencies of her own," Will said, just before he deepened the kiss.

High above them, the last of the shower of sparkles died away, replaced by the glory of the eternal stars.

The summer air was pleasantly warm; they had no need to seek the cabin below and a great incentive not to do so. A flower-draped canopy adorned the center of the deck and beneath it was a bed sprinkled with rose petals—the connivance, Clio suspected, of Faith, Hope, and Charity who had disappeared for several hours and returned giggling.

"It's beautiful," she said softly as her husband led her to the bower. There, beneath sky and stars, to the rhythm of the sea, they came to each other. He removed her gown with hands at once gentle and just a little clumsy. She laughed and helped him, but left the flowers in her hair. When she was naked, she stood before him, bathed in the heat of his gaze, and carefully undid the silver and diamond brooch at his throat.

"Where did this come from?" she asked as she laid it aside.

"An ancestor," he murmured, his hands tracing the curves of her waist and hips. "He was given it by a queen."

"Was he?" His frock coat and vest had been discarded somewhere back on the lawn. She undid the buttons of his shirt and drew it off over his head. Beneath the shirt, his skin was tight over hard bone and muscle, warm to her touch and tantalizing. She bent her head, tracing the arrow of soft hair that angled down his chest, to disappear beneath the band of his trousers.

He did not wait but made short work of the rest of his clothes. Clio lay on her back on the petal-sprinkled bed, surrounded by the fragrance of roses, one leg bent gracefully, and held out her arms to him.

Will went to her, finding in her embrace a haven of love and security he knew would be the touchstone of his life through all the years and beyond. With his hands and mouth, with all his body, he cherished her. The night wrapped around them, and the sounds of their passion joined the lapping of the waves against the gently rocking boat.

Fire leaped between them, hot and fierce. Clio could

not wait but reached down, cupping him in her palm and drawing Will to her. He rose above her, his powerful arms braced on either side of her head, and moved first slowly, then more swiftly as her hips rose to meet him. In the starlight, she saw his face, taut with the surging waves of pleasure mounting in them both. Her hand curved around the back of his neck, drawing him down, her mouth taking his as the force of life itself claimed them both.

"My love," she cried, *"my dearest love."* Her breath mingled with his as she was swept away with release so intense, so transforming, that for a seemingly endless moment all physical barriers dropped away and they were truly one.

Slumped on top of her, the cool sea air soothing the heat of the inferno through which they had passed, Will raised his head and gazed down into the face of the woman he adored. Her eyes were closed, the thick lashes fanning over her cheeks. But she was still awake enough to hear him when he murmured, "As you are my love, wife, the completion of myself, all I have ever dreamed of and more than I knew could be."

Her smile was replete with joy in the moment but far beyond, for all the moments to come, strung one after another like pearls on the necklace she still wore around her throat.

Sleep took them, there on the petal-strewn bed, as the ship rocked softly in the cove beneath Holyhood from where, so many years before, a stolen bride had been taken and so much had begun.

IN THE MORNING, THEY WENT TO HAWKFORTE. THE voyage took them a few miles down the coast, past high white cliffs and stretches of verdant fields. Seabirds accompanied them, their raucous cries rising above the deep murmur of the wind filling the sail.

Clio had never been to Hawkforte before, but she had heard stories of it. Unlike Holyhood, which had been rebuilt many times over the centuries, very little of Hawkforte had ever been torn down. In this, it reminded her of Akora, where the past lingered around every corner and down every street.

Even so, she was not truly prepared for the first sight of the towers of Hawkforte rising above them. They looked like something out of a dream, the ancient stones gleaming in the sunlight, proud and powerful as though to defy all danger.

They left the ship in a little cove and hand-in-hand, climbed the path that led upward past tangles of wild roses and fragrant sea grass, the sand warm beneath their bare feet, until they came to the gates of Hawkforte. These stood open, framed by stone walls softened by lichens, moss, and tendrils of ivy.

Beyond lay a vast courtyard paved with precisely-cut blocks of stone to keep down mud and dust. They paused to put on their shoes before continuing. Clio shook her head in amazement as she took in all the many buildings within the courtyard, some large, some small, all intended for specific purposes.

"This place looks as though it could be completely self-sustaining," she said.

"It was for centuries," Will replied. "And I don't doubt it could be again, if it ever had to be. The armory alone could equip a good-sized army."

The great hall of Hawkforte simply took Clio's breath away. It towered fully thirty feet high, the walls covered with shields, banners, and weapons. Yet for all that, it had a pleasant, even homey air in the arrangement of seating areas near the fireplace, which was large enough that a tall man could walk into it unimpeded.

There were servants about but they were well instructed, seemingly with the ability to make themselves virtually invisible. In the hours and days that followed, Clio and Will found their every need fulfilled, usually before they thought of it.

Food and wine appeared, baths were drawn, fresh candles lit the room high in the oldest tower where they slept, when they were not further weaving the spell of love and passion that was uniquely their own.

On the third night after their arrival, Will woke to find himself alone in the enormous bed. He rose, threw on a robe, and went in search of his wife, discovering her at length in Hawkforte's library.

It was a very large room in the darkness of the

night, seeming to fade off in all directions. Clio was sitting at a round table, a single lamp beside her, lost in her perusal of what appeared to be a very old manuscript.

Will startled her by coming up directly behind her and dropping a light kiss on the back of her neck. She yelped, jerked around, and bestowed upon him a chiding glance accompanied by a smile that instantly made him think they should be back in bed.

"What are you looking at?" he asked, for after all, a man did not want to appear *entirely* single-minded and uncivilized.

"David told me where to find this." Clio indicated the manuscript. It was written on what appeared to be sheets of vellum, the ink pale but still legible. On the pages Will could see, the capitals were beautifully illuminated and there were small, intricate sketches on the margins. The pages were stitched together on the left side, to form a book. Beside them on the desk was a wooden box, seemingly very old, that appeared to have been made to hold the pages.

"He believes it is the oldest book here in the library," Clio said, "and was probably made in one of the great scriptoriums established by Alfred the Great almost a thousand years ago."

"Made by whom?" Will asked.

"That's the truly incredible part. From what David told me—and from what I've been able to read so far—the book was written by a woman. Her name was

Fawn and she seems to have been the daughter of a Viking warlord and the Saxon woman he married."

"How would such a book have come to be here at Hawkforte?"

"David says there was a family connection between the woman who wrote this and Hawkforte."

"What does she write of?"

"All sorts of things, but mainly about her family. She seems to have had stories she wanted to tell."

Will hid a sigh. "I suppose they're fascinating stories."

"They are, from what I've made out so far. Apparently, her father was involved in an effort to forge peace between the Norse and Saxons, and then her husband—"

She broke off when she saw that Will's attention was elsewhere, specifically on the curve of her breasts just visible beneath the frothy peignoir she wore.

With a soft laugh, she gathered up the book and very carefully returned it to the box. Placing both on the shelf from which she had taken them, Clio said, "It has waited almost a thousand years, I daresay it can wait a little longer."

She went to Will and together they returned upstairs to the high tower and the wide, welcoming bed.

The next day, they took a picnic basket and explored beyond Hawkforte's walls. They found glens filled with wildflowers, springs of crystal-clear water, hidden places where shy deer eyed them without fear.

And they spoke of the future.

"We've had a letter from Melbourne," Will said as he lounged on his side, watching Clio set out their lunch from the picnic basket. He had only to look at her to feel a degree of contentment he had never believed could be his.

The sun shone on her red-gold hair and the smattering of freckles across her nose as she asked, "What does he want?"

Will chuckled. He reached out and twined a strand of her hair around his fingers. "What makes you think he wants anything, other than to congratulate us again?"

"He is Melbourne." Concern for David still tinged her view of the Prime Minister and she was not about to pretend otherwise.

"He reminded me that Akora and Great Britain are in the process of establishing formal diplomatic relations for the first time in our mutual histories."

Clio nodded. "As we are with the United States, where my brother Andreas has been appointed ambassador." She stopped what she was doing just then and looked at Will. "My cousin Amelia has married an American who is to be their ambassador to Akora."

"But no British ambassador has yet been named," he reminded her even as his smile told her far more.

"Will—?" She scarcely dared to hope, had not even allowed herself to think it, but if it were possible— "You have great responsibilities here in England."

"So I do, but Melbourne has expressed his confidence that I can manage more, specifically as British ambassador to Akora."

She was in his arms, laughing with delight, when he cautioned, "It will only be for part of each year. I will have to spend some significant amount of time in England still."

"That is fine, better than fine, it is perfect! There is so much I want to do right here in England. Holyhood is wonderful and I think, with just a little effort, so much more of the past could be discovered there. Your grandmother—no, she is *our* grandmother now—told me there are plans in the library that show the earlier houses at Holyhood. It may still be possible to find their foundations. Truly, it's amazing what you can find if you just dig deep enough. And our children—oh, Will—our children will be able to know both places, both parts of their heritage."

Their children. He had not thought of them, not yet, but as he drew his beloved wife to him, the picnic temporarily forgotten, Will found they were very much on his mind, for they seemed to beckon, out there somewhere beyond the present, only waiting for their own time that would surely come.

About the Author

JOSIE LITTON lives in New England with her husband, children, and menagerie . . . mostly. Her imagination may find her in nineteenth-century London or ninth-century Norway or who knows where next. She is happily at work on a new book and loves to hear from readers.

Visit Josie at www.josielitton.com.

Read on for a peek at
the next two enticing romances
in the Fountain series . . .

JOSIE LITTON'S

and

On sale now from Bantam Books

On sale now

LIGHTS SHINING IN THE HIGH WINDOWS OF THE mansion's ground floor appeared and disappeared among the leafy branches of trees that swayed in the steady breeze off the river. The hour was shortly before midnight. In the walled park surrounding the house, an owl swept soundlessly from its perch. Wings barely moving, it soared over the open ground before descending rapidly to pluck a hapless mouse.

The man waiting in the dark shadows of the bushes saw the catch and smiled faintly. He, too, would hunt soon. Several hours before, he had gotten close enough to the house to confirm that the family was at dinner. He watched them briefly through one of the windows—Prince Alexandros; his wife, Princess Joanna; their nephew, Prince Andreas; and their daughter, Princess Amelia, were all relaxed and in good humor. They had no inkling that their privileged world was about to be shattered.

He had withdrawn to wait and now stirred a little, flexing muscles that would otherwise cramp as he remained concealed behind the thick bushes just inside the high stone walls. The night was cool and damp, but he scarcely noticed. He had known far worse.

He was a tall man, lean and very fit. For this night's work, he was dressed in the garb of a London office worker, a respectable man who earned his portion in a counting house, perhaps, or as a solicitor's secretary. A man neither poor enough nor rich enough to attract attention. His dark trousers and jacket, of plain but sturdy wool, made him all but invisible in the shadows. He had turned up the jacket collar for further concealment and pulled the brim of his felt hat down close to eyes that some had likened to the color of steel.

He was without weapons, although, to be fair, he would still have the advantage against most armed opponents. If the guards found him, he wanted to appear a harmless drunk who had wandered where he should not. For that purpose, he had rubbed dirt on the jacket and trousers such as would result from an inebriated climb over a stone wall, and he carried a half-empty bottle of whiskey in the pocket of the jacket.

By the look of it, the ruse would not be necessary. While it might be true that there was no residence better guarded in all of London, the patrols were at regular intervals, therefore predictable. That was expected. The security around the manor was intended to insulate its inhabitants from the waves of popular unrest that roared through London periodically, not from a lone man intent on gaining access.

Gray eyes flickered in the darkness. He waited, patient and watchful. The lights were extinguished on the ground floor as other lights appeared on the floor above. The family retired early by the standards of society. They preferred one another's company to the customary round of balls, routs, masquerades, assemblies, and the like. According to his information, they had no social commitments on this night. That suited his purposes perfectly.

The patrol was good; he scarcely heard it coming even though he was expecting it. The three men passed within a dozen feet of him. They did not speak and their steps were almost entirely silent. They were, he knew, part of the military force that was among the most feared in all the world. The warriors of Akora, the Fortress Kingdom beyond the Pillars of Hercules, had maintained that mysterious land's freedom and sovereignty for centuries. Ancient, legendary, and only recently beginning to emerge into the modern world, Akora fascinated many, but not him. He cared nothing for the place and hoped most sincerely to have nothing to do with it.

The patrol passed by him. He took a breath, cleared his mind, and ran across the open space of lawn. In little more than a heartbeat, he reached the bushes beneath the ground-floor windows. Crouching there, he paused and listened intently.

No sound from the house or the surrounding grounds suggested that his presence had been detected. Cautiously, he stood and looked into the now dark dining room. The servants had finished clearing the table and would be going to their own rest soon. Only the guards on patrol and on duty in the hall would be awake.

He moved again, around a corner to the back of the house, and looked up. Directly above him were the windows of what he had already confirmed was Princess Amelia's bedroom.

The patrol was returning. He pressed against the wall of the house, blending into the contours of stone and shadow, waiting.

When the patrol was gone, he took a length of black cloth from an inside pocket of his jacket, put it over his face, and tied it at the back of his head. Only his eyes remained visible.

He grasped the stones an arm's reach above him, his fingers digging into the mortar between them, and hoisted himself up smoothly and easily. His feet found the narrow indentation that was just deep enough for him to balance on. Steadied, he reached up again. Swiftly, silently he climbed the wall.

There was a stone balcony outside the princess's

windows. He swung onto it, dropped, and listened again for any sound that would warn he was detected. When none came, he slowly eased the French doors open.

The room was dark, but he could make out the placement of the furniture, particularly the bed hung with gauzy curtains.

His quarry lay on her side. He could not make out her features, but he knew well enough what she looked like, having observed her for several days as she went about London. She was not precisely beautiful, but her face had a certain unique appeal and, so far as he had seen, there was nothing lacking in her figure. He had also noticed her to be an exuberant woman, confident and outgoing, given to frequent smiles and ready laughter. That seemed at odds with her reputation, namely that she was cold and proud, an unfeeling breaker of hearts, a spinster at twenty-five despite her family's wealth and power.

If the lady's unmarried state troubled her, there was no sign of it. Lost in sleep, she breathed slowly and deeply. For just an instant, he felt . . . not doubt precisely, never that. Just a twinge of regret that he hadn't been able to come up with a different plan.

But he wasn't a man to linger over his shortcomings. In a single movement, he brushed aside the curtains and seized hold of her. She woke instantly with a gasp that was smothered by the covers in which he quickly rolled her. Although she struggled fiercely, within seconds he had the gag in her mouth and a hood secured over her head.

Far from being cowed, her efforts to escape redoubled. She was surprisingly strong. No match for his strength, of course, but still she proved more than a handful.

He might have cautioned her to stop, but he could not risk her recognizing his voice. Instead, he tightened his grip warningly. But not, it seemed, quite enough. To his astonishment, his squirming, struggling captive got an arm loose and promptly landed a solid punch to his jaw.

Only a lifetime of self-discipline stopped him from cursing out loud. He wrapped her ever more tightly in the covers and moved quickly to the door.

The inside of the house was not patrolled. That, too, he had confirmed during his surveillance. The guards were stationed only in the central hall.

He avoided them by using the back stairs frequented by the servants. The going was difficult because the squirming bundle in his arms refused to desist. Trussed as securely as a Christmas goose, the princess continued to struggle. It was all he could do to keep hold of her without actually causing her harm.

He reached the ground-floor landing and paused.

She could not escape him, of that he had no doubt. But neither did he underestimate his potential peril. If she managed to get out more than a muffled cry . . .

The Akorans would take him prisoner, but he

doubted very much that they would turn him over to the British authorities. Everything he knew about them suggested they would handle the matter themselves in their own way, presuming they didn't just kill him outright.

She'd damn well better be worth all the trouble.

He opened the door and stepped outside. If his calculations were correct, he had not quite five minutes before the patrol passed again. Enough time to cross the lawn, get through the trees, and scale the wall.

Or it would be if Shadow was on post.

He was, as evidenced by the large shape concealed in the foliage of the upper branches of the trees, and by the rope dangling down the near side of the wall. With an inner sigh of relief, he dumped his unwilling burden into the sling at the end of the rope, secured her firmly, and tugged to signal Shadow. Immediately, the sling began to rise. He watched long enough to confirm that his captive was still struggling fiercely, before climbing the wall himself. Settled beside Shadow, who gave him a quick nod, he helped hoist the sling.

Scant seconds before the patrol was due to return, it was done. With his quarry slung over his shoulder and Shadow following close behind, he ran down the road and around a corner to a waiting carriage.

The wheels were turning even before the door was closed.

Fountain OF SECRETS

On sale now

"TAKE OFF YOUR SWORD," THE WOMAN SAID again. She spoke clearly and firmly, with no hint of fear.

He damn well would not. Indeed, it was all he could do not to draw his blade. He had to remind himself that she was a woman, never to be harmed, according to the most sacred of all Akoran creeds. Summoning patience, Gavin said, "What are you going to do if I don't, shoot me?"

The arrow whooshed past his shoulder, missing him by no more than inches before striking the ground. She had another notched and ready in less than a heartbeat.

"Understand," she said, "I don't miss. That was a demonstration. Take off your sword."

"This is ridiculous." He was genuinely angry now and in that anger, he began walking toward her. "Unless you're a madwoman, you're not going to murder me in cold blood." Of course, there was always a possibility that she was mad, in which case he might be enjoying his last few moments in this world. For a man with a reputation for being unfailingly calm and controlled, it would be supremely ironic to die because of a fit of temper.

All the same, he truly was angry and his mood was not improved when he moved close enough to see her more clearly. She wore not the ankle-length tunic of a woman but the short tunic of a man, ending above her knees. Her hair was golden brown, braided and tightly coiled around her head. Her skin was deeply tanned, suggesting she lived much of her life outside. She was slender, but her bare arms, holding the bow, were sleekly muscled. He eyes were large and thickly fringed, her nose surprisingly pert, and her mouth—

Her mouth was full, lush, and positively enticing for all that it was drawn in a hard line.

He was still staring at that mouth when she said, "I am not mad."

"I am infinitely relieved to hear it."

"If you come in peace, why do you need a sword?"

"Well . . . the truth of that is a little embarrassing." As he spoke, he continued closing in on her. "When I put on this kilt this morning, I realized it was missing a clasp. I was in a hurry and I figured my sword belt would hold it up fine. But now you want me to take the sword off and I'm thinking that if I do that, my kilt's going with it and the fact is I'm not wearing anything under—"

Her eyes were growing saucer-wide. They were also, he saw, a deep, rich brown lit by fragments of gold. Rather more to the point, she was startled and distracted just long enough for him to close the remaining distance between them, take hold of both her arms, and twist the bow from her grasp.

"Damn you!" she cried out, struggling fiercely.

Gavin let her go at once, partly so as not to hurt her but also mindful that she might very well feel no similar prohibition where he was concerned. All the same, the brief contact was enough to inform him that for all her dressing as a man and acting as one, she was most definitely a woman, lithe and slim but perfectly rounded where it mattered most.

Kicking the bow beyond her reach at the same time he tried to dispense with such unwonted thoughts, he said, "The first lesson of warrior training is that you do not draw a weapon on an opponent for any reason other than to kill."

She watched him warily but still showed no sign of fear, he duly noted. Indeed, disarmed, she held her ground with courage and spirit. "Are you saying I should have shot you?"

"I'm saying we should both behave like civilized

people." This despite the fact that the feelings she provoked in him were anything but civilized. First anger and now something altogether different for all that it was no less hot and raw. That was absurd. He was a gentleman—cultured, educated, a man of science and reason. Women were marvelous creatures, to be sure, and passion was one of creation's great gifts in the proper place and the proper time, always properly controlled.

He was not feeling in control now, far from it. With an effort that should not have been necessary, he said, "My name is Gavin Hawkforte and yours is—?"

At the mention of his name, she drew back a little further. Did he imagine it or did she pale slightly? Looking at him, she said, "Your mother is the Princess Kassandra of the House of Atreides and your father is the Hawk Lord, is that not so?"

This recitation of his lineage caught him off-guard. He understood that he and his family were public figures not only on Akora but also in England and elsewhere. Even so, the degree of awareness about them invariably took him by surprise. "He is called that here. In England he is the Earl of Hawkforte."

Her eyes flitted to the bow, but to her credit, she did not attempt to reach for it. Returning her gaze fully to him, she asked, "Why have you come here?"

"In due time. I have told you my name. Now, what is yours?"

She hesitated, but after a moment said, "I am called Persephone."

It was a strange name for anyone to give a child, recalling as it did the legend of the daughter of the Earth stolen away to the underworld. All the same, Gavin merely nodded. "Persephone . . . what brings you to Deimatos?"

"I was about to ask you that. I saw what you were doing. What need have you for surveying instruments?"

There was no mistaking the challenge of her words. Even so, he answered calmly. "I'm just taking a few measurements."

She frowned and again glanced toward her bow but still held her ground. "Do the Atreides intend to build on Deimatos?"

"Build? Of course not."

"The question is not so foolish as you would make it sound. What reason is there for surveying unless one intends to build?"

"There is no such intention. I'm merely following up on an earlier survey, doing some measurements for purposes of comparison. That's all."

Her laugh was dry and scoffing. "A prince of the House of Atreides doing the task of an artisan? That is difficult to believe."

"Why would it be? My brother, cousins, all of us do all sorts of tasks. Even so, I have told you why I am here. Now I ask you the same." And woe betide her if she failed to answer. Lovely though she might be, for all her unusual garb and manner, not to mention her decidedly unorthodox behavior. And lovelier she might seem with each passing moment. Even so, he would have his due, which meant courtesy and no more nonsense.

She was silent long enough for him to think she truly did not mean to answer and he considered what he really could do about that. Finally, she said, "I live here. Deimatos is my home."

THIS TRULY WAS NOT POSSIBLE. SHE COULD NOT have been in the midst of what seemed a perfectly ordinary day only to find herself confronting so extraordinary a man. Such things did not happen in her simple, solitary life.

She had drawn an arrow on a prince of the Atreides and lived to draw another breath. That alone was remarkable. As for the prince himself—

She must not! Just keep breathing, keep walking beside him, keep pretending that everything was all right. He had scarcely reacted to her announcement that she lived on Deimatos but she was not fooled. He was a warrior, bred and trained. Such men were unfailingly dangerous, not in the least because they did not toss their thoughts around like crumbs for birds but kept their own counsel, awaiting the most opportune moment to strike.

He had returned her bow. Having disarmed her, seemingly effortlessly, he had given her back the bow as they walked together toward the cave.

He had not hurt her. He could have easily, for though she was tall for a woman, he was taller yet. Moreover, the broad sweep of his bare chest and shoulders, rippling with muscle, mocked any thought that she could hope to challenge him and win.

He was, she guessed, about her own age, which would make him twenty-four or perhaps slightly older. One of the golden youth that the people of Akora enjoyed so much, the children of the royal house of Atreides in its many branches. His hair was dark blond, very thick and brushed back from his forehead to fall almost to his shoulders. His eyes were deep-set above a blade of a nose. The skin of his face was burnished by the sun and stretched tautly over hard bones. He was, she realized, supremely masculine in a way she had not encountered before.

But then she encountered so very few people in her life, preferring to keep her own company.

"I really am just taking measurements," he said when they reached the entrance to the cave. "And I mean you no harm whatsoever."

It would be so much easier to believe him, but doubts lingered. She did not know the Atreides but she knew of them, had studied their extraordinary history as described in her precious books. For three thousand years, members of that family had ruled Akora in an unbroken line that spoke of their courage, tenacity, and, when necessary, ruthlessness. That one should appear here now could not be mere chance.

"All right . . . " she said slowly. "What are you measuring?"

"The elevation of various points around the island."

"To compare, you say?"

He nodded. "There was a survey done about a hundred years ago. I found the records of it in the palace library."

Despite herself, she smiled. "Oh, yes, the library."

"You know it?"

"I go there from time to time." The palace and its magnificent library dominated the royal city of Ilius, the city she shunned except at those times when the weight of solitude became crushing or the hunger for knowledge proved intolerable. That city to which she had thought shortly to go, and tell the people she feared what she had learned. Now it seemed one of them had anticipated her.

"But you say you live here?" Gavin asked.

"I do live here," she corrected.

"With your family?"

He was bound to know, there really was no preventing it. Already, she sensed he had a strong, seeking mind that was no easier to stand against than was the strength of his body.

"I have no family," she said even as she spied the instrument in the open bag. "Is that a sextant?"

"Yes, it is. Everyone has a family."

"That statement is obviously incorrect since I don't."

She thought her logic irrefutable but it did not appear to impress him. "There are just over three hundred and fifty thousand people on Akora," he said. "With the exception of *xenos,* strangers newly arrived here, we are all related to each other in multiple ways. You are clearly Akoran, therefore you must be part of that web of relationships."

"If you say so. I say I have no family, at least none known to me. Why would you choose to retrace a century-old survey of this island?"

"How can you survive here alone?"

The question amused her, hinting as it did at an underlying belief among Akorans that she had discovered in her readings. Akora was the place "where warriors rule and women serve." Women, it must be assumed, who were not capable of living or acting independently but who instead were dependent on their benevolent masters, the men, to care for them. The mere thought of such an existence made her skin crawl.

"I am very good at taking care of myself," she told him and let a little of her pride show.

"Apparently so. How long have you lived here?"

"A long time. You ask too many questions, Atreides prince."

He ignored that and went on, all the while watching her with disconcerting intensity. "Then you must know this island very well."

Persephone nodded. "That is so."

He hesitated as though coming to a decision. Casually, as though the question was really of no importance, he asked, "Have you seen anything unusual happening here lately?"

She knew then, in a way she had been coming to know since realizing who he was and what he was doing. A prince of Akora come to Deimatos. Come to measure the earth and search for answers.

She had thought she would have to go to them, persuade them, convince them, but now she knew that would not be needed.

All she had to do was show him.

"I have seen what I think is the real reason why you have come here."

She looked up into his eyes, seeing in them wisdom and strength, praying her vision was true.

Around them, the island lay wrapped in stillness. The fronds of the palm trees hung motionless, the scarlet blossoms of the jacarandas did not stir. Sunlight glinted off the azure sea and the golden beaches, over the green hills and the black outcroppings. Time itself seemed not to move, but it would, inevitably and relentlessly. There was no escape from it. They would be carried along to whatever fate awaited them and have to endure it as best they could.

Best then to confront the truth and hope this man could somehow help ease the horror she feared was coming.

Quietly, into the stillness of the golden day, she said, "The volcano that tore Akora apart three thousand years ago is awakening."